SKAGIT

SKAGIT

Robert M. Miskimon

Writers Club Press
San Jose New York Lincoln Shanghai

Skagit

Writers Club Press
an imprint of iUniverse, Inc.

For information address:
iUniverse, Inc.
5220 S. 16th St., Suite 200
Lincoln, NE 68512
www.iuniverse.com

Any resemblance to actual people and events is purely coincidental.
This is a work of fiction.
©Robert M. Miskimon©
10912 107th Ave. SW
Vashon, Wash. 98070
(206) 567-4834

ISBN: 0-595-22092-4

Printed in the United States of America

No man is an island, entire of itself;
Every man is a piece of the continent, a part of the main.

—John Dunne

VOLUME I
Breakaway

CHAPTER 1

Skagit Island rises from the fog-enshrouded waters of Puget Sound like a green glacial fortress, a calling-card from the last ice age that carved out the entire swath of water and land between the Olympics and the Cascades and left islands like crumbs from the banquet of creation scattered up and down a 100-mile corridor from Seattle into Canada. From the bow of the lumbering Whatcom ferry somewhere between Seattle and the quickly-approaching isle, Rex Armistead could just distinguish its thickly-forested outlines, and his heart raced as he hurried down to the loading deck from the over-heated passenger cabin. The cold beads of driving rain that pelted his face felt adventurous. Like a true pioneer, he held his back straight and his head upright as he strained for a better view of the island. Behind him on the platform, regular commuters were huddled close together in their cars, heaters running full blast. Even though it was only 5:30 p.m. on a Friday in February, it was practically dark and the big ferry navigated the last few yards of its approach by fixing on the floodlights of the dock. Just as the boat nosed into its huge slip, there was an immense roar of reverse-thrust propellers and the bow shuddered with a thunderous flapping.

"Arriving Skagit Island!" Rex whipped his head up around toward the public address speakers and caught a glimpse of terror in the eyes of the captain on the bridge.

There was a groaning, creaking sound as the huge ship plowed into the pilings and lunged to one side. Rex was thrown to the deck, with several other ferry crewmembers, and slid several feet across the cold wet steel. One of the cars broke loose from its wooden chocks and rolled into the yellow cable draped loosely across the bow. The ferry then lunged in the opposite direction, whipped back by the rebounding pilings like a ping pong ball, as Rex and the crewmen clutched for something to hold onto.

Rex grabbed the chromium fender of a battered old Mercedes-Benz to halt his slide. When the ferry finally stopped its flagellation, Rex pulled himself up in the rain and noticed a white-haired couple sound asleep in the Mercedes. He tried to brush the oily wet slime off his clothes, but it was pointless.

"Sorry about the bumpy ride, folks!" The captain's goofy, good-natured voice sounded like the disembodied laugh of the Fat Lady in the circus.

With a handful of other battered passengers, Rex dragged himself off the ferry and trudged up the loading ramp to the still-shimmying dock. Tall and bony, Rex still looked and moved like the high school track star he'd once been. A shock of light brown hair across his thin features gave him a preppy look, accented by a residual tan emblematic of his penchant for getting outdoors whenever possible. A figure in a dark purple raincoat with umbrella waved at Rex as he entered the waiting area.

"You must be Mr. Armistead?" A gnarled hand thrust forward and grabbed him Rex by the shoulder, pulling him up onto the platform out of the rain. "Rayne Fountaine with Island Realty. Won't be able to see anything tonight, but we can get an early start tomorrow morning. My car's right over here…had anything to eat?"

Rex grunted and pulled the collar of his coat up around his neck. "Those ferry captains take drugs?"

"Oh, they're always banging into the dock. That was a pretty good landing, actually. Not long ago they plowed into the ferry dock at the other end of the island and completely destroyed the slip. Took them a month to repair it!"

"I need a drink."

"Why don't you come over to my house, meet the wife, then we can go have dinner at Quarterdeck Harbor?"

Rex was in no humor to resist, and slumped into a silent heap in the front seat of Fountaine's car as the windshield wipers slurped back and forth.

"So what kind of a place you looking for?"

"My wife and I have three kids, and we really want to get out of Seattle. Something with a little land maybe—but someplace quiet and safe."

"Wanna view?"

"I don't really care about that. Just something…away from it all. Someplace that's quiet where the kids can play and my wife won't get mugged or raped."

"Well, there isn't any place on this island where that's likely to happen!" Fountaine sniffed.

Rex drank in the deep green wetness of this place in the rain, and it was soothing in a strange kind of way. The heavy pine and cedar trees provided an anchor to the earth, so that all within the sweep of their branches could never be lost. It was a huge garden afloat in Puget Sound—a retreat for humans. Rex liked the idea of Skagit Island as a kind of refuge for humans, a wildlife preserve for the endangered species *homo sapiens*.

"What's your wife do?"

"Advertising. She's an account executive with an agency in Seattle. But she'll be working a lot at home once we move to the island."

"I've met a lot of people who have businesses at home since I've been selling real estate. Yeah, one guy I sold a house to is a stockbroker. Does all his trading by computer at home. Another guy is a neurologist in LA and his wife's a writer. She comes up here in the summer and he commutes by plane every weekend to see her."

"That sounds wonderful." Rex was tired and sullen and had no patience with this barrage of happy talk.

"Isn't that what you do? You a writer or something?"

"Something like that," Rex smirked. "I'm a freelance science writer and editor. I'll probably be working at home too, if we can find a quiet place away from the kids."

"So I guess you need a place with at least…what?…four or five bedrooms?"

"Nah, hell no! Not that many. Three would be plenty. We're a close family."

Fountaine wrenched the steering wheel suddenly to the left and slammed on the brakes to avoid hitting a deer that jumped into the road. By the time the car skidded to a stop the deer had disappeared into the bush again.

"Jesus! Never seen one just leap right out like that. That was a close call."

Rex ran his hand nervously across his face. "Got a cigarette?"

Fountaine rummaged through his glove compartment and handed him a crumpled old pack of cigarettes that looked as if it had been submerged in salt water several times and dried in the fetid fumes of the car's heater. Rex hadn't smoked a cigarette in more than 20 years, but now was the time. As he lit up the twisted cigarette and inhaled, he began choking and gasping for air like an adolescent who chuffs on their first cigar.

"How much further to your house?" he gasped.

"We're almost there. I'll get you some fresh cigarettes if you'd like."

"No, never mind. Just some water would be fine."

Zack Beale had tried many times to leave the island but always came back—sometimes in resignation but more often with a sense of deliverance. When his wife deserted him and moved to Alaska to be with her fisherman friend, he finally put the house they'd built on the market and moved south to Oregon where he'd been told the weather was milder and jobs were plentiful. After one bleak, drunken winter in Coos Bay when he tottered on the brink of suicide for several months, he finally quit Oregon in a fit of disgust and made his way back to Skagit where at least the place was familiar and he still had friends. With most of his possessions stuffed into his battered blue Chevrolet pickup, and his faithful collie dog Blazer riding in the front seat, Zack sighed deeply as he drove onto the ferry from Tacoma that would deposit him on the south end of the island so he could drive its full length, savoring the rich canopy of greenness and the captivating contours of the hills and ridges along Quarterdeck Harbor.

Despite all the heartbreak of the world and its manifold disappointments, Skagit was still a place where Zack could find peace and a tantalizing reminder of the innocence that once had flooded his world in bright childhood sunlight. Although not a literary man, Zack liked the sounds of words and sometimes turned them around in his mind for days, comparing their colors and shapes. Even words he didn't understand, such as "antiphony" and "megalomania" held a distant fascination for him. But words that were almost alike were his favorites. Whenever he tried to think of why he liked the island and kept coming back, Zack compared "heaven" and "haven" in his mind, trying to decide whether Skagit was a little of both. When he first came to the island as a young man, it seemed like heaven because work in the strawberry fields was plentiful, the girls in town were both beautiful and friendly, and he could fish and clam practically anywhere. Nowadays, with the end of his marriage, the fact his hair was mostly gray and he could no longer work in the strawberry fields since they'd been taken out years ago, the island seemed like a haven for his broken spirit.

Zack carried himself on a wiry, long frame that ambled loosely and left people with the impression that he was quite carefree. With his easy smile and quick handshake, Zack was well-liked in the town and had no shortage of friends and odd jobs he could perform to eke out a living. Survival on the island was for him a known quantity, but life in the outside world presented a bewildering palette of choices, decisions and discomforts. Sometimes he wondered if he wasn't a coward, as his wife had so often told him, afraid to meet the world on its own terms "like a real man." Then, after thinking about it for a while, he wondered if everybody else in the world except himself wasn't crazy. After all, why beat your brains out for money, prestige and possessions when sure as hell you couldn't take them with you? No, Zack had become quite comfortable with himself in his "rut," as the dear departed Lureen had called it. Maybe he wasn't a business tycoon, but he still knew how to make fresh blackberry pie and could maneuver his kayak clear across Puget Sound alone when the weather was nice. How many people—especially men his age—could do that?

Now he was back again, this time forever. Should he throw the renters out of his house and move back in or find another place to live and hope to sell it soon?

Hell, I could live in my truck. What I really need is a bunch of cash and I could just live off the interest for a while. I ought to just sell the house…too many memories, anyway. Every time I go outside and look at her garden, I get upset and angry.

Not worth it.

By the time Zack reached town, the sun was shining brightly and the air was warm. On that corner, right there, he'd met a woman from Seattle one summer at the Skagit Strawberry Festival who slept with him that very night. Gone the next day, too, but what a night! Twenty years later, he could still feel her sunbaked skin and smell her sandy brown hair. What was her name? … Whitney, or Courtney, or some college sounding name like that. She was a doll. Definitely not an islander, though. As the warm sunshine beat down on his face, Zack felt a sharpness in his lower abdomen. He'd forgotten about the ghosts that also go with the island. *Damn, why is life so hard?*

Then he thought about the cemetery where his parents, brother and cousin lay side-by-side on the rolling grass hillside dotted with collapsing concrete crosses and shattered sarcophagi. Beale was one of the oldest names on the island, but not as powerful or important as Lanscombe or Tuffing. Those families had entire compounds to themselves, separated from the island commoners by iron link fencing. Orchids and lumber could buy that sort of thing, but working for the men who sold orchids and lumber could afford naught but a hole in the ground. Zack decided to visit the graveyard and pay his respects to his parents, once he'd stopped at the Island Bar & Grill for a beer and some friendly conversation.

"Well look what the cat dragged in!" The voice from behind the bar was the unmistakable raspy-throated roar of Nell, surrogate mother to half the wayward men on Skagit—the half that hadn't already ended up in prison or dead. Zack waved his arms in the air before clamping them hard around her too-ample chest.

"What the hell are you doin' here, boy?"

"Came back. Got tired of Oregon. Gimme a draft beer, OK?"

"Somebody was askin' about you just the other day," Nell said, rolling her protuberant eyes and searching the floor for a clue. She rubbed her chin vigorously for a moment, then popped her head up suddenly. "Yeah…Charlie Rector. He said he was tryin' to get some investors together for an apartment building or somethin'. Might want to look him up."

"Yeah, I will…just as soon as I hear how my favorite gal is doing!"

"You've always been a charmer, Zack. How come you're not married yet?"

Zack gulped his beer, then set the glass methodically on the counter. His mouth would not form the words that could express the pain and longing inside, and he looked helplessly at Nell who regarded him with a gentle smile.

"Oh, I guess you're still pretty sore all right," she said offhandedly, trying to dismiss the subject. "Don't worry, though. Someone will come along...when you least expect it."

Zack relaxed and allowed himself to smile. "If there was another woman on this island like you, Nell, I'd marry her in a New York minute!"

"Well, there's only one of me," she shot back gamely. "And I'm spoken for."

Zack got up and walked briskly toward the door, then turned back quickly.

"Then I guess I'll never marry again."

Nell waved her hands dismissively. "Go on! Never say never." They both coughed with laughter as he swept outside.

Allison Koorie wanted to paint an orgasm. She'd wanted to paint one ever since the time she'd gone to bed with two teenaged boys in her studio near the Offney Ranch just south of town. Her problem was that she could vividly recall the experience of having two boys at once, and the multiple orgasms that she experienced, but couldn't quite figure out how to translate that to the canvas. As she stood in front of the canvas with her paintbrush, skinny-legged and busty with her blonde hair encircling her head like a tumbleweed, she paused for a moment and sucked on her lower lip. In the corner of the studio her previous attempts to capture that moment of ecstasy were piled high like so much colorful refuse. Garish colors peeped out of the pile of discarded canvasses, testament to her dilemma. She sucked once more on her cigarette, tossed it on the concrete floor and squished it with her thong as she squinted her blue eyes.

A medieval scene with dragons, swords and dark caverns might capture the mood. A brooding moon spills its light down on a scene of incredible carnal lust...pleasures unspeakable juxtaposed with a Bible or a cross...something for stark contrast. A busty woman being ravaged by a horse? By a black knight?

Allison felt she'd at last gotten on the right path, and paced excitedly as she ran through the images in her head. She squeezed paint from three tubes onto her palette and started to swirl her brush about, mixing colors frenetically. Then she placed her brush on the canvas and made a quick swirl of paint, followed by several jabbing motions. As she worked, she could recall that afternoon in the studio and felt a warmth throughout her stomach and pelvis.

All art is erotic, so why shouldn't this be the same? The trick is to disguise it with a bunch of symbols so people think it's somehow edifying. But the true sensualists, the real artistes, will know right away that this is a canvas about sexual excitement. Once that's established, the challenge is to render that excitement with full intensity by using the right colors, composition, lighting…

She jerked her hand as the telephone rang, and set her brush down with a muttered curse. When she turned toward the kitchen to get the phone, Allison stumbled over a coffee can filled with brushes and tumbled onto the concrete floor, hitting her head. The last thing she remembered was the pleasant coolness of the concrete against the side of her face as the warm blood pooled around her mouth.

When she awoke in the Skagit Health Clinic, Allison was stretched out on a gurney with a scant white sheet draped over her chest. The room was oyster white and noiseless, littered with an assortment of medical instruments, and as she looked around at her surroundings Allison felt her heart race. She gasped for breath and sat up quickly to figure out where she was. She felt disconnected and disembodied. Her head was reeling from some kind of anesthetic, and her stomach was queasy, so she laid back down and closed her eyes.

"Pretty nasty little bump there!"

Allison opened her heavy-lidded eyes wide enough to recognize Dr. Frank Bleeker. With his impish smile, prematurely balding pate and horn-rimmed glasses, Dr. Bleeker was a well-known and revered figure on Skagit Island.

"What happened?"

"You fell in your studio and got a hairline fracture of the skull. Just a small one on the right side of your face above your eye. We've X-rayed it, stitched you up and given you antibiotics. You should be fine. You'll need several days of rest once you get home. Is there anyone to look after you, Allison?"

Allison's head felt like melting Jell-O, but she was reassured by Dr. Bleeker's presence. "Nobody at home," she mumbled. "Only me and the cat. I'll be all right."

Bleeker frowned and pursed his lips. "Just to be sure, I'll stop by after work on the way home and check on you. Do you need some help getting home?"

"Oh, I'm fine," Allison muttered. "I don't need any help."

"I want gold lamé...don't you have any at all?"

"No, I'm sorry. We never get any requests for it. I might be able to order some from one of the other stores for you."

The diminutive woman with gray-streaked hair and a bejeweled cigarette holder was clearly no one to be trifled with. Cerise Bagoth was a tough little Jewess from Chicago who came into the world as Gladys Shorenstein, but assumed the name of a forgotten Gypsy dancer when she moved to Los Angeles in the 1960s and became a free spirit. Now, into *her* 60s, she flounced about Skagit in flowing sheer scarves and posed as an author, using her husband's wealth to intimidate anyone—especially variety store clerks—whom she chose.

And Dean Fongalong was just the sort of wimpish, effeminate store manager who seemed to provoke the worst in people. Barely five feet tall, his black Filipino hair was combed neatly back in a boyishly cute manner that went along with his overall demeanor as a boy/man/fagbait/transsexual innocent moron who only wanted to drape sale banners across the store and file pleasing monthly reports to the corporate headquarters of QuikSave. His saccharine manner invited acidic intercourse.

"I have this silver fabric if…"

"I didn't ask for silver did I?"

"Well, no….I.…"

"I suppose I'll just have to go into Seattle. Can't find anything worthwhile here. So you're….Mr. Fongalong?" Cerise said, squinting her eyes at his plastic nameplate. "I'll have to remember that." And she marched out of the store clasping her cigarette holder in front of her face, without looking back.

"Who was *that* bitch?" asked Carolyn Chester, the first employee of QuikSave who started as a sales clerk when the store opened in 1970. Although a native of Skagit Island who rarely left, she had somehow achieved the same grizzled look as dime store sales clerks all over America, so that she would have seemed equally at home in a Woolworth's in downtown Pittsburgh.

"You don't know who *she* is?" Fongalong seemed chastened, out of breath. "Probably one of the wealthiest women on the island. Her husband had tons of money…she lives in this huge house overlooking Quarterdeck Harbor. Every time she comes in here, I cringe. She's always so mean to me."

"Don't worry about her, honey," Carolyn said in a raspy voice. "She's just looking for somebody to inject her venom into. It's not your fault."

"I hope not!" Fongalong sniffed and shuffled some papers nervously. "I get a stomach ache every time she comes in the store."

Cerise marched across the parking lot to her red Jaguar XKE and revved up the engine. With a throaty roar, the wheeled missile thrust her out onto Skagit Highway in the direction of the White Eagle Art Center where an exhibit of her watercolors was scheduled to open that evening.

Zack pulled his truck out onto the highway at the precise moment that the Jaguar appeared on the horizon. The old Chevrolet lumbered out of the parking lot and into the roadway, and as he reached for second gear the engine suddenly quit, causing the heavy truck to slow—then stop—in the middle of the highway. As he cranked the engine and cursed under his breath, Zack could hear the high-pitched whine of the sports car somewhere in the distance.

Cerise put her cigarette holder to her lips and drew a quick breath, before getting ready to execute a quick turn around the stalled pickup. The hot ash from the end of her cigarette dropped free and burned into her scarf, igniting a flash fire that roared quickly around her head. In her fury to put out the flames, her hands slipped off the wheel and the XKE slammed directly into the rear of Zack's truck. Skid marks measured after the crash indicated she had applied the brakes only a few feet from impact. Her estimated speed at the moment of the collision was 68 miles per hour.

Whipped back and forth like a paddleball on a rubber string, Zack was thrown forward onto the steering wheel then hurled back against the seat. His head and chest felt as if they were broken, and he sat motionless for a moment while his head spun wildly about. He heard a "WHOOSH" from behind his truck, and through the rear view mirror Zack could see a huge curtain of flames and smoke rise from the XKE. He pulled himself out of the cab and staggered back to the car, which was half-wedged under the bed of his truck. Panting furiously, Blazer leaped out of the cab and nervously circled the truck. The door on the driver's side was partially open, and he could see Cerise slumped down in her seat, unconscious. Zack tasted the contents of his stomach in his throat as he quickly reached into the rising ball of flames and pulled her arm until she slipped out of the car onto the pavement. Then he bent down and hoisted her over his shoulders and ran as fast as he could away from the truck, until they reached a wooded knoll on the far side of the highway. As he started to lower her to the ground, a terrific explosion went up as the truck and car were joined in a single roaring fireball.

"Holy shit!" he muttered as he slowly lowered Cerise to the grass. Zack noticed that her left arm seemed to be rather badly burned, and that there were singed areas of her dress around her neck. He checked her breathing, placed his ear against her chest, then sighed with relief when he heard a heartbeat.

Jesus, how can I get some help? Can't leave her here but afraid to move her.

Zack felt like someone had dropped a piano on his back.

Approximately the same size as Manhattan, Skagit Island is home to some 10,000 golfers, punkers, loafers, bikers, boozers, potheads, yuppies and two black lesbians. Oldtimers, like Zack, generally resent the newcomers—who just want to be left alone to enjoy their solitude—and the social fabric is stitched together more with loose-knit mutual indifference than with the tightly woven threads of community. Cradled at the southern tip of Puget Sound about equidistant from Seattle and Tacoma, Skagit Island hides from the view of mainlanders in sheets of sea smoke in the winter. In the summer, when the days are sunny and long, the island is overrun with tourists who quickly discover there is hardly a place for them in the scant bed 'n breakfast economy of the island, which requires that they hop a ferry back to the mainland by nightfall.

Although Native Americans had lived on the island for centuries, the first white settlers didn't arrive until after the Homestead Act of 1860 promised 160 acres of land to any man who lived on it for five years and filed a proper claim. Orion Lanscombe, rumored to have been a lieutenant in the Army of the Confederacy, established the first lumber mill on Skagit shortly after the Civil War. To carry his lumber to market. Lanscombe also bought and operated the first regular ferry service to the mainland—a steamer called Piccadilly. The men who worked in his mill traveled back and forth each day between Tacoma and Skagit Island with their product, thus inaugurating the first island commuter service.

Once some of the land had been cleared, the European settlers noticed that wild strawberries abounded on the island. They quickly established strawberry farms that made Skagit Island the premier strawberry-growing region of the United States by the turn of the century. The cool sea mists and warm summer days produced berries that were plump, sweet and delicious. In 1926, Skagit Island's strawberry farmers shipped 274,000 crates of berries across the United States. The strawberry economy provided abundant summer jobs for islanders as well as anyone in the Puget Sound area willing to perform the backbreaking labor. But by the 1930s, the fruit maggot had decimated Skagit's strawberry fields forever. The harvest dropped precipitously and within three years had dwindled to nothing but a memory kept alive by the annual Strawberry Festival.

By the time the strawberries disappeared, Skagit Island had been "discovered" by a certain breed of rugged individualist unafraid of either the ferry commute to jobs in Seattle or the isolation of the island in winter, when storms frequently knock out power for several days and telephone connections with the mainland are sometimes severed. Stories abound of couples moving to Skagit in a state of connubial bliss, parting each morning to travel to jobs off-island and uniting in the evening for sweet candlelight dinners…until one or both partners tires of the rigors of this island life. High divorce rates and frequent real estate turnover also are as characteristic of Skagit Island as winter rains. The ideal profession for an islander, it's often remarked, is a combination of marriage counselor and real estate broker.

6:35 a.m. Tuesday morning—a fog-swept early spring day—as Rex Armistead stumbled bleary-eyed into Paul's Pastries for a Danish and coffee before racing the remaining five miles to the ferry dock to make an 8 a.m. appointment at DigiTek. Happy, rocking sounds of "Jimmy Mack, When Are You Coming Back?" broadcast through the damp morning air from the bakery's open door as Rex approached to see a pony-tailed man in shorts and brown uniform shirt of a Puget Transit bus driver swaying his hips and shuffling his feet to the Motown beat. It was, indeed, an infectious beat but the bus driver's effeminate movements betrayed more clearly than his hairstyle his homoerotic proclivities. Rex stood motionless at the pastry counter as the smooth-skinned young man danced dreamily around the bakery, eyes closed.

"The party's back there," he said in a drag queen baritone, suddenly opening his eyes and looking directly toward Rex. Then he sashayed behind the counter, grabbed the aging flower child waitress around the waist and executed a merry jitterbug figure in front of the oven.

"Oh, stop it!" she protested with a smile. "This gentleman is waiting for me."

"No…go right ahead!" Rex smiled, tapping his foot. "He was here first, anyway."

"Why don't you order first? I'm just getting off work and you seem in a hurry."

"Well, thanks. I'd like one of those blueberry Danish things and a cappuccino."

When he sprinted back to his car and drove off into the fog, Rex could see the two still dancing vigorously in the soft yellow lights of the bakery. *Yeah, I think this is the place.*

"I'm sorry it's so late, but I just wanted to stop by on the way home and look in on you," Frank Bleeker apologized to the head-bandaged Allison when she opened her door. "I would have come sooner, but we had this bad accident and I had to do some surgery."

"Oh no!" Allison said. "Anybody seriously hurt?"

"Not really…just some cuts, scrapes and burns that will heal. Our patient was a very lucky woman. But I came by to see how you are faring. Taking your medicine?"

"Yes! Can you come in for a second?"

Bleeker stepped inside and smelled fresh oil paints. His eyes quickly scanned the old farmhouse where Allison lived and worked. It was a hurly-burly of stacked cardboard boxes, canvases, riding gear and books.

"Want something to drink, Frank?"

"Sure...got some tea?"

Allison poured herself a large glass of red wine and put some water on the stove.

"I could get my son and help you move some of these boxes so you'd have more room," he offered.

"Are you offended by my chaotic lifestyle?"

"No, not offended, just concerned. As your doctor, I feel a responsibility to look after your safety and welfare."

"Well, it would be a treat if someone did. Sure, Doc! I'll take you up on that offer. When would you like to come and help me organize my life?"

"Saturday?"

"Uh...OK. If it's in the afternoon. I paint in the morning. Around 2 o'clock?"

"Wyndham is big and strong...played football and basketball both last year."

"Mmmmm...a hunk like his daddy!"

Allison gulped her wine and slinked toward Bleeker, his cup of tea in her hand. As he sipped the hot brew, her fingers found their way to his hair and gently stroked his neck and bald head.

"After we're done, why don't you take the football player home and come back here for a touchdown?" she crooned.

Bleeker smiled wickedly. "We'll see."

CHAPTER 2

*O*nce aboard the ferry for West Seattle, Rex ambled out of his car into the pre-dawn chill air of Puget Sound and scampered topsides into the galley for a coffee refill. As he climbed the metal stairs, he could smell the tart aroma of French roast mingled with the saccharine scent of hot donuts. He moved toward the former and tried to ignore the latter. Fortified with a full plastic mug of java, he strolled around the passenger deck peering into the darkness for a glimpse of sunrise. Instead, he encountered a news rack with copies of the latest edition of the *ClamShell*, the island's own weekly, with screamer headlines:

"BRIDGE PROPOSED ACROSS SKAGIT ISLAND"

The newspaper reported that officials of the Washington State Transportation Department had once again rolled out their perennial proposal for a bridge across Puget Sound by connecting Skagit Island to the mainland. The behemoth project would link the area just south of the Seattle airport to a swath mid-island, then continue across the sound to Kitsap County where it would provide direct highway access to the Olympic Peninsula—and Olympic National Park, plus ski and golf resorts under development by Japanese investors.

A citizens' committee was being formed to organize resistance to the bridge proposal. There was a meeting Thursday night at the Skagit High School. All were invited. Rex scalded his tongue as he read of the scope and brazenness of the state's proposal, matched only by the swift and forceful response of islanders. Evidently, someone had heard of a state report about a possible bridge mentioned on an Olympia radio station and had the presence of mind to make a few phone calls. Citizens on Skagit Island knew about the threat before any of the large Seattle newspapers or television stations had gotten wind and were already in motion to plan their counter-assault. Between gulps of his hot coffee, Rex gleaned that a petition already had been drafted to the Skagit County Council opposed to the bridge and was in circulation. Volunteers were needed for various tasks—fund raising, publicity, and governmental liaison.

He pulled out his appointment book and crossed off the evening he'd scheduled at the Seattle Art Museum and wrote in the words "bridge meeting—MUST GO." As the ferry lunged and churned across the sound, its huge prow slapped against the wind-whipped waves. The ferry, probably 200 feet or more in length, wide and stable at its water line, was obviously built for stability rather than speed. And yet, even on this relatively calm morning, its hull was being slapped around like a coolie in a cowboy bar.

The DigiTek "campus" was really a sprawl of modern-looking glass enclosures flung here and there on a hillside just off the Eastside Freeway connecting Seattle, Mercer Island, Bellevue and the other tony suburban shopping malls that resembled Southern California more than the Pacific Northwest. Expensive red BMWs darted in and out around silver Mercedes-Benzes while Rex tried to find the entrance from DigiTek Way. Once inside, he noticed that everyone wore blue jeans, was in their late 30s and seemed to have just gotten out of bed. Its resemblance to a college campus stemmed from its "student body" rather than its buildings. It was casual yet intense. The nerve center of American telecommunications capitalism seemed more like an endless fraternity party than the savagely competitive predator it actually was.

Rex approached a reception desk and watched his image on a TV monitor overhead.

"I'm here to see Allegra Burgstrom...my name is Rex Armistead."

"Would you sign in please?" the pleasant Asian woman said, pointing to a computer keyboard. Rex typed in his name and the name of his appointment. "Allegra will be with you in a moment."

The coffee table in front of him was a large, looping glass amoebae with neatly-folded copies of the *Wall Street Journal*, *New York Times*, and *Forbes*. Behind him, a firehouse-style metal staircase ascended into the heavens, or at least into the executive offices where cyberpunks and magneto heads made decisions about what kind of email half the offices in the world would have next year.

"Mr. Armistead? I'm Allegra."

She wore her smile like a masque, concealing rather than revealing her true feelings. Although her mouth was arched upward through years of autonomic training, her eyes betrayed something altogether different. They were haunted, glazed, as if they had seen something too shocking for words. She had the air of one who had lost something terribly important a long time ago, but had been so shaken by the experience that she could no longer remember what was lost—only the feeling of emptiness and terror remained. Her face, thus contorted with a forced smile and a distant, unfocused gaze, was unsettling rather than inviting. Everyone knew this except her. An outstretched hand covered in a Saks Fifth Avenue jacket thrust itself toward Rex, who grabbed it and shook with a light grip. (*How firm a grip should a man use when shaking hands with a women? Is it different according to the degree of masculine dress?*)

"So you've done some technical writing before?"

"Well, yes and no. I've done lots of general news writing over the years and have specialized in the last few years in science and medicine. I don't think it would be very much of a transition to technical…"

"The placement agency said you were a technical editor," she interjected. Her eyes regarded Rex coldly, like a cobra deciding whether to strike.

"The medical writing is quite technical…"

"It doesn't matter," she burst in again. "This project is medical writing for an online computer product. May I see some of your medical samples?"

Rex' gut wrenched tighter as he opened his portfolio on the oaken conference table. His samples looked battered and shabby in this high-tech, sterile corporate setting. Mistakenly, he grabbed a yellowed copy of the *Peninsula Pennyroyal*—the California weekly newspaper he'd edited for a decade before moving to Skagit. The world it came from, and the ideas it expressed, seemed now impossibly remote from this silicon sleekness populated by power suits and blue jeans. Quickly recovering, he remembered to produce a copy of the hospital magazine he'd edited after leaving the newspaper. Glossy, graphically appealing and filled with pertinent medical copy, he thrust it toward her to divert attention away from the newspaper. He sighed when she lay down the latter and inspected the former carefully.

"This is fine, but it's not technical writing."

"Do you mean technical writing…about computer software?"

"Well, yes. I think that's a good background for the kind of thing we're doing here. I can't tell you how many people I've interviewed already with newspaper clippings." Her distant eyes came suddenly into a cold, close focus.

Yeah, but none of them are from a black newspaper. None of them put their life on the line for their beliefs. None of them endured threats against their children. None of them won awards and the confidence of the community…

"Mr. Armistead?"

"Yes?"

"We'll give you a call when we make a decision."

Numbly, Rex fumbled with his samples and left the room. Everyone at DigiTek seemed 30 years old, unwrinkled by time, and smiling smugly as he walked again through the lobby toward his car. He felt as if he had finally seen manifest what his college buddies used to laugh about when exams were over: an all-nighter that never stopped. The frenetic grind before a ball-buster of a final that came anew each day was the core of the DigiTek experience. The pizza, soda pop and long hours betrayed themselves in baby fat, nervous laughter and a kind of artless narcissism.

"Fuck you all," Rex snarled as he drove off. "I don't wanna work for a bunch of yuppie computer faggots anyway!"

The Skagit High School Auditorium heaved and panted with the combined breath, enthusiasm, anger and fear of 3,000 islanders who had assembled for a single purpose: to defeat the state bridge proposal. There were bearded artists in berets, mothers in muumuus with children running asunder, artfully attired attorneys, mud-caked cowboys and uncomfortable commuters looking slightly dazed. Crouched behind a row of tables at the front of the room was a group of suited state flacks, slick in their choreographed arrangement of overhead projections, bound engineering studies and infrastructure inspeak. Their very lubricity made them an even more appealing target for the islanders' rage. As each islander rose to spoke, they were greeted with cheers and applause.

"I'd like to know why the State Transportation Commission has brought this discredited bridge plan back after it was rejected 10 years ago as unworkable." Stan Ewert, owner of Island Lumber, stood tall and erect, his teal eyes flashing anger. "I'm beginning to think we can't trust anyone in state government. What has changed that makes this now a viable project?

"Every engineering study I have seen that is not prepared by a firm friendly to this commission says there is no way to safely build a bridge across Puget Sound," roared Rod Matthews, a freelance computer systems consultant. "Our lawyers have told us that those studies would make excellent supporting evidence when we go to court."

"I don't want a bridge because it would make all the blue herons leave the island and make a lot of noise and pollution," iterated a precocious blond-haired young man of about 10 years old. "I've been learning in school about how much damage humans have already done to the environment. Isn't this a disaster we can prevent from happening?"

"When I was a commercial seaman for 37 years on Puget Sound, I made hundreds of trips past Skagit Island—in all kinds of weather. Let me tell you, ladies and gentlemen of the state who work in office buildings, that the weather out there can get pretty nasty," said Luke McLoskie, a grizzled sea captain with foghorn baritone voice. "If I had to pilot one of those supertankers up the sound through a bridge across Skagit, I wouldn't do it unless weather conditions were perfect because of the danger of hitting the supports. And we all know how often the weather here is 'perfect.' And I know plenty of other merchant marines who feel just the same way. This is a stupid idea!"

A gorilla-suited man leaped from the audience, handing out bananas to the roaring crowd as he loped toward the podium. "The State Transportation Commission must think we're a bunch of apes, if they think we're gonna fall for this idea! Take your monkey business with you back to Olympia," he snorted, then placed a banana in front of each of the seated commissioners.

"I have here a petition signed by 7,000 residents of Skagit Island opposed to a bridge," said Wyn Dashett, head of the Island Residents Against Trans-sound Egress (IRATE). "That represents more than 75 percent of the registered voters on Skagit. I know of several people—myself included—who will personally place ourselves in the way of the bulldozers if you try to go ahead with this."

"We will not allow Skagit Island to become a quaint pit-stop for wealthy tourists on their way from the airport to the Olympic Peninsula to play golf," boomed Arthur Ashton, a rotund, bearded metal sculptor who rode Harleys and led Audubon bird-watching expeditions in Fern Cove Bog. "Your bridge would not only destroy the quality of life here for humans but would endanger the habitat for at least six species of rare and threatened birds. This is an ecological nightmare that future generations would have to live with. But, believe me, we will not leave our children this legacy."

The islanders went on for more than three hours hammering home their message in a tidal wave of outrage, each speaker more incensed than the previous one. By the end of the hearing, the commissioners looked stunned and crestfallen, ashen with the weight of so much hostility. Their breezy air of officialdom had evaporated under the laser beam of strident island militancy.

"Bastards!" someone shouted at them as they drove off in their state cars after the hearing closed. Repeated thumps against their cars reverberated from hard kicks administered by islanders' boots and fists. "Carpetbaggers!"

Rex walked into a room of about 50 islanders for an impromptu strategy meeting of IRATE. A day later, the energy and anger among islanders were still palpable. The rebels had congregated at Island Edibles, a hippie-style restaurant with wooden beams and window casements that looked out onto an enclosed green garden ringed with bright daisies and geraniums. There was a light mist in the air when Rex arrived, and the smell of fresh espresso wafted to greet his nostrils.

"Hi, I'm Zack Beale." A large, grizzled, hairy hand reached out to Rex as he sat at the table. "I'm Rex Armistead. Nice to meet you."

"I noticed your name on the sign-in roster this morning. You're just the guy we've been looking for. You've had experience working with the media?"

"Well, yeah. Lots of it, actually."

"We need a good writer who knows their way around the news media," Zack said. "There's a lot of people who write here on the island, but not many of us know how to get our message across with the media. Can you help us?"

"Of course. What can I do to help?"

"We need a position paper, a press kit, some news releases and maybe even a press conference. That's part of why we're here today."

"It would be good if you could go with me when I visit the news media, if you have the time," Rex said. "It's always more impressive if there's a couple of people who show up in the newsroom. Demonstrates credibility."

"Not a problem. Just let me know when you're ready."

When Rex arrived home, exhausted and anxious to see his family, he noticed a foul smell near his house—the unmistakable stench of sewage. Sniffing the air gingerly, he tried to locate the source. But since there was no breeze, it was impossible to tell from which direction the odor emanated. As soon as he went inside, he quickly deduced the source by the distraught look on his wife's face.

"What's that smell?"

"The septic tank has overflowed," Cynthia Armistead replied, thrusting a nervous hand through a thick shock of black hair. "It's been smelling like this all day."

"Migod…it's not even habitable with that smell! Where are the kids?"

"They're at the movies. I have to go pick them up in a minute."

"Well, did you call anybody?"

"Yes, I did. I got two estimates from our local septic tank contractors. The consensus is that we have a plugged drainfield that will cost anywhere from $500 to $5,000 to fix. They won't know until they start digging tomorrow."

Rex dropped suddenly onto the sofa and stared blankly out of the picture window at the ships passing on Puget Sound. His head was reeling, and he felt slightly nauseated. *If they built a bridge, would that mean the island would get a sewer system?* He heard his wife say something unintelligible in the distance that sounded like "I'm gonna go move now" before she left the house. The sky was lead gray and the light mist had turned to a drizzle. Water droplets dripped rhythmically from the edge of the roof overhang onto the freshly painted deck, and a couple of brown and yellow slugs nuzzled on the railing.

CHAPTER 3

On the same day that he received a bill from Skagit Septic Systems for $4,750, Rex got a letter in an official-looking envelope from the Skookum County Planning Department inviting him to become a charter member of the Skagit Island Governance Committee—an appointed panel of 10 islanders charged with the task of studying various forms of government for Skagit Island, including retaining the existing status as an unincorporated part of the county. He recognized most of the names of the other committee appointees as fellow members of IRATE.

"We used to call this co-optation in the 60s," Rex explained to Zack over coffee. "What do you suppose the county really has up its sleeve?"

"Hard to tell. This could be just a smokescreen to draw our attention away from the bridge. Having a bridge would only bring more tax revenue into the county. So something tells me there's folks in the county who'll stop at nothing to get this thing built."

"Yeah. Divide and conquer. We've got another six weeks before the state is supposed to decide on the bridge—long enough for people on the island to lose interest. I suppose the county figures if they could get the 'trouble-makers' interested in some kind of diversion like this, it might drain the energy out of the bridge opposition movement."

The waitress at the Dirty Dog Café returned to fill their cups. From under her mop of blonde hair, she gave Rex a double take.

"You look familiar to me," she said. "Were you at the bridge hearing at the high school the other day?"

"Yes. We're both part of the group that's fighting it."

"I thought so...my name is Allison. I'm an artist. If you need a logo or anything, I'd be happy to donate my time."

"Really?!" Rex and Zack eyed each other gleefully. "Matter of fact," Rex said, "we do need a logo. Where can we reach you?"

She handed him a business card with a broad smile. "Call me. I'm busy, but I'd like to help out any way I can."

"Hmmmm. One of the advantages of living in a small community," Rex mused.

Allison had a certain carefree way of swinging her hips that reminded Zack of his ex-wife. His eyes followed her for a moment, then gazed blankly out of the window. Rex slurped his coffee loudly. "So are you gonna join this government committee?" he asked.

Zack's eyes were ringed with a faint tinge of red as he looked at Rex.

"Yeah. I want to know what those bastards are doing so we can stay one step ahead of them."

"One thing I learned from living in California is how to wage guerrilla warfare with the government...how little it takes to gum up the gears of their system. A small group of people with a mission can question their motives and facts, cause procedural delays, demand more studies and generally jam the wheels of bureaucracy for years—to the point that sometimes projects just get abandoned."

"That's what we need from you—some of that experience. Most of us here on Skagit have been far too trusting of our elected officials for far too long. We've always assumed they were looking out for our best interests, but I think this bridge thing has shaken us out of *that* fantasy." Zack coughed and lit up a cigarette.

Rex left the Dirty Dog Café and drive directly to Lighthouse Point, on the east side of the island, a bent-knee shaped protrusion of land that juts sharply into Puget Sound. The old lighthouse was maintained in pristine condition and its huge lens still swept powerful flashes of light across the water to guide mariners, although it had been supplanted in recent years by the installation of a tall steel tower with a radar dish. The beach was soft, sandy and covered with chaotic driftwood sculptures. Rex walked northward where the trees sloped and slouched crazily over the edge of the embankment because of constant erosion, dodging the water-spouting geoducks on the rocky tideline and the tangled tree trucks on the other side. In the distance, jet aircraft circled as they approached the Seattle airport on the north end, and swooped with a takeoff roar into the gray air on the south end. Rex could also make out a small stretch of I-5 where commuter traffic was slowly and tediously moving into the city, whose skyscrapers rose defiantly into the gathering clouds. *Be fruitful and multiply.*

He tried to imagine a bridge spanning the sound. Rex had driven the Golden Gate Bridge, Bay Bridge, Chesapeake Bay Bridge Tunnel, George Washington and Brooklyn Bridges, but none of those would compare with the engineering miracle that would have to occur to bring a cross-sound bridge into existence. For one thing, it would need to be anchored solidly in bedrock more than 700 feet below the surface of the water. For another, it would need to be elevated in the center to allow maritime traffic passage. The supports would have to be widely spaced to allow sufficient berth for those large vessels to pass through with any degree of safety, which would create real problems of support for the structure. A suspension bridge was out of the question because of technical reasons. A floating bridge would never be considered because of Washington State's horrific record with floating bridges suddenly sinking. The whole purpose of the bridge was fast and unfettered transit from the mainland to the Kitsap Peninsula and the planned vacation golf resorts. A bridge that opened to allow ships through would slow traffic and hardly be worth the effort and expense, and yet that was the only kind of structure that had a chance of passing engineering standards. Rex drew a deep breath as he walked along the beach, then chuckled at the absurdity of the situation. But he knew that—given enough political pressure from developers—planning, engineering, safety and even common-sense considerations would be thrown out the window in a flash. So, even as ridiculous as the idea seemed, there was really no reason to give up or give in. The only alternative was to fight to the conclusion.

When did it first dawn on the Sammamish that they should fight the white man? Or did it ever dawn on them? When this island was home to a handful of displaced Mongolians from Central Asia who trekked across the Bering Straits, suffered in caribou skins down the whole western slope of North America on down into Canada, Washington, California, Mexico and all the way down to the tip of South America, what was there to fight except buffalo, caribou, reindeer and antelope? Would they have laid down this green gem in Puget Sound for a few silver bracelets and some whiskey? Will these white Europeans now lay down their island for the same things? Money can buy you anything—including men's souls, not to mention their land the future of their unborn generations. Why is it any different now, 100 years after the Sammamish?

As he walked off the beach, Rex noticed something glinting in the afternoon sun. His fingers reached instinctively for it and pulled it up closer to his eyes. It was a large, rounded agate. He held it up to the sun to be sure. The warm afternoon light shone through it brilliantly, and he stuffed it in his pocket with a sigh.

From his childhood in Piedmont, a primal memory sprang to his mind as he drew in deep draughts of the sea air. It was a chill autumn in his hometown, and his mother was several years into her second marriage to a deranged monster who hid rusty Arab daggers and loaded Army pistols in his closet and brandished them when he wanted to strike fear into Rex' pre-adolescent heart. Deep also into her alcoholism, his mother was all but blind to the ravages this beast visited upon not only Rex but his brother Charles and sister Millie. As the oldest, Rex received the brunt of this man's twisted rage because he bore his father's name—a name uttered like an oath, with pungent loathing, around his his household. In that chill autumn, Rex had signed up for a paper route with the Piedmont Dispatch because it got him out of the house in after-school hours when he was most likely to confront the monster who went by the sobriquet Boozoo, gave him some pocket change and a feeling (illusion) of independence. Fingers hammered into bloody spindles by the weight of paper stacks balanced on his bicycle by twine, Rex made his rounds each afternoon, enjoying the casual encounters with retired little old ladies and stay-at-home mothers, if not the occasional hostile loose dog. As part of that newspaper route, Rex passed each day by a large overgrown lot, snarled knee-deep in grasses, ivy, berries and bushes between the high sycamore and pine trees. This wild territory he designated "the Outback" and found his way around within it, whenever he had the time after delivering his papers. Rex had established a couple of secret entrances to this foreboding and lost piece of property, and had dragged a large section of plywood inside where he made a rough lean-to shelter. This was his sanctuary, his hiding place, where he could run or ride to escape the cruel violence of Wookie, that Marine Corps-warped, square-jawed deviant with booze-reddened nose and bloodshot eyes. The Outback was a land of mystery and romance, a place to hide from the world, and it belonged completely to Rex. So far as he knew, none of the other boys in the neighborhood ever ventured there because of the dense undergrowth, and he felt safe and protected there. But on that chill autumn afternoon, as he made his afternoon paper deliveries, Rex rounded the corner to discover the Outback completely swept away. All that remained was a muddy lot criss-crossed with tractor-trailer tracks, and two or three huge piles of debris. A sign in front of the lot proudly proclaimed "Another fine home under construction by Wilson & Watson Builders, Inc." Rex' heart stopped beating, and he dropped his load of papers in the street. The Outback was now nothing more than a memory. His safe haven had been taken away forever, and he had nowhere to hide. It was that same afternoon that Boozoo administered the cruelest, and last, beating he ever dealt to Rex before being sent to prison and divorced by his mother. And, as a final afterthought, his mother sent him to live with his father that summer and he never again saw Boozoo, the Outback or his red bicycle again.

But Rex carried inside him always the yearning for that haven, a place where kindness and gentleness could flourish, a place where violence was not allowed, a place where fear could not intrude. For many years he found that solace in alcohol and its calming euphoria, but that too only evaporated over time like the security of the Outback. His search continued into adulthood and through the writings of St. John of the Cross. Rumi, Thomas Merton, and Ecclesiastes, the musical ecstasies of John Coltrane, Sun Ra, Albert Ayler, Bird and Monk, and women who thought they understood or in many cases knew they understood and whom Rex understood he could take to bed, and through a thousand nights of writing poetry searching always searching for the word that would bring the spell cast the magic shudder the spine in sympathetic vibration with the universe. None of those came close to serenity and Rex continued his wandering into the cities of America with their din and dirt, neon-lit nights, steel monuments to greed and fouled air that choked the lungs as the food bled the body and spirit. New York, Boston, San Francisco, Phoenix, Denver, finally Seattle. Rex longed for the darkness of a country road at night in midwinter, stars shimmering in the clear dark sky, the cold clear air of the country and the sweet singing gurgle of a mighty river gnawing its way through the silent forest of night with a happy confidence. There was no city, no book, no music and not even any woman who could give that to him. No, nature alone could heal that open wound in his heart and it was unadorned nature that he wanted, desperately needed.

I get ahead by staying put. I enrich myself by giving to others. I make new discoveries by opening my eyes to the world around me. I discover God by going inside and entering the darkness. I escape the world by going through it. Four score and 10 are man's days on earth, and not a minute more. How long does it take to learn the lesson, hear the music, see the picture, become lost and then discovered? I sought you in a thousand places, O my Lord, and found you here in the dust of a winter afternoon. Found you in the black night sky, in the roar of the ocean and the heat of the sun.

And in the howling streets of the faceless city, where men clamor over each other like starving rats, I have heard your voice calling to me, saying:

This time, this world, this place will never last and all will pass into nothingness. It is not without considerable forethought and enormous compassion that your lives on earth are numbered, for you could not bear to know the final outcome of this world or the next. You are time-limited and space-bound because of your mortality, and will only know of the world beyond when you leave your mortal body and the world behind. Only in the faint shadows of color on a waning autumn afternoon, or in a snippet of faintly heard sweet music from some faraway place, or in the glow of your beloved's eyes can you glimpse the next world. But have faith and do not be afraid, for all things have been considered, and it is well. When you follow your heart, you follow me.

CHAPTER 4

"**D**o you remember me?" Cynthia Armistead squinted through the evening light at her husband as he approached the house. She was tall and bony in an aristocratic sort of way, plain but elegant with her sandy hair and green eyes—like an expensive but understated silver Bentley with red leather upholstery. Her friends at Vassar used to tease Cynthia by warning her not to close her bank account when she married Rex, for fear it would cause the town's economy to collapse. Old money, solid East Coast family. Understated sarcasm.

Rex lowered his head like a guilty child, and skulked slowly toward her. "Hi, dear. Sorry I'm late…I was talking to Zack and then I went for a walk on the beach. I guess I just lost track of the time." He gave Cynthia a gentle kiss on the cheek, and she sighed heavily.

"Do you want to tell the kids goodnight, while I warm up something for you to eat?" Her voice sounded weary, but conciliatory.

"That would be wonderful. Let me go and see them…I'll catch up with you in a minute."

After hugs, giggles, tickles and bedtime stories, Rex found Cynthia sitting alone at the kitchen table with a cigarette in one hand and a glass of wine in the other.

"When did you start smoking again?"

"About three minutes ago."

Rex fixed a sober gaze on Cynthia. "I wish you wouldn't."

"Well, I wish you wouldn't come home so late without ever telling me where you are or when you're returning."

He sat down next to her at the table, gently took the cigarette out of her hand and stamped it out. She looked at him with surprise, not anger, as if realizing by his action that he really did care about her. Rex kissed her on the lips, ignoring the musty tobacco scent of her mouth.

"I know I've been selfish lately. I've gotten so caught up in this bridge thing I've ignored my own wife. You are much more important to me than any bridge"

"Really?!" Cynthia arched her eyebrows in mock surprise.

"OK. I deserved that…thank you for making me aware of just how I've been treating you."

Cynthia pulled a plate of warm Mexican food from the oven and set it down in front of Rex. "Want some wine?"

"No, thanks."

"It looks like I'll be teaching an art class at the White Eagle," she said, pouring out a cup of hot coffee for Rex.

"Really? When did this happen?"

"It's been happening for the last three weeks, only you haven't been around to hear about it. The director called me today to say that there's an opening for someone to teach a watercolor class in the fall, and she's recommending me to the board. They're meeting tonight and I should know for sure tomorrow."

"That's terrific," Rex mumbled as he shoveled a very hot chili relleno into his mouth. "At least one of us has something remunerative to do!"

"How did the interview at DigiTek go?"

"Not very well. They want someone who is a real technical writer, which I'm not. You know, somebody who understands computers and can write owner's manuals…that sort of thing. Hell, I only graduated from a manual typewriter to a computer a few years ago. I

don't know squat about computers. Mmmmmmm....great chili relleno!"

"Well, I hope you find something soon so we can pay for the septic tank repairs."

Rex didn't hear a word she said, but gobbled all his food and went
for seconds. By the time he'd filled his plate, Cynthia had gone to
bed. He clicked on the evening news to witness a talking head from
one of the Seattle stations doing a "standup" about the looming
bridge battle at the Skagit ferry dock, where commuters raced to
catch their boats. The reporter was a young, smiling blonde woman
with perfect teeth and painfully obvious network ambitions. Her
story was upbeat, good-natured, saccharine. Rex turned off the television in disgust as he calculated the odds that a bunch of ragtags
from Skagit Island could actually prevail over the county planning
bureaucracy and the state transportation agency. His model for the
struggle ahead had been set by César Chavez in his successful efforts
to organize farm workers in California, against overwhelming political and economic odds, by a direct appeal to the consciences of con-
sumers. There was clearly no point in arguing ethics to bureaucrats,
but by shifting the focus of the bridge fight to an environmental
arena, public support was inevitable. Whether that would translate
into any sort of effective political power was still an open question.

"I know you think we're crazy for ever moving here," Rex mumbled as he climbed into bed. Cynthia mumbled softly, as if speaking
from a far distant planet. "We decided that it wouldn't be easy for a
while, but we were here to stay no matter what. If we can make it for
the first three years, then we're OK. This is probably the riskiest thing
either one of us has ever done, you know, but we decided we were in
this together. Once we're established here, in a few years we'll thank
our lucky stars..."

Rex realized that Cynthia was fast asleep, pulled the covers gently
over both of them and laid back quietly next to her warm, soft body
as rain steadily pelted the roof.

When Zack got home, half-tanked with beer, the lights were still on in the kitchen and he could hear his two renters holding an animated discussion. His stomach tightened as he entered the house and began his quest for some peace and quiet. Sally, the tall, weather-beaten redhead was standing near the refrigerator with a beer in her hand, gesturing as she spoke in a bombastic tone to Kevin, a slightly-built gardener and handyman who scratched his head sleepily under his tilted-back baseball cap. He bent forward in his chair as if paralyzed by fatigue, although obviously irritated by the verbal barrage that assaulted his ears. Sally was expounding about one of her house-cleaning clients who had a different theory of the monetary value of her work.

"Could you hold it down, I'm going to bed," Zack said wearily.

"We're just having a friendly little chat," Sally sallied. The set of her jutting jaw was confrontational.

"That's fine, if you can keep it down to a dull roar."

"We pay rent to live here. Why can't we talk when we want to?"

Zack pulled his shoulders back and set his dark eyes on the woman like a predator fixing a cold death gaze upon its prey. "I want you both moved out by the end of the month. I've decided I don't want to rent any more, and I want you both out of here no later than the last day of this month. Got it?"

He turned on his heels and stamped his feet loudly as he plodded his way upstairs to bed. "Who the hell does that bitch think she is?" he muttered as he threw his clothing down on the floor. "For a lousy two hundred a month, she thinks she owns the place!"

In his dreams, Zack floated on a warm sea atop a gently bobbing raft, adrift in golden sunshine and gentle ocean spray. For as far as the eyes and ears could reach, there was nothing but quiet, peace and beauty. The soft rocking of the raft seemed to melt his cares and worries away, and they arose heavenward with the evaporating sea mists.

Allison splattered the paint on her large canvas with great swoops of her hand, as the putty knife spread the gooey purple tint flat in the center and bulging at the edges. Here and there, she twisted the knife suddenly to give a different effect, sometimes going back over the same swatch again to lay down a deeper layer of paint. Her fingers were long and blonde, like the rest of her body, and they held the brush with a firm, loving grip. As they covered the canvas, her thoughts raced to Rex' eyes and held them in drenching sensuality. It was a feeling that had slowly crept up upon her. She'd resisted it at first, then acknowledged it for what it was, and finally recognized the hopelessness of her desire while deciding to exorcise herself of it by putting it down on canvas. This particular canvas, a wild symphony of colors and shapes, was "abstract" in the sense that Allison knew of no other way to express her chaotic feelings. And abstraction was surely the safest way to release them without clearly revealing their wellsprings.

Allison had married young and foolishly, like all artists. Her husband made a comfortable living as an importer of African fabric, and they had lived peacefully in Los Angeles until her daughter was three and was diagnosed with cystic fibrosis. Unable to face the prospect of years of sickness and an early death of his daughter, her husband escaped into the arms of another woman. Unable to accept her husband's unfaithfulness, Allison divorced, returned to school to earn her master's degree in fine arts, and took a teaching position at UCLA. When her daughter graduated from community college, Allison sold her house and moved to Skagit Island, sight unseen. During winter months, she spent much of her time in Los Angeles teaching and schmoozing with gallery owners. But during the golden summers on Puget Sound, Allison reveled in the delights of her Skagit Island studio and supplemented her income with occasional stints at the Dirty Dog Cafe.

"Jeeezus," she mumbled as her hands worked over the canvas. "I should start seeing that shrink again if I can get this screwed up over some married guy. Get a grip, girl! I gotta be nuts for even thinking I need a man in the first place. And that Dr. Bleeker, whoa! That's another devil in a pair of trousers. I must be having a second adolescence or something."

As she talked under her breath, her eyes grew wild with excitement like a kid trying to burn fleas on a dog's belly with a magnifying glass. Her fingers worked faster and the paint built up into deeper gullies and higher peaks. If anyone had walked suddenly into her studio at this moment, they would have assumed Allison was possessed by the devil and was trying to perform some sort of self-exorcism. She paused for a moment, and stepped back from the roiling canvas. Then her eyes lit up mischievously. In the upper left corner, she painted a small suspension bridge, spinning eerily in space.

"This one's for Mr. Armistead!"

Zack fought his way out of sleep to answer the telephone in the orange sunlight of the Skagit dawn, muttering under his breath about the mess left overnight in the kitchen.

"The State Transportation Commission has slipped the bridge item on their agenda for Thursday's meeting," Rex announced abruptly. "I got an anonymous telephone tip from someone in the state bureaucracy this morning. We need to be there in force. Can you drive up to Olympia with me?"

Zack scratched his head. "On the agenda? For what?"

"They're gonna decide whether to approve the goddamn thing…in secret."

"Jesus! Yes, of course I'll go with you. We need to get a lot of people there."

On the way to Olympia, Zack lit up one of his Cuban cigars, which made Rex feel nauseated. But he didn't want to protest because he valued Zack's friendship and he knew this rough-hewn man could be very useful in carrying the political message in a way that he—a recent transplant—could never be. Rex rolled the window all the way down and stuck his face into the airstream.

"Wassamatter boy? This stogie too much for you?" Zack laughed heartily.

Rex coughed, and gagged. "I'm...I'm just not used to it."

Zack rolled down his window, and tossed the cigar butt into a puddle on the side of the road. "Damn good cigar."

"You didn't have to do that for me," Rex lied.

Zack smiled sheepishly. "If I'd have quit sooner, I might still be married."

They drove on in silence while Rex cleared his lungs and tried to quiet his roiling stomach. "If we were smart, we'd support the bridge and then go into the tourist business," Rex said breezily, trying to recover his equilibrium.

"You better take a few more deep breaths before we get to Olympia," Zack said. "No more smoke-filled rooms for you!"

They found the State Transportation Commission meeting tucked away in a dim crevice of the Capitol, in a small meeting room with seats only for a half-dozen people. But Skagit Islanders crowded the room, practically looking over the shoulders of the commissioners as they began their deliberations with expressions of shock and amazement crossing their faces, as if unaccustomed to conducting their business exposed to public scrutiny. A lengthy discussion of the engineering feasibility studies of a cross-sound bridge ensued, droning on until the lunch break without so much as any acknowledgment that members of the public wished to be heard on the issue. Commissioners filed back into the cramped room later to confront an irate bunch of islanders.

"When is the public hearing?" came a shouted challenge from the back.

"We can't afford to sit around here all day...we want to be heard!"

Reluctantly, the commission opened the hearing and listened for an hour to the objections of islanders then voted unanimously to approve the next phase of engineering studies for construction of the bridge—a far bolder move than had ever been taken in the 40 years the state had entertained the idea of a bridge.

"Jesus! This would never happen in California," Rex sputtered. "How can they get away with this? In California, they would already be defending themselves in court over the environmental impact report. I remember when the City of Carmel kept a big land development in Carmel Valley tied up in court for years just over a defective hydrology report."

"This isn't California," Zack answered sullenly.

Before driving back to Skagit, they stopped at a roadside espresso stand and sat in the front seat of Zack's pickup truck, sipping their coffee.

"One thing that has been bothering me since I moved here is how much people here seem to resent Californians," Rex mused. "I mean, I'd heard about it before I moved here but I never imagined that it was so pervasive. I guess I thought it was a case of Northwesterners just being closed to newcomers, or something." Rex paused and noticed that Zack was nodding faintly, but steadily, to his cadence.

"But it's almost impossible to get a job here, the prejudice is so thick you can just feel it when you enter the room, and I've even heard people discussing 'Why don't they all just go back to California?' when I'm waiting for the ferry. I mean, I'm not a native Californian or anything, but what the hell! I thought this was a free country. Did it ever occur to any of these lumberjacks that maybe people from California will help develop their economy, that maybe they have a few ideas they could use…?"

Zack jerked his head back abruptly, and fixed his liquid blue eyes on him.

"It's not that," he said softly. "We've just seen so many people come up here with so much money and buy all these expensive houses, then get some low-wage job. The sell their homes in Los Angeles, then buy some waterfront property here and live for a few years on what's left over. I think a lot of people resent it because it seems unfair. And, of course, they do use the roads, sewers, schools, ferries."

Rex sipped his coffee again, slowly.

"I think my experience in dealing with land development in California can be very useful here. I've seen some of the tricks they can pull, and maybe I can help us to avoid getting screwed."

"Maybe you can."

When they reached the Chimacum ferry dock at the southern end of the island, they waited in line to board while a snorting diesel lumber truck rumbled off the ferry and up the hill with its payload of freshly-cut spruce and cedar, a few unmolested green leaves still clinging to the massive trunks.

"Looks like we may already be too late to save the island," Rex sighed.

They drove in silence up the leafy Skagit Highway that winds around Quarterdeck Harbor with its neatly painted sailboats and above Motherskill Beach. A light rain started to coat the windshield and the road, making both slick and shiny in the oncoming headlights. When Zack pulled up into Rex' driveway, he leaned toward him with a broad smile.

"Wanna go fishin' tomorrow?"

Rex looked at the rain and wind whipping the tree limbs, and pulled his collar over his neck. "Sure! What time?"

"I'll pick you up in the morning about 8."

"OK, pal. See you then."

The weather-beaten lorry that Zack's rusty trailer dragged behind his battered blue four-wheel drive personal assault vehicle was cause for alarm. Because it hadn't been painted in what seemed a century, the caulking between the planks was hanging out like the innards of a party-whipped piñata. There were a few remaining flecks of paint here and there, evidence that the craft had once been painted ochre.

In general, the lorry was like Zack—worn, battered and of dubious reliability. But, also like Zack, it had a certain rough charm that was inviting, if not reassuring.

"Ever been out fishing in this thing before?" Rex said.

With a hurt look on his cowboy face, Zack managed a limp smile. "What do you mean, have I ever been out? This boat is my salvation. I go as often as I can and get all kinds of fish. I've had it for 15 years and never did any repairs. I'm afraid if I took a hammer to it, my luck would turn."

Rex stared blankly at the lorry, wondering just how long *his* luck would hold.

Propelled by a sputtering five horsepower Johnson, they reached the middle of Puget Sound where they were bounced by the wakes from passing ferries and cargo ships.

Zack cut the engine and started rifling through his tangle of fishing tackle, with wind-hardened fingers that were both clumsy and nimble. He placed a limp squid on the burnished aluminum top of the cooler and sliced it quickly with a hunting knife, lancing the pieces with a rusty fishhook and tossing his line overboard with a casual backhand. Then he did the same for Rex' line, opened the cooler and pulled out a couple of cold beers.

"Here ya go, pal." Zack tossed one to Rex and opened his, swigging down a hearty draft as the cold rain pelted his face. Then he pulled the hood of his parka over his head and lit a cigarette, sighing heavily as he exhaled a thin plume of smoke. "We may have missed the tide, but we'll see what happens anyway."

Rex normally found cigarette smoke repugnant, but for some reason on this wet, frigid morning in the middle of Puget Sound it was pleasant and reassuring. He placed the unopened beer carefully beside his seat and tugged on his line. "What do you suppose we'll catch?"

"Pneumonia," Zack snorted, then broke out into a belly laugh.

As they rocked peacefully in the boat, Rex remembered fishing with his grandfather on Carter's Creek in the Chesapeake Bay, anchoring the boat and swimming over the side in the warm salt water. The terror of what lay below, waiting to swoop up and attack his feet, legs, belly had kept Rex swimming frantically about, always close to the boat so he could scamper aboard if danger struck. Whereas the depth of the water when he fished with his grandfather had been about 30 feet, here it was something like 600 feet, and Rex sat up straight as the realization dawned. He felt a tug on his line, and yanked it vigorously.

"Pull it in! Pull it in!" Zack yelled.

As the end of his line appeared at the surface of the water, Rex could make out a huge crab hanging from one claw. As he gave the line a final jerk, the crab released its grip and quickly disappeared into the murky depths.

"Damn! Couple of those and we'd have our dinner."

"That's the hard way to get crabs," Zack commiserated.

As he turned to bait his line again, Rex noticed a rainbow-hued film glistening atop the slush of seawater in the hull of the boat. And the pungent smell of gasoline wafted past his nostrils.

"I think we may have a problem," Rex said, pointing to the gas tank.

Zack immediately flipped his cigarette into the sound and sniffed. "That don't seem right," he snorted, as he wrestled with the rubber fuel line that connected the tank with the rusty outboard engine. He quickly pumped the pressure gauge, then threw the hose back down into the boat in anger.

"Shit! We got ourselves a gas leak, and most of the tank is now sloshing around in our boat. And I didn't bring any kind of tape, either!"

"What do you need tape for?"

"To tape the gas line so's it don't leak while we go back in. We got no pressure in the tank, either, so the engine can't get what gas we do have. We're fucked."

Rex remembered his grandfather's red face as he wrapped his starter rope around the flywheel on his old outboard engine, cranking it endlessly in the hot summer sun until it finally started. He remembered, too, pumping the pressure on the gas tank that supplied the engine.

"What if I hold the gas line tight with my hands so it doesn't leak and keep pumping the pressure, while you steer us in?" he offered.

Zack ran an oil-smeared hand quickly through his hair. "OK. It's worth a try."

Rex squeezed the split section of rubber fuel hose as tightly together as he could, while Zack pumped up the pressure. When there was resistance to the pump, he quickly started the engine and headed for Skagit Island. They had stopped the boat somewhere near the middle of Puget Sound, but winds and currents had carried them a mile or more further out since they started their fishing expedition. It was anyone's guess whether they had enough gas, since the fuel gauge on the tank had never worked anyway. But Rex held the severed fuel line as tightly as he could, occasionally reaching with one hand down to work the pump. He could feel the cold gasoline oozing out onto his fingers and smell the fumes. The engine ran smoothly and they were grateful for the cold rain that pelted their faces, as they raced against time for the island.

Eventually the mouth of Quarterdeck Harbor opened ahead of them, and they shot each other knowing glances. Rex' hands were cramped and sore, and he was sorry he'd ever agreed to go out on Puget Sound in Zack's lorry. But he kept pumping and squeezing and the boat kept going, somehow. Finally they were within sight of the dock and the engine sputtered briefly, but continued to hum. When the boat was no more than 10 feet from the dock, the engine abruptly died and they both let out an ear-splitting shriek, pumping their fists skyward in defiance and exhilaration, as the lorry coasted nicely into the dock where Rex jumped off and secured a bow line. Then Zack climbed off and tied up the stern. They stood on the dock in the rain for a second, stunned at the miracle they'd just witnessed. Then they embraced and hugged each other heartily.

"Damn! That boat must lead a charmed life!" Rex said.

"Like I said, it's never let me down before. Guess it's time for a new gas line."

"Awww...I wouldn't spend your money frivolously. Just get some duct tape and wrap that sucker up!"

They shared a laugh and the fellowship of the delivered.

*R*ecovered from the cold and damp, Rex rifled through his bookshelf looking for a slim paperback on the fishes of Puget Sound, when his fingers came across a red covered, hardbound volume that had been his grandfather's—"Robert E. Lee: Man and Soldier." One of a collection of Civil War books published in the early 1930s, this publication had been a favorite of Frank Armistead, MD, and Rex thumbed through its still-pristine pages marveling at the high quality of the paper and the photographic reproductions. The book somehow conveyed the sense that the Confederate cause was too just and too fine for this world, that defeat was nothing more than the triumph of the many over the few. As Rex replaced the book, he gasped suddenly. *Secession. Our own government. Our own land use decisions. No bridges. Skagit Island takes control over its own destiny!*

The thought was like the first slug of tequila on a hot summer afternoon. Rex paced around in circles for a moment as the full implications of the idea seeped down through his cortex, intoxicating him. The organizational structure was already in place in the form of IRATE, and the motivation clearly was also in place because of the threatened bridge. There was no time to waste in floating the idea with other islanders.

Rex called the county elections department and learned the particulars of government by petition—a minimum of 1,478 signatures of registered voters would be required within 90 days of the start of the petition process. The petition itself would merely be a request that the county place the issue of self-government on the ballot for islanders to decide. An actual election, if forced by petition, was at least a year away. Undaunted, he quickly made a list of names of people likely to help gather signatures. At the top of the list, naturally, was Zack.

"Personally, I think you're nuts," Zack said. "But I guess I owe you one for getting us in safely the other day."

"Good. We have to get over to the elections department tomorrow, pick up the paperwork and kiss some bureaucrats' asses. You up for that?"

"Everything except the ass kissing. It wouldn't make any difference anyway. They don't care about Skagit Island."

"I'll bet they'll care about us once we get the signatures and file for an election."

"They just care about the tax revenues from the island."

"That's right…and that's exactly how we're gonna get this thing passed. By demonstrating that we can operate our own island government more efficiently than the county."

"We need to do some homework, and we need to get the other IRATE people to help us. Why don't we call a meeting when we get back with the papers?"

"Great idea! Strike while the iron is hot, and all."

The White Eagle Arts Center, as the oldest community arts organization in Washington State, was dedicated to maintaining its long tradition of promoting artists from Skagit Island—regardless of their artistic merits. Noble in its objectives, the White Eagle often found itself in the position of declining a show by a nationally-known Seattle abstractionist in favor of an exhibit by an islander who welded together garden trowels, chains and shovels to fashion fanciful animals suitable for decorating flower beds. Thus the center became an agent for perpetuating a comfortable insularity within the arts community on Skagit, and its board members frequently wrung their hands in despair because art critics from the Seattle daily newspapers could not be lured into giving White Eagle exhibits space in their columns.

Having completed six new canvases, Allison arranged for a one-woman exhibit in the cramped gallery space originally designed as a meeting room in the Skagit Grange Hall before it was converted into the White Eagle Arts Center. Located on Skagit Highway just south of town, the gallery was open weekends so visitors from off-island could browse and occasionally purchase original art works at prices considerably less than those asked in Seattle galleries. Friends and fellow artists packed into the gallery for the artist's reception, feeding on whole-wheat crackers and tart white wine. "Discoveries" was the sufficiently vague name she picked for her collection of canvases, to disguise its patently erotic origins.

The new paintings were arrayed sequentially on one wall, displayed with single names such as "Bart," "Will," "Timothy," and "Phydoe." They were great splashes of vivid colors—oranges, yellows, whites—abstract in their conception and arresting in their presentation. Simply as decoration, the canvases would delight even the most jaded eye and bring cheer into any rain-saturated soul. Allison's erotic intent would remain, she hoped, merely her own secret as these vivid paintings found their way into people's living rooms and offices.

On another wall were Allison's masks—large, leering primal faces from the id that represented her attempt to capture Jung's theory of the collective unconscious. Some were totemic and tribal, wrapped in rough swatches of leather, with smaller obscene heads that protruded out of a larger face where a nose would normally rest. Others were absurdly self-satisfied, smiling countenances that looked like various hallucinatory states passed through on an LSD trip. She worked intensely with copper and kiln-fired ceramics to give these masks a disturbingly battle-ready aspect.

Rex strolled through the cramped crowd, trying to get a glimpse of the masks, when he felt a friendly nudge from behind. He turned to encounter a broadly beaming Allison with a glass of wine in her hand.

"What do you think?"

"Very nice," he said. "But who's 'Phaeton Alice'?"

"That's me! I've changed my name. Do you like it?" She wagged her blonde hair and smiled rakishly.

"Yeah…I do. Uh, where did you get the name? Are you hiding out?"

"No, not hiding out. Phaeton was my mother's maiden name, and Alice is just a variation on Allison. I thought it was time for a change," she said with the offhandedness of a precocious and willful child. "I may change it again if I don't like it."

Rex raised his cup of coffee and took a long gulp in silence. "I had no idea you were so versatile. Is this your first exhibit?"

"Oh, heavens no! I've had tons of them in LA, but this is my first one here on the island. This gallery space sucks."

"Well, I suppose they do the best they can with what they have. Like most of us."

"Can I have a ride home when you leave?" Allison moved closer to Rex. "My car is on the fritz and I got a ride here but don't have any way to get home."

"Yeah, but don't you think you should stick around?"

"Right. But if you're still here in about an hour I'd sure appreciate it."

"That's a deal," Rex offered, immediately wondering how he could entertain himself for an hour. When Allison moved away to talk to some other guests, Rex slipped off to buy a boating magazine from the supermarket and read it in his parked car until the appointed hour. There were the same ads for hydroplane kits, plans for racing sailboats, and specialized brass racing propellers that could soup up any workhorse outboard to the ferocity of a Mercury Quicksilver racing engine that he'd encountered when he was a teenaged boy with his first boat on the Chesapeake Bay. He could see his father on that hot August afternoon walking down the dock with the stubby package in his hands from the Michigan Wheel Company containing the two-bladed, high-pitch racing prop he'd ordered for his 15th birthday present. The heavy-duty brass weighed like lead in his hands, and was covered with a veneer of industrial grease. It was easy enough to remove the standard, three-bladed aluminum prop from the 12-horsepower Johnson outboard he'd managed to talk his grandfather out of. Then the dazzling new prop slipped on with tight precision. A turn of a cotter pin transformed his lightweight run-about into a hotrod of the bay, pouncing in great sprays of sea foam past lumbering sailboats and even other outboards. The engine took on a high-pitched drone as it revved up to its maximum capacity, and his little plywood craft skimmed the waters at upwards of 45 miles per hour. Once he added grain alcohol to the fuel mixture and thrilled as the engine roared even louder, pushing his boat up to 50 m.p.h. and giving him dreams of entering the Labor Day races at Indian Creek. Those dreams were shattered when his car—a 1949 Dodge—broke its transverse axle while stuck in the sand at Fisherman's Bay and he had to sell his boat to finance a new car. Ever since those lost boyhood days, Rex had fantasized now and then about building his own hydroplane someday. The clean sturdiness of fresh wood cut, glued and screwed into tight formation as the hull of his new racing boat took shape would ease all the slings and arrows of the world. That moment, if ever it arrived, would be more precious than any woman or any bank account he could ever imagine. As he closed the pages of the magazine and looked off wistfully into the black night, Rex wanted nothing more than to be that teenaged boy with his shiny new brass racing prop on that hot August afternoon, his heart filled with joy and his life drenched with sunshine.

He tossed the magazine in the back seat of his car and drove back to the White Eagle, where the guests were still declaiming in loud voices as they moved past the exhibit. As he entered, he was met with a wall of stale, warm air from the compacted bodies inside the cramped, airless space and he felt dizzy. Allison appeared from the crowd, took him by the hand and led him quickly outside into the cool darkness.

"I have to get out of there! Those people are driving me nuts." Her voice had a truly frantic edge that alarmed Rex.

"Just to show you what a nice guy I am, I've waited all this time to give you a ride home. My wife probably wonders where the hell I am."

"Well just zip me home and then hurry back to your house as quick as you can. Want me to call her and tell her that you're on the way?"

"No, I don't think that would be a particularly good idea."

They drove in silence down a winding, tree-overgrown side road to Allison's house. The silver moonlight cast a thin veneer of magic over the rusted, abandoned farm equipment in the field next to her studio. They sat in the car, surrounded by the silent field, the brooding trees and the luminous moonlight. Allison leaned toward Rex, put her lips on his for a second or two longer than just "thank you," opened the door and walked inside. As he drove back to the highway, the warm yellow lights inside her house reached out to him like the aroma of bread baking in a winter oven. He drove home in a stupor, like a man mortally wounded.

CHAPTER 6

❦

Creepy little bastards look like Martians with their hair all dyed and sticking up. Before the fuckers expect anyone to follow their program they oughta get a job and see what the world is all about. They're against capitalism, globalism, corporations, pollution and they'll tell you in no uncertain terms while they puff on a cigarette and drink a diet cola. If they really wanted to do something revolutionary, why don't they all tell the tobacco companies to take a flying fuck? The lazy little buttholes don't know what work is, or even capitalism for that matter. They can't even read and write, but they want to stop the spread of American ways all over the world. They go into Seattle and raise hell, smashing windows, throwing shit in the streets, lighting fires—for what? So their mommies will see them on the tube and feel the need to nurture them some more? What the flaky bastards is a swift kick in the ass. The creeps.

Zack's face contorted with anger as he pushed his lawn mower around the yard and contemplated Rex' suggestion that they enlist young "activists" to help in the petition campaign. He was so absorbed in thought that he didn't notice Allison approach through the driveway and stand in the middle of the yard—until he was practically on top of her. Zack jerked back, killed the engine, wiped his sweaty forehead with the sleeve of his shirt and exhaled with relief.

"Damn! You could give a guy a heart attack."

"Sorry. I just wanted to come right over and give you the news. Apparently the state Supreme Court has ruled that the Growth Management Act does allow for the creation of some new incorporated areas in Skookum County. Rex went over to town to get a copy of the ruling, but he wanted me to give you the word. So I guess this is one more reason to push really hard on the petitions."

Zack plunked himself down in the freshly mowed grass. His green eyes sparkled against his sunburned freckles.

Allison bent over him, searching his eyes. He couldn't help noticing her silken breasts dangling inside her sleeveless blouse. "There's more," she said. "I think we've found the perfect person to help organize our teenage helpers. He's the son of a friend of mine"

Zack rolled his eyes back in his head.

"Can you come over to my car and meet Seymour?"

"Seymour?!"

She took him by the hand and led him out of the sun to the patch of shade where she'd parked. In the front seat a lanky young man with close-cropped hair and horn-rimmed spectacles was absorbed in *The Atlas of North American Butterflies*. Allison rapped on the top of the car to get his attention. Seymour lowered his book, startled.

"Seymour, this is Zack Beale. Zack, please meet Seymour Creighton," she said politely. Seymour thrust his hand out of the window to greet Zack, who tried awkwardly to execute a handshake. *Limp-wristed sissy. This oughta be good.*

"So, what are you reading there?" Zack inquired.

Seymour put his book on the dashboard and slowly climbed out of the car. When he stood erect, the youth was a few inches taller than Zack—but thin and reedy. His eyes, enlarged by thick glasses, peered owlishly about.

"Did you know that the habitats for 67 species of birds, 24 species of butterflies, 12 mammalian species and eight species of reptiles could be wiped out if the bridge is built?" he asked, ignoring Zack's question. "The birds include the blue heron, red woodpecker, and pheasant. Some of the mammals include the otter and muskrat. They really don't have any reason to like humans, I guess."

Zack shot a puzzled look at Allison.

"Seymour is kind of an expert on local ecology," she said, trying to fill in the spaces. "He's president of the Skagit Island Junior Audubon Society and is organizing a branch of the Sierra Club at the high school. Isn't that just incredible?"

Seymour was once again encouraged. "That bridge would use 397, 450 cubic tons of concrete and 1.7 million tons of steel girders," he continued obliviously. "It would require 200,000 man hours for construction and would cost approximately $500 million—assuming that the contractors didn't run over budget, then there's the insurance costs and…"

"Wait a minute," Zack burst in. "Are we gonna stand here all day citing facts and figures or get to work organizing some petition signing?"

Seymour gulped down his words. His eyes seemed to blaze with fright behind his thick glasses.

"I, uh…there's just so much to consider," Seymour stammered. "I already have some other kids lined up at school to help. I just thought you'd like to know about how bad this bridge would be."

Allison smiled approvingly. "Seymour was telling me on the way over here that he's already got—what, a dozen?—students who've volunteered to help," she intervened with a motherly tact. "I think that's terrific!"

"Yeah, that's great," Zack agreed, aware once again of his own clumsiness. "I guess we'd better get some petitions to circulate. Come on inside and I'll find them."

They followed him into his messy house and sat down in the kitchen.

"Want some lemonade?"

Zack placed a chilled carton of lemonade on the table and rummaged around in the cabinet for clean glasses. Seymour picked up the lemonade and studied the label.

"Hmmmm…water, sucrose, dextrose, artificial flavoring, preservatives. Don't see any lemons anywhere in here."

"Well, I'm sure it will be refreshing," Allison said *sotto voce*, removing the carton from his hands and replacing it on the table before Zack could notice. "Let's try to be polite."

Seymour once again assumed the hypervigilant, wide-eyed stare of an owl in daylight.

"Here's about 25 petitions to get you started." Zack thumped a wad of legal sized papers on the table, as Allison poured him a glass of lemonade. "Only thing is, I'm not sure whether we can let kids circulate these things, legally."

"I'm 18 years old, if that's what you mean," Seymour said. Most of the students who are interested in helping are also 18. Do you want me to call the county elections department and check on that?"

"Yeah," Zack sighed. "That would be fine. I just want to make sure we're legal so's all our work doesn't get thrown out just when we think we're OK."

"Seymour is very responsible," Allison added, with a wink.

"During the French Revolution, 6,355 people were guillotined," Seymour said abstractly. "Currently there are 3,816 people awaiting execution on Death Row in the United States. In Finland, the death penalty is levied against drunk drivers, and in some parts of Africa…"

Allison stood up abruptly. "Perhaps we'd better be going now."

Zack shot her another sideways glance, then led them silently out to their car. The sun was hotter and he'd lost all motivation to continue cutting the grass. As they drove off, he scratched his head wearily.

The island was in full summer bloom. Thickets of blackberries lined the sides of the road, punctuated by purple lupines and white sweet pea blossoms. Crows swarmed and cawed wildly everywhere, as if they owned the place. And the days were long and sunny, suffusing every living thing with energy and drive.

"I like the way you know so many things," Allison said, placing one hand on Seymour's leg as she drove. He looked puzzled. "Do you read a lot?"

"Sometimes. Why are you putting your hand on me?"

"Because I like you."

"That's funny."

"Do you have a girlfriend, Seymour?"

"No, do you?"

Allison cackled, and moved her hand slowly up his leg.

"What are you doing this afternoon? What to come and help me in my studio?"

"Help you with what?"

"I could use some help moving canvases around, just getting my studio organized. What do you say? I'll pay you, if you'd like."

"How much?"

"Mmmmm…how about $10 an hour?"

"OK. But I can only stay until 4 because we're having a Sierra Club meeting this afternoon."

"That's OK…we can work fast."

Seymour opened his butterfly book and buried his face inside it.

When Rex reached the Skagit ferry dock, he noticed two teenagers in iridescent yellow vests canvassing the waiting motorists with petitions. One had a bumper sticker plastered on the back of his vest: "Free Skagit Island." A cursory glance as he drove past in a convoy of cars exiting the ferry seemed to indicate a receptiveness on the part of drivers, or else it was just relief from the boredom of sitting in line and waiting for the next ferry. Either way, the petition circulators were smiling and enjoying themselves, which seemed to bode well. He drove on through town in he bright sunlight, even though it was

8:30 in the evening. As he drove up to his house, he sensed something strange: the front porch light was on but the inside of the house seemed still and empty. And Cynthia's car was nowhere in sight. *Probably took the kids to a movie, or up to the malt shop.*

He strained to lift an enormous pile of papers from the back seat of the Volvo station wagon, and precariously balanced them under his chin as he made his way to the door, which he wrestled open with one finger dangling down like a bad circus act. Once inside, he plopped the pile down on a hair juxtaposed with the front doorway. Rex wiped his had across his brow and scored a cold beer from the refrigerator before sitting down at the kitchen table to sort through the mail. A note in Cynthia's hand jumped immediately into his line of vision.

"R—Dinner is in the fridge, just pop in the oven. I've decided to take the kids and go back to visit my folks for a while. I need some time to myself to think things through. Please do not try to contact me. I will call you when I'm ready. Take care of yourself.—Cyn."

Rex swilled the cold beer in great gulps, put the bottle down on the table and read the note again and again. He pictured Cynthia packing the car, loading the kids inside and hastily scrawling the note. He swiped his had angrily at the pile of papers, and they scattered all across the floor. Then, exhausted and remorseful, Rex put his head down on the table and wept like an abandoned child.

"I ain't signin' any petition 'cause it'll just raise taxes." The blue-haired granny waved her arthritic arm dismissively as she approached Zack outside the supermarket, where he stood in the doorway with his clipboard and petitions.

"No ma'am, signing the petition doesn't cost anything. The only thing signing the petition does is let islanders vote on whether we want our own government. Then the county has to put the issue on the ballot—and *then* we vote."

"Don't trust none of them politicians anyway," she croaked. "Besides, what's wrong with staying in the county?"

"I'm sure you're aware that the state is trying to build a bridge between the island and the mainland?" Zack said politely.

"Oh, they'll never build that stupid thing! Costs too much money. This has come up every few years for as long as I've lived here on Skagit Island, and they ain't built it yet. What makes you think they're gonna build it now?"

"Well, this time there's a lot of money pushing it through—some of it from out of the country. There's a lot of political pressure to get this built, and there's nobody to stand up for us. Besides, we've studied the issue of taxes and found we could actually provide the same services as the county for about the same cost—maybe a little less—if we set up our own government. And we'd have self-determination, the right to decide ourselves what gets built and what doesn't."

"Nah, I ain't signin' any petition. Anyway, I ain't even a registered voter."

"I can take care of that right now, ma'am," Zack said with a smile.

"Nope…see you later." And the crusty little woman waddled off briskly to her car.

Zack rifled through his sheaf of papers. *Ten signature in an hour ain't too bad. At this rate, it will only take three years before we get enough names…*

A thin young woman in loose-fitting clothes, beaded necklaces and long curly brown hair approached. Her bright blue eyes caught notice of Zack, and she immediately headed in his direction.

"What's going on?" she asked with a slightly devilish grin.

"I'm collecting—or trying to collect—signatures on a petition to put the question of independence for the island on the ballot. Do you know about the recent efforts by the state to build a bridge…?"

"Where do I sign?"

She executed her name in great swirls of script that Zack couldn't decipher. But when she printed it, her name was easy to read: "Sally Smyth."

"I'm so upset with the county and its parochial attitude toward this island! I'd do anything to get them out of our lives. Thanks for doing this." She smiled sweetly, winked at Zack then turned and walked into the grocery store leaving behind a faint whiff of patchouli.

Those hippie chicks just break my heart. They're so sweet and kind. Too bad they weren't around when I was younger. Zack shook his head in bewilderment and longing.

Another small-framed woman with silver-gray hair approached, but this one was dressed stylishly and seemed to know her own mind. She emerged from a tan Jaguar coupe and strode confidently across the parking lot. When she noticed Zack, she turned and reached for a petition to sign. As she affixed her name, Zack remembered—Cerise Bagoth.

"How are you recovering from your injuries?"

She squinted at Zack behind her dark glasses.

"Well, I'm better…do I know you?"

"Yes, ma'am. I'm the fellow who pulled you out of your burning car a few months ago when you had that nasty accident."

Cerise gasped, then threw her small arms around his large frame. There were tears in her eyes.

"I've been meaning to thank you, Mr…?"

"Beale—Zack Beale."

"Forgive me for not contacting you sooner. I've just been in so much pain until recently. This is God's will—that we should meet like this. I'm so incredibly grateful to you for saving my life!"

"I'm so glad that you are OK." Zack shuffled his feet awkwardly.

"So now you're involved in this battle, huh? I've been reading about your group in the papers, and I totally agree with what you're trying to do. In fact, if I were younger and stronger I'd be there fighting with you."

"Yes ma'am."

"Well, you are very modest. I want to make a cash contribution. To whom should I send it, Mr. Zack Beale?"

"That's very kind of you…we could certainly use the support. You could contact Rex Armistead. He's the head of our group. I can give you his telephone number."

Cerise smiled wisely. "I believe I know Mrs. Armistead through the White Eagle Arts Center. I will look them up and write a check this week. And thank you again!"

"My pleasure…and thank you for signing our petition."

Zack trudged home, sipped some cool iced tea and counted the signatures. When he reached 200 and was still counting, he picked up the phone to Rex the good news. After getting no answer, he jumped into his Jeep and headed to Rex' house. As he knocked on the door, he could hear music coming from inside but no one answered. Finally, he forced the door open and stepped inside.

"Rex? Rex?"

Except for the strangely disconnected music from a radio in another room, the house was deathly still. Zack walked slowly into the living room, then back into the hall and headed for the kitchen. As he turned into the kitchen, he jumped with fright at the sight of Rex sprawled out of the floor, face down in a pool of vomit. On the table, on the floor and on the counter were beer bottles—some empty, some half-full, some overturned. Zack bent over him and gently shook his shoulder. Rex made a faint gurgling sound in his throat. Then Zack pulled Rex completely over so he was face-up, and shook him harder.

"Rex! Anybody home in there?"

Once again, Rex gurgled and moaned. Zack noticed, though, that he was breathing.

"Shit!" Zack picked up the phone and called 911 for emergency ambulance service, and set about cleaning up the mess on the kitchen floor. The ambulance crew slapped an oxygen mark on Rex' face, a blood pressure cuff on one arm, and an IV tube in the other—then hurried off to the Seattle Regional Trauma Center. Once they'd left, Zack sat down at the table to catch his breath and found the note from Rex' wife. "Shit!" he said, as he balled it up and tossed it into the garbage.

CHAPTER 7

✿

*R*ex lingered in the limbo of unconsciousness for nearly a week. Always cautious in their prognosis and careful in their choice of words, the neurologists wouldn't say whether he was likely ever to regain consciousness—or recover normal functioning if he did. Allison and Zack came to the hospital and sat beside him, talking among themselves, sometimes speaking directly to him about recent developments in the petition drive.

"We have more than 300 signatures already, and we've just started, Allison said brightly. "The high school students are working really hard."

"We should be getting a donation from this woman that I pulled out of her burning car after an accident," Zack said. "A big one!"

Rex moved his lips silently, but said nothing. Zack and Allison gave each other a pained look and left the hospital. They drove in silence to the ferry dock, and did not speak until the boat had almost reached the island.

"Did you know that his wife left him?" Zack said.

"No. I'm surprised to hear that."

"Found a note from her in his house. That's what started all this."

"Think so?"

"What do you think?"

"Well, I'm not sure. Not everybody whose wife leaves them, drinks themselves into a coma."

"Well it doesn't much matter unless he snaps out of this, I guess."

"The only thing that matters is whether he decides to get sober and stay that way—if he survives."

"You seem to know something about this."

"Yeah, I guess so. I'm a recovering alcoholic myself. Takes one to know one!"

"How long you been dry?"

"You mean sober?"

"Yeah. Whatever."

"I'll have 10 years on the first of next month. But it took me 20 years to get those 10 years."

"How's that?" Zack seemed genuinely mystified.

"Well, my mind was ready to quit drinking but my body just kept telling me to keep going. It was awful…I almost died from the disease. I was living in LA then and luckily I found a good AA group with a lot of supportive people. I must have gone to more than 1,000 meetings in my first year. I had a few relapses along the way because I stupidly got into a relationship before I was ready."

They drove off the ferry into the darkness, a brilliant canopy of shimmering canopy of stars overhead.

"Sometimes I wonder about my drinking," Zack said, almost to himself, as they approached town. "It's not what it used to be. I don't really enjoy it any more."

"Ever gotten into any trouble with your drinking" Allison asked bluntly.

"Nothing serious, I mean no problems with the law or anything. Never got a DUI. Never got into the fix that Rex is in, for damn sure! I just don't seem to be able to get high or have fun when I drink."

"We never tell anyone they have a drinking problem in AA. If you want to drink, that's your business. If you want to quit, that's AA's business."

Zack seemed to be lost in concentration as they approached Allison's house. He got out and opened the door for her.

"So Rex will have to decide for himself whether he has a problem?"

"Yes. We can't, and shouldn't, try to convince him of it—assuming he gets better. Thanks for the ride, Zack."

Rex could feel his dog's cold, wet nose against his cheek. Bootsie, the little Cocker Spaniel whose affections had been alienated by a lonely old lady down the street while Rex was away at boarding school, had come back to lick his face. He raised his hand to stroke Bootsie's muzzle, and felt…an ice pack wrapped in a towel.

"Bootsie…?"

"Does that feel better, Mr. Armistead?" The nurse's platinum blonde hair almost blended into her white uniform to produce a startling, otherworldly apparition.

"What the…? Who are you?"

"My name is Karen, and you've been sick. Excuse me while I page your doctor."

Nothing made any sense. Rex was confused and more than a little frightened. He could remember nothing, and was especially puzzled by his physical weakness. He could barely turn over on his side without exhausting himself. Rex closed his eyes and started to doze off again.

"Mr. Armistead!" An officious male voice boomed from the doorway. "Are you related to Dr. Peyton Armistead of Piedmont Medical College?"

"Yeah…he was my great uncle." Rex squinted to focus on the face with the voice, but he could barely make it out.

"I studied pediatric neurology with him—toughest course I took in med school. Quite a brilliant doctor, your great uncle."

"Uh, thanks. Do you know why I'm in here?"

"A miracle," he said, drawing closer so that Rex could read his nametag: Kurt Jaeger, MD. "You've been given another shot at life. After being admitted in an alcoholic coma with seizures, you've come back to the land of the living. We're glad you're here."

"What?"

"Apparently you drank a little too much beer the other day."

"I did?" Rex scratched his head, but it was empty.

"Acute alcoholic toxicity. Luckily, we were able to pull you back before there was any brain damage. But we'll need to run some more tests on you to make sure you're OK before we can release you." Dr. Jaeger placed his hand gently on Rex' shoulder. "You're a very lucky man."

"Lucky? That's an interesting way to look at it. My wife left me and I nearly committed suicide…"

"But you're still alive. Have you considered going into a treatment center?"

"Not really. I never thought I had a problem, until now."

"A social worker will visit with you before you're discharged to discuss some options for you. And I'll be back to see you before you leave."

Allison walked slowly with Rex into the sunny Seattle afternoon and led him to her parked car where Abby—her frisky Airedale—waited for them in the back seat of the purple Mazda station wagon. When Rex got into the front seat, Abby leaped into his lap and covered his face with wet kisses. "Wow! What a love bug! I've always wanted an Airedale."

"OK," Allison deadpanned. "Take her home with you." They both chuckled as Allison directed Abby to the back seat.

"Before Cynthia left, we had a little of Scotties. There was one I was particularly fond of, but she sold him just before she left and took the others with her. So I have no dog now."

"She did what?"

Rex shook his head. "The mother was a pedigreed AKC dog that he brought with us to Skagit, and Cynthia paid for the breeding and all. So I guess she figured she owned the whole litter. I pleaded with her to leave one of the puppies for me, but she just ignored me."

"What a bitch!"

"Yeah, I've often thought the same thing myself."

"Well, you can see Abby any time you want. She loves to walk on the beach."

"And, so do I. Maybe we could take a walk after we get back to the island?"

With Abby running in wild arcs before and after them, Allison and Rex walked on the soft white sands of Dolphin Point. The sun cast golden ripples on the waters of Puget Sound as it slid behind the deep purple of the Olympics to the west.

"I'm going to an AA meeting tonight," Allison said. "Want to come with me?"

"You, too?" Rex stammered.

"Yep. Me too."

The next day, Rex opened an envelope from Cerise Bagoth with a $10,000 check made out to IRATE, and a letter from Cynthia. The former he attached to his refrigerator door with magnets; the latter he threw in the trash. Then he drove to Zack's house and found him working in his garden, a red bandana wrapped around his head. Rex approached, waving the check in his hand.

"Boy, what did you say to her to get such a big donation?"

"I just told her that she could have an appointment to a high government position when we incorporate the island," Zack said, stamping out a cigarette butt. "Was that the right thing to say?" His eyes twinkled with the tease.

"Sure, as long as you didn't promise her the mayor's job!"

"Nope. I thought you had your eyes on that one."

Rex chuckled. "How many signatures already?"

"Well, the high school kids haven't checked in with me for a couple of days, but the rest of us have more than 500 names already."

"So we're about a third of the way there," Rex calculated. "The timing of this thing could get hairy."

"How's that?"

"Suppose we file for an election just when the county is ready to vote on the bridge. Do you really think they'd postpone a vote on that until after the special ballot on our secession?"

Zack rubbed the stubble on his chin. "No. I think we need to get a lawyer or two to help us, don't you?"

"Exactly. That's what this check is for!"

"Well, we should try to find someone who's willing to donate their services and save the money for any lawsuit we might have to file, or defend."

"Do you know anybody?"

"Actually, I got a call from some attorney fellow the other day who said he'd been on the island a long time and wanted to volunteer his time and expertise. I think he's with some big law firm downtown. Here's his card."

Zack pulled out a crinkled business card from his wallet, perfunctorily tried to straighten it, then thrust it toward Rex. "Pittor Dragoneth," Rex said aloud. "What kind of name is that?"

"Beats me…sounds kind of Russian or something."

"Or something, is right. I'll get in touch with him."

When Rex got home, he thumbed through the Skagit and Seattle phone directories for Pittor Dragoneth and found no listing. A check with information also revealed nothing. And there was no listing for the law firm on his business card—Dragoneth, Arkan and O'Soullivain. When he dialed the phone number, a voice with a faintly Slavic accent answered immediately.

"This is Pittor. May I help you?"

"I'm Rex Armistead with IRATE. I believe you spoke with Zack Beale the other day about possibly helping us with the petition drive. So I'm calling to see if we could all meet and discuss strategy."

"Certainly. When did you have in mind?"

"The sooner the better…"

"How about tonight?"

Allison, Zack Rex and Seymour huddled in Rex' living room and exchanged stories about collecting signatures. For every grouchy old lady who didn't want to be bothered with a petition, there seemed to be an enthusiastic young man—and the other way around, too, so that things achieved a sort of crude balance. In the pauses between conversations, there was a heavy stillness in the woods and a quiet that was profound. Save for frogs chirping happily, the night was dark and silent as obsidian. During one of those quiet moments, there came a knock on the front door.

"Hello, you must be Mr. Armistead. I'm Pittor Dragoneth."

"The figure at the door was a tall, gaunt, red-haired man of inde-terminate age. He thrust out his hand and Rex noticed the thick growth of bushy red hair on the top of his muscular palm.

"Welcome, thanks for coming. Please come and meet the group."

As he entered the house, Dragoneth removed his straw hat cere-moniously and bowed several times toward the group as he approached. His shoulders were slightly stooped but he moved with a charged gracefulness that seemed to defy his otherwise humble demeanor. His aqua blue eyes sparkled whenever they met someone else's.

"There's much that can be done to discourage the county from building a bridge," he said, refusing a cup of tea. "None of the envi-ronmental studies I've seen are any good. None of them even men-tion that the bridge would run directly across an old pioneer cemetery, for instance.

"Really?!" Rex was energized.

"There are a couple of old family plots almost directly where the bridge abutment would be built. They're all overgrown and most people don't even know of them."

Zack stroked his chin. "Oh, yeah. I know what you're talking about. I used to sneak out there when I was a kid. Kind of creepy."

"So, if you'd like, I can go to court and ask for a temporary restraining order to stay the project until the environmental impact report can be redone."

"Why didn't we think of that before?" Rex looked amazed and bemused. "How much will you be billing us for your services?"

"Nothing," Dragoneth said, insulted. "This is my service to Skagit Island. I'll keep you informed of how things progress."

Rex showed him to the door and returned to the group. The silence that surrounded them revealed no sound of a car or any other kind of mechanical noise as Dragoneth departed into the night. Rex wondered to himself whether Dragoneth had walked all the way to his house from town—about five miles away—with no directions.

"You know, it's really odd that Pittor knew about that old pioneer cemetery," Zack said. "I haven't been there for probably 30 years and I'm not even sure exactly where it is any more. I haven't heard anyone mention it, either, since I was a kid. How do you suppose he knows about it?"

"Isn't that what lawyers are supposed to do? Find out about stuff like that?" Allison said. "I mean, there must be maps or something."

"Well, I'm certainly glad he *does* know about it," Rex added. "The shock value when he files his court papers should blow the county and state right away."

CHAPTER 8

*I*n response to a petition filed by Pittor Dragoneth, Skookum
County Superior Court Judge Iris Thalheimer issued a 90-day
restraining order prohibiting any further action on the bridge. The
order stopped the project so the environmental impact report could
be amended to assess the costs and feasibility of relocating the bridge
abutment to avoid disturbing the cemetery. Nevertheless, the petition drive dragged on slowly, and Rex began to realize the extent to
which islanders functioned with self-imposed blinders in the political arena. Pleased to be out of the mainstream of mainland life, most
residents of Skagit Island seemed to operate on blind faith—or mis-
placed hope—that the county would forever protect the rural environment of the island. Whereas most islanders would readily sign a
petition opposed to construction of a bridge across Puget Sound,
many balked at the prospect of creating a new government with new
taxing authority. So in the minds of county and state bureaucrats,
Skagit Islanders were viewed as reactionary isolationists with only
narrowly defined self interests. It was a sort of have-your-cake-and-
eat-it-too attitude that not only caused mainlanders to shake their
heads, but also caused Rex and other IRATE members to question
whether their drive for self-determination could ever succeed.

"Here's 500 signatures, and there's more to come," Seymour smiled impishly as he handed the papers over to Allison. "I got most of them myself."

"Wow…that's awesome! You deserve some kind of reward."

Seymour's face lit up. "OK, how about a cheeseburger and milkshake at the Burger Bin?"

"Sure. By the way, do you drive?"

"Well, I still have my learner's permit but I'm supposed to get my regular license any day now."

"Why don't we ride over to the Burger Bin in my MG? I keep it parked in the garage for special occasions—and this is definitely one. I'll let you drive, if you want."

"The MG is a British-made sports car first imported into the United States in the early 1950s. It was designed as an affordable sports car for people who couldn't afford a Jaguar, and now it's been copied a million times. Other British cars include Austin Healey, Rolls Royce, Bentley, Triumph…"

"You certainly know your foreign cars!"

"Yeah, I read about them all the time. Never driven one though. But I think I'd better let you drive, because I don't know about insurance and my father would kill me if I got into an accident."

The old MG let out a plume of bluish smoke, sputtered, then ran smoothly as they bounced up and down the tree-lined highway.

"You were born and raised here on the island, right?"

"Yes, unfortunately."

Allison chuckled under her breath. "Why do you say that?"

"Oh, sometimes this place is really boring. That's why I memorize all this stuff. It keeps me entertained."

"Oh, really? Well have you ever heard about an old pioneer cemetery somewhere near the north end?"

Seymour screwed up his face for a second. "Nope. But I'll find out."

From his father's bookshelf, Seymour pulled down a spiral-bound booklet titled "Graves and Gooseberries: A History of Skagit Island," published in 1948 by the Skagit Island Historical Society. He noted with pride that his grandfather was listed as a founding member of the group in the overleaf. In the back, there was a roughly-drawn map of the island as it existed at the turn of the century, showing the location of the original churches and their attached burial sites, as well as three known graveyards of original settlers. Near the north end of the island was a burial site simply marked "Reveille," after homesteaders who had started logging on Skagit in the 1860s and owned the original cemetery—now undoubtedly overgrown with blackberries and madrona trees. A footnote explained that most of the residents of the original pioneer graveyards had been displaced and moved to the new island cemetery around 1901, although some could not be moved because of lack of consent from surviving family members. The graveyard was directly in the patch of the proposed bridge right-of-way. Seymour took the fragile booklet to the Skagit Library and ran off 10 copies of the map to distribute to IRATE members, then returned it carefully to his father's bookshelf.

"We now have about 1,100 signatures—thanks to some hard work by everyone—and about another 500 to go," Rex announced happily to an assembled group of IRATE members. "Do you think we can get those additional names with the approach we've been using, or does anyone believe we need a change of tactics?"

Zack rubbed his chin. "Strawberry Festival's coming up. Maybe we should have a booth there—if we can still get some space."

"But wouldn't that reach mostly off-island people?" Allison wondered.

"Not necessarily. I know a lot of folks who never go anywhere much, except at festival time. It's their one big event of the year."

"Well, if that's the case maybe we could get all 500 signatures in one weekend," Rex mused.

"Yeah!" Seymour chimed in. "Why don't we do an all-out blitz at the festival? I'll get all my friends out to canvass the crowds while everyone else runs a booth."

"Makes a lot of sense to me," Zack said. "I think we need some kind of brochure or something to hand to people when they sign the petition."

"Your command is my wish," Rex agreed. "Perhaps we can get Allison to do us some original art work—like the logo that was supposed to be ready three weeks ago?"

She shot him a knowing smile, then nodded her head.

"OK, I'll see about getting a booth at the festival," Zack volunteered.

"And Allison and I will get the brochure done," Rex said.

"And I'll make sure my friends will be able to work the festival," Seymour added.

After the group left, Rex stayed to help Allison clean up. She put on a Modern Jazz Quartet recording, which gave notes to the cool fog blowing in off Puget Sound. Despite all that, he felt a steady warm glow inside his head and chest that seemed to bubble up even stronger as he started to leave.

"You know, I've really enjoyed working with you on this campaign—no matter what happens," Allison said. "And I feel bad that I haven't done the logo yet."

"Don't worry about it. We really haven't needed one until now."

She moved closer to him as he stood in the front doorway, absorbing her warmth through every pore.

"After I was divorced, I thought I never really needed a man—until now."

Rex moved his face close to hers and looked directly into her blue eyes. "Until you knew me?"

She looked longingly at him for a moment, then cast her eyes downward and nodded her head imperceptibly. Rex placed his hand under her chin, raised her head back up and kissed her deeply, wildly. She softened and sighed in his arms. He noticed tears running down her cheeks.

"Wow...am I that bad of a kisser?" he chuckled.

"No, not at all. Maybe even too good. I...I guess I'm afraid. I don't ever want to hurt you, Rex. I'm just an emotional wreck."

"What is that slogan in AA? No romancing and no financing?"

Allison giggled under her breath. "Yeah, I suppose so. But honestly that's not the reason at all. It's just that I'm not sure I'm ready, and I'm afraid of losing you."

Her tear-filled eyes overflowed with desire and fear, and Rex could feel her tremble.

"Is anyone ever ready for love?"

Allison smiled pertly, then sniffed. "It's funny, isn't it? We always talk about love and dream about it and then when it comes along we're afraid. Go figure."

Rex held her tightly in his arms and kissed the top of her head.

"Hell, I'm no more ready for it than you."

"Kiss me," Allison said impetuously. "I just know I want you and nothing else."

As he kissed her. Rex swung Allison around slowly as if they were dancing. The precise, shimmering tones of the MJQ glowed in the night air and it was too late to go back. Too late to go back for both of them, because their warmth had become fused and had started a chain reaction that would burn all the available fuel within them to become white hot. Allison closed the front door, locked it, turned off the porch light and gently led Rex by the hand to her upstairs bedroom to stoke the nuclear reaction.

With more than 1,600 signatures of Skagit Island registered voters, Rex and Zack filed their petitions with the county elections department. A week later, an election was certified for the November ballot with 1,543 valid signatures on the question of whether Skagit Island should be incorporated as a rural city—a previously nonexistent legal entity. Constitutional law professors at the University of Washington said such a jurisdiction was theoretically possible, but had never been created in the U.S.

"Let's have a victory celebration," Allison beamed.

"Definitely," Rex agreed. "Shall I make the calls?"

"OK, but let's pick a date and time first!"

In his carefully organized Rolodex file, Rex had the names, addresses and telephone numbers of all the members and active supporters of IRATE. For Pittor Dragoneth, he had a business card with only a telephone number stapled to his files. When he called Dragoneth's number, a digital voice informed him that it was no longer a working line. Directory information had no listing for Pittor Dragoneth in the greater Seattle area, or on Skagit Island. He rummaged through all his current and outdated copies of the Skagit phone directory, searching in vain for Dragoneth's name.

"Do you have any other phone number for Dragoneth?" he asked Zack.

"Nope. Just the business card. Why...can't reach him?"

"Not only can I not reach him, there's no trace of him anywhere...except in the history books."

"What do you mean?"

"No listings anywhere. Where did you get this guy's card?"

"When I was out collecting signatures, I talked to lots of people. Some of them offered to help...I can't remember them all by name. But when I got home, I was sorting through my papers and his card just fell out."

"You won't believe this," Rex' voice quivered slightly. "I called the state bar association and the only information they had on Pittor Dragoneth is that he was admitted to the state bar in 1889."

"WHAT!?" Zack shrieked.

"No lie...1889. This is getting a little creepy."

"Yeah, he's awfully well preserved. I want some of his magic formula."

"First we have to find him!"

"OK, the best place to start is the cemetery." Zack's eyelids twitched. "Are you in?"

"Yeah, I guess so."

"I think we should be able to find the place. But don't tell anyone about this…we don't want to scare anybody off."

Down a steep slope that dropped abruptly to the east of Skagit Highway they climbed, bracing themselves against the thick birch and pine trees to break their steep descent. Within a few hundred feet, Zack and Rex found themselves in another world undisturbed by humans. The thick forest carpet of pine needles and decaying leaves bore no trace of human tracks and the sunlight reached the interior of this netherworld only obliquely, shaded and refracted by a million leaves and branches overhead. The stillness of the forest was so profound they found themselves whispering to each other as they negotiated the tortuous route down, down to the tiny meadow near the water's edge where the maps and Zack's memory indicated the graveyard could be found. Even a single twig snapping underfoot seemed a transgression. A sense of excitement and danger filled the quiet air. The nattering of a woodpecker shattered the silence as they broke free of the thicket and approached the meadow, bathed in sunlight ahead.

"Oh, yeah. I remember this place now," Zack said with amazement. "When I was a kid, we used to walk along the beach at low tide, then climb the banks to get up here. I think that's a much easier way!"

"Look directly over at the mainland," Rex pointed across the eastern neck of Puget Sound. "See the airplanes over there? It's a direct line from this point to the airport, and the bridge abutment would connect right here—directly in front of the meadow."

"And then continue on to the other side of the island and over to Shomamish County, and then on out to the Olympic Peninsula,"

Zack completed the thought and the geography. "It's like somebody took a slide rule and just drew a straight line from the airport across the water to this point, without even considering what might be here on this side."

In the center of the meadow stood a couple of old oak trees, their heavy branches bowed down with the weight of years.

"So you really think there's a graveyard over there?" Rex said.

"I know there is. Follow me."

On the water side of the oak trees, Zack noticed a small row of evenly spaced bumps in the grass. He pointed silently, and they approached slowly. As they got closer, Rex felt a surge of energy unlike anything he could remember. A small bit of his wild creature-hood seemed to awaken and he felt stronger.

"Those look like they could be headstones buried under some kind of erosion from the hillside, maybe. See how it kind of builds up on one side of the bumps? What do you think?"

"Could be," Zack said. He pulled out a pocketknife and cut the thick weeds away from one of the lumps. The blade scratched something hard and rock-like. "Maybe we'd better dig one of these out and see what it is."

Using a small, collapsible Army shovel, Rex dug carefully around the edges of the lump until to revealed a grave headstone. He dug deeper so they could read the inscription: "Matthew Reveille, 1839-1890, Requiescat in Pace," he read aloud. "Do you think it's OK to dig around these stones just to read the names without disturbing the graves?"

"I don't see why not," Zack replied. "Looks like there's about a dozen of these things. Maybe we should check them all out, as long as we're here."

"When Rex tired of digging after a few more headstones, he handed the shovel to Zack, got up and walked around the meadow trying to imagine a homestead or two on the spot. The twin oak trees would make perfect places to hang rope swings for children.

"Holy shit! Look at this…quick!"

Rex ran over to the simple headstone that Zack had unearthed, and they stared in silent amazement at the chiseled inscription:

Pittor S. Dragoneth
1870-1910
He loved God and Skagit Island

Zack furiously shoveled the dirt back around the headstone and they both ran out of the meadow and back up the hill, emerging again at the roadside bloody and breathless. They jumped back into the truck and roared off, sending up a rooster tail of dust as they raced back to town.

"I…I don't know what to think about this," Rex said at last. "We're both reasonable people, we both saw the same thing. What do you make of it?"

Zack just shook his head slowly. "I don't remember seeing that headstone before, but it was a long time ago when I used to play down there. Anyway, if I did see it I'm sure it wouldn't have meant anything to me."

"Is it possible there are *two* Pittor Dragoneths?"

"I doubt it. How come you can't find him anywhere? Isn't that just a little weird?"

"A *little* weird? It's got me freaked out! I'm gonna stop at the *ClamShell* and see if I can look through their morgue. Why don't you just drop me off there, and I'll get a ride home later."

"Morgue?" Zack's eyebrows twitched.

"Oh," Rex chuckled. "It's a newspaper term for the library where all the old stories are kept on file. If I'm lucky, there may be an obituary on Mr. Dragoneth. And if they don't have one, then I'll try the Seattle papers. See you later!"

The *ClamShell* nestled in a cubbyhole between the bakery and the hardware store, and doubled as stationery and office supply outlet. Editorial offices for the weekly newspaper were crammed into the rear of the small retail space. Visitors were led on a labyrinth between rows of manila envelopes and fax paper to reach the "newsroom," a converted storage area where two desks piled shoulder-high with papers literally jammed into each other. John Jaybeck, former flak for a major Seattle lumber and paper firm, had run the *ClamShell* for more than 15 years in his inimitable and often inscrutable style of community journalism. Like the store, he led a double life and when not excoriating county officials editorially, was pleased to dispense staplers, mailing envelopes and ink wells.

"Dragoneth? Doesn't sound familiar." Jaybeck scratched his bald head as he rummaged through some papers on his desk. A small man with a squeaky voice, Jaybeck could barely reach the top of the paper stack. Rex wondered what might happen if the pile ever shifted and crashed onto his head while he was working at his computer.

"But maybe you'll get lucky. Just last week, my wife finished inputting the last of the old copies going back to 1865, when the paper was started. You can sit here and look through the old obits, if you like."

Gingerly, Rex took a seat at Jaybeck's computer and followed his instructions on how to search the back issues. For a moment, the old excitement of the newsroom pumped through his blood and he felt a familiar rush of adrenaline as he began to look for the elusive Mr. Dragoneth, working forward from January 1910. In April, he hit pay dirt:

PITTOR S. DRAGONETH

Pittor S. Dragoneth, son of a pioneer Skagit Island family and a self-taught attorney, died last week at home. Services are pending at Island Mortuary.

Dragoneth was the only son of Dmitri and Annija Dragoneth, who immigrated to Skagit Island in 1866 from Romania to become homesteaders. Pittor was born in 1870.

The Dragoneths operated a berry farm on the north end of the island, and Pittor studied law books when he wasn't helping on the family farm. He was admitted to the bar in 1889 and practiced law in Seattle until stricken with cancer.

A staunch defender of the rural character of Skagit Island, Pittor Dragoneth sued Skookum County in 1908 over plans to build a road through his family's homestead. During a tense standoff between the Dragoneths and county officials near their property, the young attorney drove the would-be encroachers off with an old sword said to be a relic of the Cossack era.

He leaves no survivors.

Rex printed out a copy of the obituary, folded it and stuffed it quickly in his pocket, hoping to slip unnoticed out of the office. But Jaybeck accosted him as he slinked toward the door.

"Congratulations on the petitions!" he hailed. "I'm supporting you editorially this week."

"Terrific! We need all the help we can get. This could be a long struggle." Then Rex quickly bolted for the door and disappeared so he would not have to answer more questions. As he scurried to find a pay phone to call Allison, he noticed that his hands were shaking.

CHAPTER 9

"We can't have a ghost for our attorney!" Rex paced the kitchen floor, as Allison watched with cautious eyes.

"Why not? You can't afford anyone else."

Rex sighed deeply, then sat down next to her. "Maybe I'm just too worked up over this. But it's got me wondering what the hell happens next. Do you know anything about this sort of thing?"

Allison nodded her head. "I was really into the occult when I was in college—took a course in parapsychology, too. The only thing I can figure is that Dragoneth is using this situation as a way to finish his old business with the county, so he can move on."

"You mean, if we win the fight and become independent of Skookum County then he'll go away?"

"Probably—provided you make sure the old Reveille graveyard isn't ever disturbed. He seems more like a poltergeist, and not something evil."

"Well, I hope so. He's only helped us so far."

"You may never hear from him again."

Rex sighed heavily. "I wish."

"Have you told Zack?"

"Not in so many words. But he has a pretty good idea, after our little trip to the graveyard and what I told him from digging around in historical records. Think I should?"

"Definitely. You need to tell him and swear him to secrecy. Then we have to go on with the business of getting the election taken care of."

"For an artist, you're pretty practical!"

"In my former lifetime, I was a courtesan of the King of Atlantis—that's where I learned all about politics."

"My name is Rex, and I'm haunted by ghosts," he announced at the next AA meeting. A ripple of laughter spread through the church basement, but Allison bathed him in a knowing smile. "I suppose most of us are haunted by ghosts. My ghosts are the memories of time I could have spent being present in my children's lives if I'd been sober, and all of the stupid things I did when I was drinking that hurt other people—and me. But I found in this program that I could be free of my ghosts, if I became willing to work the 12 steps, starting with the admission that I'm powerless over just about everything."

On the way home, Allison snuggled close to Rex on the front seat. "I hope someday we can both be rid of our ghosts," she said wistfully. "And I'm not talking about Pittor Dragoneth. I'm afraid I still carry a lot of resentment about my divorce. It makes me sad that I can't get rid of it."

"Is that what they mean when they speak of karma? I have the same wish, but it's only slightly different. I wonder what it would be like to just drop all of my worldly attachments and heaviness. Do you suppose we're always grieving our losses all through life?"

"If that's so, then it's even more reason to celebrate the good things we have right now—like each other." She pecked him sweetly on the cheek, and he put his hand firmly on her thigh. "You know, for the first time in my life I'm glad just to be who I am, where I am."

The night sky split open with a flash of lightning, followed by a huge rumble of thunder like a thousand freight trains hurtling through the darkness. Then another, and another followed by a torrential rainstorm. Rex had to slow down so he could regain some visibility.

"The obligatory summer squall," he said. "I remember one Fourth of July when there was thunder, lightning and hail the size of marbles."

"I love it. It's so romantic!"

They raced between the raindrops into the house and buried themselves under the bed covers, snuggled together and listened to the cataclysm outside until they fell dead asleep.

Zack was awakened by a crashing sound downstairs—a huge, rib-rattling concussion that rocked the house as if someone had dropped a grand piano on the floor from the height of the ceiling. The thunderstorm had started to fan fierce winds, but Zack usually had no trouble sleeping in a rainstorm. Shaken, he jumped out of bed and raced down the winding staircase and turned on the light in the living room. Everything was in perfect order and there was no sign of a disturbance. He checked the kitchen, storage room and office—not a sign of any intrusion or damage. But he did notice that the wind had picked up strength, puffing and howling against the windows so the panes seemed to bulge and weep with the storm's fury. As he turned off the lights and started back to bed, he heard a giant crackling, snapping sound followed by an enormous crash upstairs. Convinced that this time something huge had struck the house, he raced back upstairs to find still-wet green leaves and the just-broken branches of a pine tree in the bedroom—in fact, on his bed. The giant old tree had snapped in a violent gust of wind, crashed through the window above his bed and slammed onto the bed itself. He quickly calculated that a few seconds' difference in either his leaving or returning to bed certainly would have meant instant death. He sat on the wet floor with pounding heart.

"Oh my God," he muttered, running his fingers through his disheveled hair. He watched the lightning flash and listened to the rain pouring into the smashed window as a chill crept over him, and he shivered. "Nothing I can do about that tonight anyway," he said at last, rising to pull a folded blanket from under the wreckage of the bed. Zack went downstairs again, wrapped himself in the pine needle and rain-battered blanket, curled up on the sofa and went to sleep.

"Can you meet with the group tonight to discuss campaign strategy?" Rex asked Zack when he called the next morning.

"Sure. Did you ever find out anything about our Mr. Dragoneth?"

"Yeah, a little bit. Apparently he was involved in some kind of fight with the county when he died of cancer. He was suing Skookum County to stop them from building a road through his family's property."

"Hmmm…did you have any damage from the storm last night?"

"Just a few things blown around outside…"

"I had this pine tree come crashing onto my bed!"

"Jesus! Are you OK?"

"Yeah, but just barely. It was really weird. I heard this tremendous crashing noise downstairs, like a meteorite had slammed into the house or something. So I jumped out of bed to go investigate, and there was nothing. Just nothing…everything was the same."

"What?"

"Just then the tree crashed through my window and onto the bed. I would have been crushed if the noise hadn't gotten me up."

"Allison says Pittor Dragoneth is some kind of poltergeist and we should be grateful he's on our side," Rex said breezily.

"You don't suppose…?"

Rex came by his propensity for language quite naturally, as if some verbal gene had been imprinted into his DNA. His great great-grandfather had been a Methodist minister in Piedmont—a circuit rider who services three congregations from the Chesapeake Bay to the Blue Ridge Mountains. Once Rex and his father had made a special trip to Armistead, a tiny village of only 600 souls named for his preaching ancestor, where they discovered the red brick ruins of his Civil War-era church overgrown with kudzu in a thicket of pine trees down a sandy road capped with crushed oyster shells. Each year, Rex' father drove to Armistead to mail his Christmas cards before the U.S. Postal Service obliterated local postmarks as its contribution to the march of homogenization in America. And for many years Rex had subscribed to the local weekly newspaper to keep track of the social dinners and church functions in Armistead. Then his paternal grandfather, growing up poor and honest in Harpers Ferry, had enrolled himself in private schools and paid his own tuition by working in a pharmacy, where he made milkshakes and delivered liver pills. Determined to have a better life, he then attended pharmacy school and within a few years of graduation was vice president of an international drug company based in Switzerland. Although the Depression took away his yacht and summer home on Long Island Sound, Dr. Armistead still could afford to send his son and daughter to Ivy League colleges and Rex' father graduated from Yale and Columbia University College of Physicians and Surgeons. As World War II raged in Europe, the second Dr. Armistead enrolled in the Navy and was shipped off as a medical officer in the invasion of Salerno. Rex had among family memorabilia photos of his father—tall, lanky, intense—schmoozing with chums in a canvas tent on the sands of North Africa just before the largest military invasion in history. In that same tent, Dr. Rex Armistead had received a telegram from Casablanca notifying him that his first son had been born in Piedmont. Meanwhile, Rex' Wellesley-educated aunt was sinking into *myasthenia gravis*, a terrible neurological disease that robbed her of the ability to play her beloved music she'd studied at Eastman School of Music. To compensate, Lucy Armistead started a live radio program broadcast from her bedside for others who were homebound because of illness, affliction or injury. "The World Inside" was soon broadcast on network radio throughout the

Northeast and was the subject of magazine and newspaper articles—as well as a congratulatory letter from President Roosevelt.

But when Capt. Rex Armistead, MD, returned home from the war with several medals for bravery pinned on his jacket, something had shifted in his marriage with Beverlie. There were two more children—a brother and sister—born in the wake of the armistice and Rex' father joined the medical practice of his father-in-law upon his return to Piedmont. Although he only knew snippets of his parents' marriage through the endless reverberations of their divorce when he was less than five years old, Rex was able to piece together a somewhat coherent picture of what had happened. The returning soldier was shunned as a Yankee in Piedmont, and his suggestions for improving the joint medical practice were not welcome. His wife grew boisterous and abusive when drinking—something Rex' father had never experienced in his close nuclear family. And she hectored him for not making enough money, as well as being deliberate about sanitation, frugality and race relations. Strains in the marriage worsened as Dr. Armistead found another female for companionship. Then the divorce followed swiftly, and years of bitterness and recrimination by Beverlie. Somewhere in the midst of that alcoholic insanity, an abusive stepfather emerged like a rattler from under a rock. Most of those days were only a blur in Rex' memory—a blur punctuated by scenes of extreme violence and cruelty, and Rex' determination to administer a brutal and painful death to the man who had brought the extra ration of suffering into his family, once he'd reached manhood himself and had the strength to do so.

The only reason Rex had never acted on that mission was his forcible ejected by court petition from his mother's home at the age of 13, followed by an awkward transplantation into his father's stepfamily. And then years of profound grieving morphed into clinical depression, for which he was hospitalized at the age of 17 and subjected to daily insulin shock therapy. Maybe it had saved his life, Rex wasn't sure. Sometimes he wondered why it mattered anyway. Soon after the psychiatric hospital visit and just after graduation from college, he married his childhood chum and progressed directly into the alcoholism that had destroyed his mother and practically everyone around her. But Allison had opened a new door, and he was ready to step inside at last.

For the first time in his adult life, he could awaken on a Saturday morning tired from a week's work but not hung over—clear-headed enough to enjoy a morning cup of coffee and a pleasant chat, a tickling match or a roll in the hay with Allison. The old howling sorrow was still inside, just below the surface, but it was magically held at bay so that Rex could at least entertain notions of sanity and even joy. Years earlier, he'd rejected the fatuous image of the Sunday school deity with white beard floating on a cloud and hadn't bothered to carry the matter much further. Now the "higher power" so much discussed in AA had become, for him, a decision to enter the darkness of unknowing and faith defined by St. John of the Cross—or "God as I *don't* understand Him," as Rex paraphrased the AA literature. Sobriety was an adventure and each day one of discovery. Some of the discoveries were pleasant: the fact that he could make love without drugs or alcohol. Some were daunting: the realization that just one more drink could mean madness and death. Some were puzzling: his discovery that the "bondage of self" slipped away the more he did work on his own recovery. And some were embarrassing: his exquisite sensitivity and sense of victimization were merely another mask for self-centered arrogance. As one of his AA friends continually remarked, "What a long, strange trip it's been!"

But what leavened all this shocking self-discovery and new relationship to other human beings and to the world was humor. The hugging, laughter and gentle self-recrimination practiced on a daily basis in AA meetings all served as tools to nudge him toward sanity. Rex recalled a story he'd read about the Kennedy family and their eerie closeness, how all the family members would gather in a circle around a relative who was having a particularly bad time and make funny bird-like noises—as if to summon their spirit back into the here and now of this world. AA was like that, he thought: the walking wounded propping each other up in the journey of life, until each could run confidently again. If AA were just another addiction, as some detractors claimed, then at least it was a healthy addiction that brought love in place of liver disease, laughter instead of tears, and faith to replace insanity.

"We are like men who have lost their legs. We never grow new ones." Bill W's graphic description of the plight of the alcoholic was strangely apt. For the first time in his life, Rex experienced unconditional love, patience, tolerance and kindness on a scale that seemed positively astral. Maybe he would never grow new legs, but he felt as if he were growing a new heart.

"You're one of the lucky ones," Allison told him. "Your bottom is a lot higher than mine. When I got sober in LA, I was six months behind on my mortgage and the house was about to be foreclosed. I'd used enough heroin that I was getting seriously addicted, and my cocaine habit was costing me thousands of dollars every month."

"What made you get sober?"

"I was stumbling along in a blackout and got hit by a car when I decided to cross the street against the light. I ended up in the hospital with three fractured ribs, a broken arm and a concussion. That's when I started to detox. The doctors were amazed at how much morphine I used, and started asking me questions. So after I got out of the hospital, I went directly into a rehab program in Santa Monica."

"It wasn't Synanon, I hope!"

"God, no! Actually, it was a county facility that was where everyone went who couldn't afford a private treatment center. There were a lot of young kids there who were really fucked up. I felt sorry for them. You can get sober, but I don't think that kind of early brain damage can ever be healed."

Rex scratched his head. "Heroin, huh? How'd you get into that stuff?"

"Oh, this stupid 'artist' I was seeing at the time was a part-time drug dealer, and he gave some to me. I thought it was fun and cool at the time. But by the time I got scared about sticking needles into my arm, I was already using it on a regular basis. It took away everything that was ugly and painful and gave me this incredible, warm glow."

"What did it do for your art?"

"Allison gave out a mirthless chuckle. "Damn near destroyed it. I thought I was creating these incredible paintings that were so 'cosmic' but when I looked at them after I got clean, they were terrible! I was so discouraged about my work. I didn't paint at all for several years."

"Isn't it strange how we both came to this island looking for peace—for some kind of deep healing?"

Allison tossed her head back. "Not really. I think of Skagit Island as a sanctuary, a refuge for humans. You know how they have wildlife preserves for endangered species? Maybe we're an endangered kind of human being—the kind that feels things too intensely."

"I'm not sure I like the idea of being some kind of exotic bird with bright feathers who can only live in a cloistered environment. We're not that precious," Rex said.

"No, not precious. That's not my point. We can both survive in the world outside but we lose our brilliant plumage. It gets torn off in the struggle to survive, by the world. Here we can be ourselves because it's safe."

"Maybe this island is just a magnet for dope addicts and dreamers who can't face reality. Maybe we're deluding ourselves that we're artists, when in fact we're just fuckups and slackers."

"That could be. But there are plenty of people off this island who delude themselves and who are also fuckups and slackers!"

As election day neared, news reporters swarmed over Skagit Island to tell the story of the picturesque little island with big notions of independence. A favorite backdrop for television crews was the ferry dock at the north end, where cameras could record the faces and comments of commuters as they trudged back and forth on the passenger ferry. The talking heads also nabbed commuters lined up in their cars, waiting for the next car ferry. The idea, of course, was to catch someone so frustrated by the long ferry lines that they would embrace with open arms the idea of a bridge across Puget Sound, thus lending an aura of hot controversy to what was practically a *fait accompli*. Except for a few irascible souls who questioned whether the financial aspects of operating a separate island government would ever make sense, there was astonishing unanimity among islanders that they should have self-determination and forever be able to hold at bay any mainland schemes of giant cross-sound bridges.

On one such occasion, a skinny young Asian woman in man-tailored business suit rushed to the ferry dock to capture the mood of commuters leaving the 5:30 p.m. boat from Seattle. Clutching notebook in hand and followed closely by a rotund cameraman in blue jeans, his hairy stomach projecting over the top of his pants, she accosted the first person off the boat. He happened to be a surly midget in a mini-sized wheelchair, electrically powered and capable of astonishing quick maneuvers. As he sped along the gangplank onto the dock, the midget's limp feet dragged in front of the wheelchair like a pair of dead fish thumping and bumping on the coarse planks. The midget was bedraggled, scruffy-looking as if he'd slept under a freeway overpass, and his small eyes had a mean look. In his lap, positioned just right, was a small hand-lettered cardboard sign that read, "Drive Carefully." He muttered to himself as he swept closer to the TV crew.

"Excuse me, sir, I wonder if you could give us your opinion of the move for Skagit Island's independence?" The reporter's voice was sweet and plenty perky, but her words broke like spun glass against concrete when they struck the midget's ears. He slammed on the brakes, spun about and faced her directly.

"Yeah, I'll give you my opinion," he said with a snarl. "That's about the most asinine idea I've ever heard of! If all these mutants from California would stop coming here we wouldn't be considering such a ridiculous scheme."

"So I take it you're opposed to the ballot initiative?" Her voice was heavy with faux empathy.

"Opposed? Let's put it this way. If I wasn't a goddamn crippled midget with MS, I'd get outa this fuckin' wheelchair and kick their asses. It's the dumbest fuckin' idea I ever heard of. And you can quote me, too!"

And he sped off to the electric whir of his battery-operated motors, leaving the young Asian reporter blushing and fidgeting with her notebook.

CHAPTER 10

*I*n the town, there were three pizza restaurants in the same block—all hoping to capture the taste buds and wallets of commuters on their way home from a work day in the city. Two of these were side-by-side, and the third directly across the street adjoined to a beer tavern with pool tables. The success of the first restaurant led to the second, and the third seemed to come along just for the ride. Sandwiched between these pizza dispensaries was the tiny office of the Skagit Island Chamber of Commerce, whose main function was to orchestrate the annual Skagit Strawberry Festival. Entrepreneurs who wanted to know more about consumer preferences, demographic information and business opportunities usually resorted to a pile of archaic studies of unincorporated Skookum County that gathered dust in the library. On the eve of the election, large plastic banners flapped in the breeze over Skagit Highway calling upon voters to approve the secessionist initiative. Ominously, one of the three pizza restaurants on the same day displayed a "Going Out of Business" sign in its front window. Within a week, the space was vacated and a new Mexican restaurant had opened to the surprise and delight of islanders. The runaway success of the new restaurant caused first one, then the other, pizza restaurants to switch to Mexican cuisine. Within three months, all had gone out of business and the only functional "restaurant" on the island was a greasy chain hamburger-and-milkshake joint. Dairy Deelite had almost been forced to shut down by county health officials after a young customer was stricken with *e. coli* after a meal, airlifted to Seattle Children's Hospital and resuscitated from the brink of death.

So it was the Dairy Deelite where IRATE members somewhat reluctantly scheduled their victory party. Zack rented the whole place and brought in a huge TV set for everyone to watch the election returns broadcast from the mainland.

"You be sure and cook everything twice as long and twice as hot as usual," he admonished the store manager as he signed the rental agreement. "We can't afford to have anyone getting sick."

By the time the dozen island "radicals" had assembled the focus of their attention was the news broadcast rather than refreshments. In an election off year, with no major state or national contests to draw voters, the fate of the initiative was far from certain. Among "seasoned" political watchers, the consensus seemed to he that a low voter turnout would be bad for all of the nine initiatives on the ballot—everything from more money to build jails to a health code professions amendment to allow chiropractors to prescribe tranquilizers. By 9:30, the Skagit Island initiative was losing by a slim margin with all precincts reporting. But within a half-hour, when absentee ballots were tallied, it had unofficially passed.

"Well, our hard work paid off!" Rex beamed. "Who wants to be on the Island Council? Any volunteers? Anyone want to be mayor?"

"I think we should call a public meeting and ask for nominations. We won't be able to vote on council members for at least 90 days, when the county schedules a special election," Zack said.

"I nominate Zack for mayor!" Allison said.

"And I nominate Rex," he countered.

"Before we start forming our revolutionary provisional junta," Rex said, "we'd better prepare for an onslaught of reporters. I'll guarantee the TV crews will be out here tomorrow, trying to track us all down."

"I'm going fishing—real early!" Zack announced.

"Thanks, pal," Rex shot back. "Can I come too?"

"Nope. You're the media guy, remember?"

"I think we should appoint Pittor Dragoneth our media liaison," Rex chuckled.

"Shhhhhh," Allison hissed, forefinger against pursed lips.

"Who's that?" asked a curious Seymour as he slurped down a large cola.

"He's, uh, our mascot. It's just the name of an old dog I once knew."

"Funny name for a dog. I've heard of Rover, Spot, Fido, Patches, Buck, Butch, Henrietta, Blanche, Killer, Sweetums, Archibald, Ruben, Blazes…"

Allison and Rex slipped out during the general hubbub following the final election results, quickly drove home, took the phone off the hook and made love like a couple of infatuated teenagers.

At Rex' prodding, members of IRATE got to work on the business of how to run an island government. Budgets for Skookum County for the last decade were scrutinized—especially revenues and expenditures for Skagit Island. The research confirmed what the committee already knew: the island had long served as a "cash cow" for the county to help offset costs of providing services in other, poorer sections of the county where property valuations were higher and the need for social services greater. They found that in the previous decade about one-third of the tax revenues collected from Skagit Island in the form of property taxes never returned in the form of services. State revenues from sales taxes were more difficult to trace, but a safe assumption was that most of sales tax revenues did not return in any form to benefit Skagit Islanders. When all of the figures were tallied and the numbers crunched, it appeared that the new government would have an annual budget of about $3 million—more than enough to maintain the roads and parks, staff and equip the library, pay for the public schools, provide police protection, issue building permits and provide planning services—with something left over. Most of the existing services could, in effect, be contracted from Skookum County while the Island Council made up its mind on which services to provide directly. With almost $1 million a year in projected revenues not yet pigeonholed, the long-dormant idea of building a first class community center arose again.

"Can't you see it?" Rex rhapsodized. "Something big enough for council meetings, lectures, concerts, exhibits…"

"And a teen center, too!" Seymour was adamant. "Teenagers on this island have nothing to do and nowhere to go. At least we could have dances or something."

"Definitely. And it could serve as a senior center, too, along with the city offices. Although in the short-run we're going to have to find someplace to rent for the offices. That's another thing we need to work on—finding someplace to rent."

"We already have the land next to the library to build the community center," Allison said.

"If we get our own animal control, I want to be the dog catcher," Seymour added. "I know animals, and I worked one summer in a vet hospital."

"Dog catcher, huh? Woof woof!!" Rex shot back.

"And we can have our own public art program, too, but better than the county's," Allison said. "I'll draw up a list of projects we could work on."

Frustrated and angered by the failure of their plans to bridge Puget Sound as a direct link to the proposed golf resort on the Olympic Peninsula, Japanese developers grew surly. Having learned that money made things happen in America, they were shocked and incredulous that their money had not been powerful enough for them to get their way. So within a month of the election results, Nippon Golf Links filed a $10 billion lawsuit against Skookum County for denial of a use permit to build a tourist "information center" at the side of the roadway that would have been constructed from the airport to the bridge across Skagit Island. In its barest outline, the lawsuit was simply an act of revenge and retaliation—not unlike the United States dropping atomic bombs on Hiroshima and Nagasaki in response to the Japanese sneak attack on Pearl Harbor. In the Seattle newspapers, developer attorneys vowed to carry their fight all the way to the state Supreme Court if necessary, even though any legal victory would merely be pyrrhic since Skagit Island was no longer within the jurisdiction of Skookum County. The object, it seemed, was to punish the county by requiring it to spend time and resources on a protracted legal defense and to inflict whatever public relations damage could be meted out in the process. In a sense, Nippon Golf Links' revenge was also Pittor Dragoneth's.

But islanders generally ignored mainland politics—which was of course the primary reason for formation of an island government. Instead of allowing themselves to be the unwitting pawns of Seattle politicians, Skagit Islanders' sense of insularity would now work in their favor. It would no longer be necessary to woo one or more county supervisors to get roads re-paved, or to have a personal friend in the planning department to get a permit processed on time. Like everything else on the island, local government would be transparent and publicly accountable in the most personal, immediate sense

Now that Skagit Islanders had their freedom, could they make the most of it? Were they more comfortable passively protesting their status as wards of the county, or would they be able to confidently assume the responsibility of governing themselves? In short, could a population that had consciously turned its back on "the world" come to face the gritty realities of life and work together successfully to secure its future?

The pioneer spirit of stoicism, self-reliance and strength in the face of adversity had worked well when the challenges were hostile

Indian tribes, starvation and the drudgery of the frontier. But now the challenges had changed, although the ideology hadn't. Survival of the independent souls who lived on the island—and indeed of the whole laid-back island way of life—now depended on communication, cooperation and teamwork. All that was very much in evidence while the white-hot frenzy of opposition to the bridge had flared, but islanders also were quick to return to their isolationist ways. The biggest challenge, Rex realized, would be to sustain and nurture a real sense of community. There had to be good reasons to work together and objectives to work for—not just threats from the outside to overcome.

Initially, the issues of a community center, teen facility and perhaps some kind of public art program seemed ideal "hooks" to get islanders involved in their fledgling government. Everyone had a stake in a community center, and lots of island artists could benefit from a public art program provided the funds were available to mount one. Both would serve as energizers to move the blood of life through the body politic. But something was needed to jump-start the process. Some sort of glue had to be found to hold the bare threads of community together for at least 90 days, until islanders could vote for the creation of their first Island Council.

"I think we should have an island celebration of some kind," Rex announced one day to Allison upon awakening.

"We just had the Strawberry Festival." Her voice was hoarse with sleep.

"I know, but that's just routine." Rex was warming to the subject. "I think we need something really special so that everybody can realize what a terrific thing we've done. We need a debutante party for the new island government."

"Where?"

"How about on the site where the community center might be built? That would emphasize the need for a community center and also bring people together to get the ball rolling."

Allison scratched her sleep-thickened head. "You're becoming quite the politician, aren't you?"

"Think so?" Rex seemed slightly offended. "Yeah, I suppose you're right. It just seems to follow logically from everything that's happened. Would you help me get it organized?"

"Wow! Where do you get all this energy?"

Rex jumped on her, pressing her shoulders to the mattress, and gave her a fierce eye-to-eye grimace.

"I'm possessed by the devil!"

After their laughter subsided, Allison sputtered: "I agree!"

"Good. I'll need you to draw up a list of people for the organizing committee..."

"I agreed that you were possessed. I did *not* agree to help you!"

Rex was stunned. His face dropped into a boyish pout.

"OK. OK. I'll help you," Allison relented.

Rod Cooke had long stringy black hair that hung down to his shoulders, a pallid complexion and several days' growth of beard that never seemed to change. Although it was obvious that he couldn't have the same barber as Yassir Arafat, the cosmetic (and comic) effect was the same. His dark wildness and jerky manner of moving somehow suggested a Charles Manson, and was frightening. As a living relic of the 60s, Rod Cooke was one of a subculture of middle aged islanders whose intellectual growth had been arrested at the moment when he "dropped out" and started to make a career of sorts as a guerrilla artist, sometime musician and full-time anachronism. Rod Cooke represented the unvarnished answer to the question on the lips of millions of parents in the turbulent 60s as they watched their children freak out, drop acid and thumb their noses at "the Establishment," which was: *Who do these kids think they are and where do they think they'll be when they're middle aged?*

Notoriety, if not fame, had come to Rod Cooke on Skagit Island because he could court it during business hours while his long-suffering wife worked diligently as a checker at the Isle-Mart grocery store. One of his projects that brought this public notice included a mural painted on the outside wall of the Skagit Movie Theater, facing the busiest part of the main highway, of "stars" from the rock culture and Hollywood in a sort of drug-induced dreamscape. Other, less visible, apparitions included occasional gigs at the White Eagle Art Center with his rock band "Unconscious Copulation" and the even-rarer poetry reading at the library. To most longtime islanders, Rod Cooke was a "character" and the jazz-loving Rex slowly began to realize the painful inevitability of having Rod Cooke perform at the island celebration—if for no other reason than to draw a good crowd.

On the appointed day, at the designated hour, in the company of about 1,000 islanders who'd come out for a good time and to support "the cause," Rod Cooke and Unconscious Copulation got down. Cooke himself doubled on guitar and saxophone, backed up by his wife on piano, with drums and another guitar. Their "music" was an insipid blend of the Grateful Dead, the Carpenters, Weather Report and Pink Floyd—all delivered with the snarling, surly attitude of a Seattle punk band. Wearing skin-tight black pants and flailing his thinning hair back and forth, Cooke also delivered lyrics into a microphone that served as some sort of ritual amulet for his puerile energies—thrust up into the air, down between his legs, to one side, and up again to his mouth in a highly-rehearsed routine that would have been laughable if the volume hadn't been turned up so loud as to cause immediate deafness.

"God! I thought Mick Jagger was bad!" Rex yelled above the din toward Allison's ear. "Next time we'll get a string quartet."

"Yeah, I brought everything…knives, forks, spoons…"

"What?"

"I thought you asked me if I brought the forks yet?"

"No, no, no…Jesus, let's get away from here where we can talk."

They fought their way through the crowds of blissed-out islanders on blankets, on foot, on bicycles and on rollerblades to a grassy knoll. The noise still rattled their brains, but at least they could converse.

"Here's some potato salad and fried chicken," Allison tried to appease.

"As much as I hate this racket, I suppose we should be grateful. We've already collected $3,700 which will buy a lot of postage stamps," Rex said brightly.

"I think it's great! Look at the turnout!"

"Let's see if we can sustain this level of interest until the elections."

"I'm sure you can think of *something*." Allison gave Rex a provocative look. "You've certainly managed to sustain *my* interest."

Rex leaned over and nibbled on her earlobe, which caused her to shriek, but the sound was lost in the general pandemonium. He said something in her ear, but it too was drowned out in the noise. Allison made a questioning face, and shook her head. He cupped his hands around her ear, drew a deep breath, and hollered at the top of his lungs at the precise moment when the band stopped playing and everyone could hear him:

"*WILL YOU MARRY ME?*"

As a chorus of applause rose from the crowd, she blushed and jumped up to leave.

"Tell the man you'll marry him, sister," a large black woman said with a merry giggle as they trudged off to the car.

"OK," Allison shouted back to him. "I'll marry you!"

Another loud chorus of applause rose as they exited, Allison beet-red and Rex puffing to keep up with her.

VOLUME II

Discovery

CHAPTER 1

*F*rom the front deck of Rex' house, you could gaze clear across Puget Sound and see the skyscrapers of Seattle, the Space Needle and the icy hound's tooth of Mount Baker on the far horizon. From the same bluff, Sammamish Indians had watched in fear as Captain Vancouver sailed for the first time into what would come to be known as Puget Sound—named for Peter Puget, an explorer friend of Vancouver and fellow Englishman. The high-rigged sails of the English ships were unknown to the Sammamish, as were the language, dress and behavior of their fair-skinned crew. Happy to share nature's bounty with their celestial visitors, the Sammamish knew nothing of property rights, commerce or money. With plenty of salmon, fresh berries, herbs and pelts, what possible reason was there for anxiety or hoarding? In summer months, the deep waters of Puget Sound often were glassy and calm. In winter, arctic winds from the north sometimes howled down from Canada until they burst upon the north end of Skagit Island and pounded Rex' house along with the rest of the hilltop dwellers. During one of those winter blasts, Rex heard a terrific cracking sound outside, as if a small airplane had crashed into his back yard. He ran out into the rain and wind to find a prized blue spruce tree literally snapped in two like a toothpick by the roaring wind. In the happier days of his marriage to Cynthia, Rex had bought a two-person sea kayak as an investment in their shared fun. Despite a few cursory paddles about the island, Cynthia finally admitted that she really didn't like to kayak and the craft sat high and dry in the garage all but forgotten—until a rare sunny day arrived and Rex stared longingly out at the water.

"I remember when a surfer got bitten in half by a great white shark at Asilomar," Rex said, trance-like, to Allison as they soaked in the warm sun and cool ocean breeze on the deck one afternoon.

"Where's that?" Allison squinted her eyes.

"California, near where I once lived. Beautiful, white sandy beach. Kids surf there all year-round."

"So what happened?"

"A bunch of surfers were riding the waves just offshore in the winter. That's when the surf is the strongest. I guess they looked around and their pal was missing…then they saw his surfboard wash ashore with this huge gaping bits out of the middle."

"God, how awful!"

"Then pieces of the surfer and his wetsuit washed ashore. It was pretty grisly. The shark just came up and took one huge chomp out of the surfboard, and the kid was gone. Just like in the movies!" Rex paused. "My kids knew him pretty well. All the surfers held a wake for him on the beach, lit a big bonfire and all."

"I'll bet that took some of the romance out of being a surfer."

"It certainly scared a lot of people—for a while. But then they got right back into it." Rex shook his head. "A few years later there was another shark attack at a beach just south of Carmel—very similar. A scuba diver on a surfboard was bitten on the head by a great white. His buddy pulled him ashore and they took him to the hospital…managed to stitch him back together after about 15 hours of surgery."

"I think I'll just stay right here on *terra firma*," Allison announced.

"I suppose that wasn't much of a segue into a discussion of kayaking, was it?"

"Kayaking? Are you nuts?"

"No…well, yes—sort of. I love to kayak and I need another person to paddle the boat. It's very safe, you know. There's never been a shark attack in Puget Sound that I've heard about since I've been here. What do you say…game?"

"Boy, you sure know how to make a girl's heart go pitty-pat!"

About halfway across the Marcos Narrows that divides Skagit Island from Badger Island, they encountered the infamous Skagit current. It formed a fairly discreet border with the calmer waters close to shore and was marked by ripples and eddies that were in a constant state of agitation and movement. Even on a sunny, calm day with no strong breezes the current pushed their kayak firmly but inexorably to the southwest in a direction sideways to their destination.

"Paddle harder!" Rex shouted. "Current's not that strong, but we have to keep paddling until we get to the other side."

"I'm scared."

"Nothing to be afraid of," he said offhandedly. "Worst thing that can happen is we'll end up somewhere on the peninsula instead of Badger Island. But we can paddle through this current pretty easily—I've done it before."

They paddled furiously, occasionally clacking their oars together as they whipped them out of the water, and successfully fought the current to the other side and calmer water. There they rested a moment and sipped cool water from a thermos as they surveyed the nearby island and its wide sandy beach. Rex scooped frigid salt water from the side of the boat and doused his steamy head, then splashed some on Allison. Then they paddled on leisurely until they reached the gentle surf, and Rex jumped out to pull the kayak to shore. As they lifted the boat from the water to carry it onto the beach, Allison stumbled and fell into the shallow water. The icy baptism brought shrieks of laughter from both Rex and Allison, as they strained their sore muscles to finally beach the craft, then dropped exhausted onto the warm sands.

As they lay wet and vulnerable on the beach, bathed in soft breezes and the gentle splashing of the surf, Rex felt really good for the first time in years. Allison had given him more than love. She had led him into AA and sobriety, and for the first time ever he felt grateful—deeply grateful to be alive and grateful for the blessings that had been bestowed upon him. It was the gratitude of a man delivered from a horrible fate even though he'd hardly earned such benison either through his words or actions. Secure in their love for each other and the goodness of the nature and the universe, they fell into a soft slumber.

"Omigod!" Rex jumped to his feet as the cold water of the incoming tide splashed over him. "We gotta move the kayak—quick."

Already, the stern washed back and forth in the surf as it gathered strength and depth in its ascent up the beach. Allison sprang to her feet, too, and grabbed one end of the boat. With a violent "heave-ho" they lifted it out of the water and jogged quickly up the crest of the sand and laid it down once again.

"Well, I'm awake now," Allison said briskly.

"Me too," Rex agreed, kissing her exposed breasts. She sighed deeply as they undressed each other slowly—teasing, laughing, giving each other corny winks and blinks—until they were as hot as the sands and as heady as the wind, blown back and forth by the gusts of desire, naked and undressed unrehearsed in the sand and open air all alone with their pulsing heat. When they were done, they once again laid back in the hot crusty sand and peered across the aquamarine waters toward the tip of Skagit Island.

"When we die, let's have our ashes scattered on the beach." Allison's whisper let Rex know she was serious. "That way, we'll always be together."

"I'd love to spend eternity here with you on this shore. People would walk on us, fish would poop on us, the wind would blow us all around—but we'd be like molecules clinging together at the moment of creation."

"I've never said anything like that to anyone before, because I've never felt this way before."

"Just for your information, I haven't either. But I think we should get going before the tide comes in and washes us both prematurely into the sea!"

Hummingbird. Finch, Robin, Steller's Jay. Woodpecker. Dove, Crow. Pheasant, Peacock. Red-tailed Hawk. Bald Eagle. Seymour mentally ticked off his own avian phylum as he watched Allison and Rex make love on the beach, through his high-powered telescope. *At least birds do it in the woods, not out in the open like that. People are disgusting. I'm glad that woman stopped trying to get me in bed with her. Gotta remember what Moolana said: "You will remember when you need to remember." Still get these damn nosebleeds, though. I know he was right about the destruction of the planet, overpopulation, environmental catastrophe. Why would they even want to breed with us, anyway? We're just like animals and they're so…so spiritual, mental. We're like insects, breeding all over the place. But so are they…walk like insects, funny eyes like a bug or something…*

"Seymour, when are you going to finish painting the deck for me?"

"Right now, mother. I was just taking a break."

Oughta levitate her right on out of here. If I could.

"You said you'd have it finished by the time your father gets home!"

"Don't worry. I'm more than halfway finished. I'll call you when it's done."

As he hurriedly picked up his large brush and dipped it into the deck stain, he noticed a large, portly peahen meandering up the gravel roadway opposite the house. At a leisurely pace, it poked along drifting from side to side as if looking for something. Seymour laughed at the silly way its head bobbed forward and back each time it took a step. The awkward bird crossed onto the pavement, stood in the middle of the road for a moment as if confused, then continued toward Seymour's house. As the fowl approached, Seymour thought he could see that its eyes were yellow and he tried to train the telescope on the bird. Sensing his sudden movement, the peahen raced wildly off into the bushes and quickly disappeared in a rustling and crunching of branches.

Wonder if you can eat them? Indians probably ate everything.

Seymour picked up his brush once again and quickly spread the deck stain. It dried fast in the hot sun but he hardly noticed as he sloshed crazily back and forth trying to cover the deck as quickly as possible. The fumes from the stain were pleasantly unpleasant and gave him a heady rush…not unlike…*the table, looking out into the dark sky, metal probe or something coming way too close, going into my neck, crunching and cracking…why are they doing this?*

"Well, isn't that a lazy kid for you!"

Seymour pulled his bleary head up off the hot deck and wiped the sweat from his brow. Through the fog, he could make out his father's stern figure standing over him.

"Did you have a nice nap?" His father smiled as he reached out a firm hand to help Seymour to his feet. Dressed in an inexpensive dark blue suit, he could easily have passed for a Secret Service man.

"Oh, wow. I don't know what happened. I was painting, and I must have passed out from the fumes or something."

"It's hot out here. Why don't you come inside and take a cold shower. You can finish the deck later."

Seymour took a quick sniff of the fumes before hammering the metal lid on the stain can. He felt warm and relaxed inside, but lightheaded once again, so he drew several deep breaths before going inside where his parents were sipping cocktails.

"Do you want milk or water with dinner?" his mother asked. Seymour heard her voice as if it came from far away, and paused for a moment to consider her words. "What's wrong, son? Are you all right?"

He rolled his eyes around in his head, then looked straight at her. "Sure. I'm fine. What did you say?"

"What do you want to drink with your dinner?"

"Nothing. I'm gonna go take a shower."

His parents stared glumly at each other. "Has he been acting like this all day?" his father asked.

"You mean weird?" His mother—a flabby woman with bleached blonde hair—chuckled harshly. "With him, how would you know the difference?"

Zack had cleaned his house completely four times, after he threw out his renters, before he discovered an old letter from his ex-wife stuck to a roofing repair bill, inside a shoebox of ancient papers he was about to discard. He carefully separated the two crusty pieces of paper and examined the envelope. The date coincided with the period of their separation before the divorce was final—a period of painful insanity and drunkenness. The letter was postmarked Barrow, Alaska and had never been opened. Zack thought carefully about whether to open and read the letter or just toss it. He put it under the light bulb to see if he could decipher any telltale words that might spare him the grief almost certainly lurking inside. The letter bore a faint scene of his wife, and the sight of her handwriting was unbearable so he tore the envelope open with an angry snarl and yanked out the contents. His eyes raced through a recitation of events that had preceded her departure, and fixed on the closing lines:

"So I guess I'll always love you, Zack, but not as my husband. I'd really like to be your friend. Do you think that's possible?"

His weathered fingers balled up the note into a small lump, and he threw it across the room. "What a fucking flake!" he mumbled under his breath. It had been almost a decade since he'd received her letter, and reading her words brought back all the raw pain of the separation. Zack could still taste the bitter tears that streamed down his cheeks on Easter Sunday after dropping Vivian off at the airport so she could fly to Alaska. And he could still see the kindly, sympathetic face of the young woman in the car ahead of him on the ferry, who noticed him sobbing and held out a baker's box with a gentle invitation: "Would you like an Easter bunny cookie?"

Why can't I find a woman who is kind and gentle. Someone with bunny cookies and smiles. Someone who is a grownup and knows what they want?

In a fury of grief and disappointment, Zack picked up his machete and went outside to attack the wall of blackberries that menaced his back yard. He hacked and whacked until his hands were raw and bleeding—then slashed some more. Great thorny green shoots dropped to the ground as he continued his assault, cutting them back even to the ground. Then he doused their roots with gasoline, splashed willy-nilly from his spare fuel container, stepped back a few yards and lit a cigarette. Once the butt was burning strongly, he tapped off the ashes and flicked it into the blackberries. A terrific flash fire flared with a deafening WHOOSH, then quickly died down to a few burning embers as the last of the blackberry stalks crumpled into the ground. Zack then went back inside the house, located the mangled letter and tossed it into the blackened area of devastation to burn with a slow, ignominious flame. Then he got into his battered pickup truck and drove to town to drink beer and play pool. Through the fog of cigarette smoke, beer and noise, Zack's attention was diverted to the huge overhead television set where a talking head was discussing the political landscape on Skagit Island and the inevitability of elections to form a new Island Council.

"Hey Zack! I want a job laying asphalt," came the cry from one corner of the dark tavern.

"Yeah…I wanna be police chief," another yelled out.

"Well, you all can kiss my ass," said Ray Fongalong, switching his effeminate ass as he bent over the pool table to make a pocket shot. "I'm gonna be the city manager!"

A great hoot and holler rose up in the tavern, whistles and cheers. Zack raised his arms in a gesture of surrender.

"OK, everybody come on down and fill out an application soon as we open our doors," he said cheerfully, raising his beer bottle high in the air. "I'm sure that all of my friends are well qualified—overqualified, maybe—but the only guarantee I can make is that I won't hire any of you! That's right...I'll let the city staff do the hiring."

Another chorus of yelling, boos and hisses went up, punctuated with great belly laughter. In the general uproar, Fongalong dinked the 8-ball into the side pocket, raised his cue stick in the air victoriously and danced a little jig around the table. His antics set off another, more caustic, round of laughter among the beer-besotted patrons.

"I'm the king! I'm the king!" he exulted.

"You're the *queen*. You're the *queen*!" came the reply.

CHAPTER 2

Candidates hand-picked by IRATE members ran unopposed for seats on the Island Council. Rex was chosen mayor by acclamation, and other council members included Zack, Cerise Bagoth, Allison and Charlie Rector—scion of an old island family, realtor and pub owner. The new council was seated at its first meeting in the Grange Hall, where more than 1,000 islanders jammed into the creaky old wooden structure to witness history in the making. Its first official act was to ratify a proclamation of independence from Skookum County. Its second official act was to vote for approval of a contract with the county to provide law enforcement services to the island for one year at roughly the same cost as before the election. With assurances to the gathered crowd that drastic economies in other areas of governmental operations would soon be evident, the council voted to advertise for an island manager before adjourning to schmooze with islanders and talk to reporters. When Rex picked up his copy of *The New York Times* the next morning, he saw his photo in a small box on the front page teasing readers inside to get the whole story on the feisty little Pacific Northwest island's declaration of independence from the mainland and mainstream of American life.

"God! I hope this doesn't make every kook in America decide to move here!" Rex snorted to Allison over coffee.

"Yeah, especially those people from California!"

"OK, thanks. I needed that. I'm beginning to sound like a Northwest redneck myself. I guess it just creeps up on you."

"You're doing fine…just wanted to make you aware of how you sound."

"It's funny. When I first got here, I couldn't believe how isolationist the people were and how indifferent—even hostile—to outsiders. Now I've surpassed even the natives in my desire to be left alone. Do you suppose it's possible to love a place too much?"

"I think it's possible to love a person too much and to get into control and emotional blackmail. So I guess it's possible to love a place so much that you want to keep everyone away from it."

"Hmmmm. Sounds pretty selfish, doesn't it? But that's exactly what we're all about here with the new island government."

"Yeah, but it's a question of degree. I think we're doing the right thing."

"So do I, but I wonder whether we can make it work."

"Mr. Mayor, you're supposed to lead—not entertain doubts! You'd better not talk like that at the council meetings. You may find yourself out of office."

Rex screwed up his face painfully. "I'm thinking of asking the council to consider allowing some limited form of commercial enterprise or even tourism here on the island—just because we're gonna need the tax revenues."

She grabbed him by the arm with such firmness that Rex was astonished by her strength. "Are you nuts?" she said in a fierce whisper. "That's why people supported breaking away from the county—so we wouldn't have business and tourism and all that."

"I know, I know," Rex shook his head wearily. "It's just that I've been doing some more research and really looking at our budget. Some of our projected revenue is based on what the county has spent on the island through the years from state funding. State funding is based on the total population of the county, and then we get a share of that for things like parks and recreation."

Allison stared at him coldly.

"So now that we are no longer part of the county, naturally the county won't give us those funds and the state won't either—until we've had a few years of experience running things on the island and then we'd have to make an application to get the funds. The whole process could take three to five years."

"How much money are we talking about?" Allison said in a hissing whisper that barely concealed her shock.

"I'd say about a million bucks a year."

"A MILLION!?" Allison shouted. "This is serious."

Rex ran his hand quickly through his hair. "Well, yes it is. But I've also been doing some figuring about how we can make up the difference. I think that if we allow a few B&Bs and just a couple of more restaurants, we'd be OK. And it wouldn't really change our rural zoning or character."

"Hmmmm. Says you. I'm really skeptical about how thrilled the council will be to hear this news. Are you certain that your figures are correct? Have you talked to the county?"

"Oh, yes. They're correct. I just need to figure the best way to let the other council members know. It might be good politics to wait a while, until everyone has settled in a bit."

Or, if you're smart, you might wait until the new administrator is hired and let him deal with it."

"That sounds fiendishly Machiavellian!"

"Not really. Just sensible."

"I like the way you think. Interested in a career in politics?"

Dudley Wharton came from a Boston brahmin family, attended Harvard and got interested in the position as Skagit Island administrator because it would give him some experience just out of Harvard School of Government in running a start-up "rural city," which certainly had an exotic ring about it in the hallowed corridors of ivy on the East Coast. Tall, elegantly dressed and courteous to a fault, Wharton was the embodiment of what every concerned mother means when she urges her daughter to find a "nice boy."

Wharton was so polite and mannerly, in fact, that some council members wondered whether he could survive the rough-and-ready political tumbles that had occasioned the birth of the new government. Clean-shaven, with thick but well-groomed black hair combed straight back on his head, Wharton had steel blue eyes that gave him the look of a haunted character out of an Ayn Rand novel. In making acquaintances of the people on the Island Council and in the community with whom he would rub shoulders daily, the young man from Massachusetts was solicitous, shy and respectful. His refinement and bearing were like a breath of fresh air in the often-coarse Northwest.

His appearance and demeanor set him apart from other islanders so starkly that he was sometimes the object of ridicule behind his back. "Faggot," "geek," and "slick-dick" seemed to follow him around like a radioactive cloud, although to his face islanders—especially council members—were respectful and pleasant. Wharton sent dramatic color postcards of the quaint island home to his mother, with upbeat messages about the nearby rain forest, smoked salmon and clean quiet environment. Whenever anyone was bold enough to ask his origins, he smiled and simply said "back east," although his Bay State accent was unmistakable.

The first task he set himself, after making connections with all the key "players" on the island, was to assess the possibilities for a new form of taxation. As Rex had discovered, revenues would not be adequate for the first few years and the pressure was on the find some other source of income. Obvious choices included a local sales tax, some form of excise tax and grant funds from the federal government to study this novel form of government. And land use approaches included provision of a zone for tourist-oriented businesses, such as restaurants and curio shops. Aware of the council's strong aversion to what Rex called "Carmelization," Wharton knew he should tread lightly in that area.

"This is not unlike the challenge facing California after the passage of Prop. 13 in the early 70s that basically wiped out property tax revenues," he explained at a council meeting. "Cities, counties, school districts and special agencies all had to get creative to make up for the tremendous loss of revenue."

"Hmmmm...I remember that," Zack said vaguely. "Seems like everyone was predicting the collapse of California for a while there."

"Exactly. And it never happened, did it?" Rex chimed in. "Why do you think that was?"

"Don't really know. Guess they have some kind of magic economy down there."

"Not really." Rex couldn't help gloating. "There are just a lot of resourceful people there, and they figured out other ways to make money."

"Exactly," Wharton emphasized. "The story of California's response to Prop. 13 was used in my civic administration textbooks as a case study. I think we can draw some lessons from their experience."

"Well, one lesson we *don't* need to learn is how to let more people move up here," Zack snorted. "That's one of the main reasons we seceded."

Rex shook his head slowly to himself, and wondered whether he'd become as much of a xenophobe as the other islanders he knew. He didn't feel exactly comfortable in his role as leader of a bunch of rebel secessionists. The ideological proximity to skinheads, backwoods militiamen and brown-shirted thugs was a little too close for comfort. He squirmed in his mayor's seat as Zack ranted.

"I move we direct the administrator to come back with a full report on alternative ways of increasing revenues, both short-and long-term," Rex said officiously. His motion was carried unanimously, and Zack's red face seemed a visible sign of the anger he'd had to suppress to make it to the end of the meeting without exploding.

"Excellent first meeting!" boomed Charlie Rector, evidently unaware of the undercurrent of tension. He walked around to each council member, slapping them on their backs and shaking hands with florid enthusiasm.

"When are we going to discuss building a community arts center?" asked Cerise Bagoth, rattling the silver hoops that encircled her wrists as she gathered up her papers. "That would be one way to get more revenue."

Rex screwed up his face, privately to Allison, as Wharton announced: "I'll have a report for the council at our next meeting."

Rex was turning off the lights to head for bed when he heard a loud knock on the front door. It was a hammering, assaultive knock that sounded threatening. He switched on the porch light to see a portly, unkempt middle-aged man with several days' growth of beard holding an envelope. Cautiously he opened the door, thinking that perhaps the fellow was lost and needed directions.

"You Rex Armistead?"

"Yes, what can I do for you?"

"These papers are for you."

The slob thrust the thick envelope toward Rex, which he accepted automatically. By the time he noticed they were from a Seattle law firm, the process server had returned to his battered miniature Honda and was pulling out of the driveway with a great clatter of disintegrating mechanical parts.

"Damn!" he muttered as he tore open the envelope to find official notification that Cynthia was suing for divorce.

"Who was that?" Allison asked sleepily.

"It looks as if Cynthia is helping to clear a path for us to be together. She's filed for divorce."

Allison rolled over and sighed. "Let's get some sleep."

The next morning, she found Rex in tears sitting on a barstool at the kitchen counter. He'd spread out photographs of his children from the various ages and stages of their lives on the counter and was staring at them as if mesmerized, while tears ran down his cheeks. Allison came up behind him and wrapped her arms around him. But before she could utter a word of comfort, Rex began to bawl like a baby. His chest rose and fell in great spasms, but Allison held her bear-hug grip and moved up and down with his grief until it began to dissipate.

"'Feel the feelings, then release them,' is what my first sponsor used to tell me," she said. "I know had badly you must miss your kids."

"It's not fair," he sobbed. "I shouldn't have to get a divorce from my kids."

"You'll see your kids. It will just take time. There's no way around the pain. You'll just have to go through it—sober."

"I'm so afraid of losing my kids. I just wonder if they think I'm some kind of ogre."

Allison turned and kissed him sweetly. "No matter what they think now, it will change. It may be a long time—until they're grown up—before they know you for the terrific man you are."

"You're too kind," he said in a whisper. "I don't feel very terrific." Rex' face was ashen and downcast.

"Dear, there would be something seriously wrong with you if you felt great when you're getting a divorce," Allison said flatly. "But it ain't the end of the world. All you have to do is just don't take a drink and work the program."

"All?!"

"Well, no. You have to keep talking about it. Why don't we go to that AA meeting you like tonight?"

"I have a hard time talking, especially when I'm in pain…"

"That's OK. Everybody in the room knows exactly how you feel."

Rex harrumphed. "Do they?"

Allison drew closer, peered directly into his weepy eyes. "They understand because that's how we all stay sober. That's our lifeline, our salvation. We must be there for each other—no matter what. Do you know of the 'body of broken bones'?"

"What are you talking about?"

"In Christian mysticism, the human condition on earth is often described as 'a body of broken bones.' I guess that's one way of saying we live in a broken, imperfect world that causes us pain and where we cause each other pain. So Christ heals the body of broken bones by connecting all the pieces—us—together in the mystical body of the church."

"Wow...I'm not sure I'm ready for Christian theology, I just miss my kids."

Allison smiled gently. "Hold on and try to follow just a moment longer. So the idea is that we all need each other to complete our destiny and purpose on earth, and to heal the broken world. And I think AA makes that old idea new every day, gives us a way to light a candle in the darkness of isolation."

Rex ran his hand quickly over his face. "Have you seen the darkness?" he asked in a hushed voice.

"I see the darkness all the time; it's always with me. It's the source of most of my artwork. I need it as much as I need the light. The light pulls me up, so I can get some perspective; and the darkness pulls me down into the earth so I can feel the pain. But I never knew this until I got sober. Until then, I was just caught in the darkness—afraid, alone, drunk."

Rex took Allison's hands in his and squeezed them hard. Then he pulled her closer. "Somehow, I don't fear darkness as much any more."

"Enter the darkness, for the darkness is light," Allison said, as if to herself. "Another mystical saying. It means we can never know God, because our senses and intellect are limited. The closer we get to God, through prayer and meditation, the closer we get to total darkness where we must operate on faith. If we actually enter the darkness, then we've found God—in the cloud of unknowing."

"I certainly have my own darkness," Rex said. "I'm sure everyone in AA knows about the darkness, too. Maybe that's what we all have in common—darkness."

"And light. We can lead each other into the light because we're all in the dark."

Rex stood and began collecting his photos from the counter. "Do you suppose our connection to the darkness and to each other continue after death?"

"I don't have a clue. Why?"

"You know, that spooky business with Dragoneth and all. I just wonder…"

"Seems to me I read somewhere that Bill W. and the early AA people used to have seances where they'd commune with the spirits of dead people," Allison recalled. "It's not generally known outside AA, and probably not well known inside either. Bill W. also experimented with LSD."

"I'm getting delirious…now I REALLY need a meeting!"

"I'll make you a bet," Allison said pertly. "If you do just what we talked about, stay close to the program and the steps, you'll get through this."

"So, what's the bet? If I don't, then I get drunk?"

"No, the bet is that if I'm right then I'll treat you to dinner at La Casa Grande. If I'm wrong, then I'll treat you to dinner at Maxim's in Paris."

"Weird," Rex mumbled under his breath. "OK, it's a bet."

"Would you like to see my latest picture?"

"Sure…what is it?"

"Follow me into the studio, then you can tell me what it is."

Since his last visit to Allison's studio several weeks earlier, the place had become littered with stacks of canvasses as if she'd been on a month-long binge of creativity uninterrupted by the need to eat or sleep. But he knew that she'd maintained the usual rhythms of her life—and taken on the additional responsibility of the Island Council. He was puzzled and amazed at her output. Allison flipped through the rows of completed paintings, found the one she sought and pulled it out to show Rex.

Stepping back a few paces from the easel, Rex diplomatically scanned the motley surface of the large canvas. Embedded in its swirls of black, brown and yellow were clumps of what appeared to be straw, scattered across the surface. The overall effect was that of a desolate landscape somehow burned and decimated. In its abstraction, the painting was frighteningly graphic. It somehow suggested holocaust, nuclear annihilation, global ecological collapse.

"Wow," he said in amazement. "That's powerful. Does it have a name yet?"

"Cryobabee."

Rex chuckled, then drew closer to examine the texture of the canvas.

"Sort of reminds me of something I saw once by Anselm Kieffer. But yours is better—of course."

"Of course. I'm glad you said that!"

"Will you be having another exhibit on the island soon?"

"Nope. I just spoke to a gallery in LA that wants to show my work, and they have branches all over the world. I think I'm just gonna concentrate on that for now."

You've been busy, and I didn't even notice. This is so much more important than anything that silly Island Council will ever do."

"Do you really think so?"

"Hell, yes. You're an artist. The rest of us are just a bunch of fools, with our own little egos and dumb agendas. In 100 years, no one will remember or care what struggles were going on with the island. But your stuff will survive forever."

"I hope you are right. But the political stuff is important too, don't you think?"

"Maybe…but it's not of any lasting significance."

Allison held her breath for a moment, then spoke in a hushed whisper.

"There's another picture I'd like you to see." She reached again into the floor filing system and retrieved a somewhat smaller canvas and placed it on the easel, with her back to Rex so he couldn't see it until she moved out of the way. Then, in a Small flourish, she stepped back.

The scene was a naturalistic—even impressionistic—rendering of the old island graveyard where Zack and Rex had found the burial spot of Pittor Dragoneth. Rising from his grave like a specter was a ghostly wisp of smoke that morphed into a red-headed man with steely blue eyes dressed in black. In its juxtaposition of the romantic with the surrealistic, the painting was shocking and strange.

"Migod! What in hell are you gonna do with this one?"

"I'm not sure yet. Don't worry…I won't show it to anyone on the island."

CHAPTER 3

*W*henever rain falls on Skagit Island, its primal peace and isolation seem palpable. Even the birds become quiet, with the exception of a few noisy crows and the occasional jay. The eternal stillness of the earth that is man's 100,000-year-old inheritance only resides intact in a few places on our raped and ruptured planet. Perhaps on the peak of Mount Everest, or in the wide expanse of the Arctic Ocean, or somewhere in the midst of the Gobi Desert, that stillness can yet be found. When weather conditions are just right, it still makes a furtive guest appearance on Skagit Island, confirming in the minds of those who have chosen to live there the wisdom of their decision—against all reason, economic sense and simple expediency. Rain—slow, steady, incessant Pacific Northwest rain—comes to wash clean the trees and skies, replenish the roots and aquifers, flush the streambeds, swell the rivers and calm the mind. Someday the truth will come out that Seattle actually receives less rainfall per year than many other American cities, such as Boston or Atlanta. It remains an open question whether environmentalists and xenophobes as a kind of cultural "virus" to discourage and slow the tide of immigrants have promoted the Northwest as the rainiest place in the United States. But the simple fact is that rain is a blessing that makes the world new and fresh and on Skagit Island it falls with a slow, steady rhythm that is soothing and healing.

When it rains on the island, the sense of separateness from the mainland becomes manifest. It is a thrilling and wonderful experience to walk through the thick green vegetation of late summer in the rain and to feel fresh cool water sprinkle about your face, smell ripe blackberries and watch sea smoke rising from Puget Sound. With every crunch of the foot on under-layers of vines, ferns, weeds, wildflowers and branches, the footfalls of the lost Sammamish Indians arise again and haunt the verdant woods. A glimpse of a muscular doe and her fauns cavorting through the foliage makes the heart race, as does the sighting of a red-tailed hawk swooping down upon its hidden prey.

The deeper one penetrates into this web, the freer one becomes from the enslaving attachments of "the world." It becomes possible to believe the random phrases from Thoreau that swarm through the brain during such an excursion and to see the earth as the great gift that it is and to sense our own abiding responsibility to preserve that gift for all generations—not just for humans but for all species.

On such a rainy day, Rex lost himself in the woods, hills and ravines of Skagit Island. He wandered like a storm cloud, tossed about by tempests over the sea, aware only of his own mutability and transience on earth. As he reached the peak of a hillock, Rex gazed across the waters of Puget Sound and realized that the steep slope of the bluff on which he stood continued its descent into and well below the level of the water and he was dumbstruck with the interconnectedness of all creation. With little effort of imagination, he could see the entire basin now filled with seawater as the mile-deep iceberg that had carved out the topography of the Northwest thousands of years before. And he wondered, with trepidation, how quickly the terrible approach of global warming would cause those waters to rise—and to what height—once again transforming the landscape and possibly even choking off life itself.

With frightening regularity, newspapers now carried evidence from all over the globe of man's destructiveness as measured by the depletion of the ozone layer, the sacrifice of the Amazon rain forest and melting of the polar ice caps. What had begun as a seemingly ineffectual outcry by a few college students in the 1970s has now become the fodder of mainstream political debate. And yet the destruction continued. Obtaining a global consensus on an effective approach to the world's environmental problems seemed as impossible as achieving a global approach to peace. Destruction of the planet, with extinction of humanity and most living species, seemed inevitable unless some ecological catastrophe occurred that pushed the world to the brink of disaster but stopped short of total annihilation. Every scenario seemed bleak beyond comprehension, and Rex felt a profound sadness as he took in the relative innocence and freshness of his surroundings.

New virus discovered in African cave! Kills humans instantly! Earth lashes out at humans for thousands of years of abuse! Mother Nature develops strange new drugs to rid herself of civilization! Medical science stymied! Obese Americans dropping dead in their SUVs. Hooray! Hooray!

As Rex walked home, the sky opened and rain fell in great gushing bucketsful. Every drop that reached his lips was sweet beyond belief. Rex found Allison painting in her studio. As he approached the extra-large canvas, he realized what the streaks and blurred colors evoked: a rainstorm over Skagit Island.

In the mail, Rex discovered a large Manila envelope containing a thick report from the makeshift Town Hall, a small cramped office above Charlie Rector's pub and pizza eatery, "Proposed Expansion of the Commercial Areas of Skagit Island." Its 200-plus pages were condensed in a 10-page summary at the front in which Dudley Wharton proposed three options for the council's consideration:

- Creation of a "visitor zone" around the periphery of the existing town, to permit operation of bed and breakfast businesses,

- Increased commercial use of the central village core, to permit creation and expansion of restaurants, gift shops and other visitor-oriented services,

- A new tax surcharge on all commercial retail activity on Skagit Island.

Anticipated tax revenues from each sector of the island's meager economy were broken down in charts, as well as projected revenues over a 10-year period if the suggested zoning amendments were made. The financial projections showed Skagit Island breaking even within five years and then building a surplus—if the commercial areas were expanded.

"Wharton says we can float municipal bonds to cover our bills for the first few years, then repay it back after the fifth year by enacting a new tax," Rex told Allison as he handed her the report. "But first we have to develop some kind of retail base so there's something to tax."

"Does that mean I can get a community development grant from the city to open a gallery in town?"

"I seriously doubt it. What it really means is that, if you want to go into business you'll have to assume all the risks yourself and pay extra taxes when you start to have an income. Pure capitalism!"

Allison screwed up her face. "What kind of backlash do you suppose we'll be facing when this comes up at the council? We promised the voters we could run this place with 'no new taxes,' remember?"

"I know," Rex said with obvious irritation. "Maybe we could just put a three-year limit on the surtax so everyone understands it's only temporary. But even that seems kind of risky. I mean, what if the revenues just aren't there?"

Allison plopped down at the kitchen table wearily. "Want some iced tea?"

Rex dropped into the chair next to her and tossed the fat envelope on the table with a "thwack!"

"Back in the days when I was a reporter, I learned not to get personally involved in politics," Rex said. "It was sort of a mixed blessing. There were plenty of times when I really felt passionately about an issue and wanted to do something. But it was also a convenient excuse whenever people tried to recruit me for their hare-brained causes." He took a long draft of the cool iced tea. "Now that I'm *really* involved with politics, I'm beginning to wonder why."

"Getting' cold feet?"

"Well, maybe that's one way to put it. I just seem to feel the weight of how hard it is to get consensus to get anything accomplished."

"That's nothing…wait until we try to get a tax approved!"

Rex wiped his hand briskly across his forehead. "Well, we're all here on this island because we're basically escapists, aren't we? I mean, we all thought we could find something here that we were missing in 'the world.' At least, that's why I came here anyway. But I'm beginning to think there's no escape. Nowhere to run…that somewhere we have to make a stand. It may as well be here on Skagit Island."

"You can run, but you can't hide," Allison said wistfully.

"What?"

"Oh, just something I remembered," she said, shaking her head. "My father used to say that all the time."

"You can run but you can't hide," Rex repeated. "You can run but you can't hide. Maybe that should be the motto for Skagit Island!"

Seymour tossed and turned in his bed, unable to find sleep. Every time he closed his eyes, startling memories and images flooded into his twilight consciousness.

Some kinda light out there everywhere in here all around me coming in bright and cold. Are they coming again? Why can't I move or scream? Is this some kinda dream or trance? And who in hell are these funny little guys with the big eyes, creeping all around me? Floating, floating up and into the air covered with light. I'm scared but I can't say any-

thing...just floating up higher. Hanging out here just floating up and up...that thing is opening and I'm going inside. It's so huge and just cold and sterile, like a hospital, and all these other people are lying on tables. What are they doing? Why are they...who are they? All these people just lying there like me, paralyzed. He...she...is looking hard into my eyes, just staring...kinda cute if they weren't so funny looking. Like asking me something—NO! You can't do that. I don't want that thing on me, in me, up inside my nose...or my butt. Stop it! Why don't they listen and pay attention? Taking something from me, taking my cum...into this metal tube or something. What the fuck are they doing? You slimy little bastards, lemme outa here!!!

He got out of bed and walked to his window, which looked out onto a moonlight-drenched meadow. The night sky was clear and he could see the crisply defined shadows of the trees in the bright moonlight. Dazed and rattled, Seymour stared for a long time into the quiet, still night. Still unable to sleep, he sat down at his cluttered desk and turned on his shortwave radio receiver. It buzzed and crackled as he wrenched the tuning dial, half expecting to find some answer to his dilemma. A cacophony of voices, languages and messages bombarded his ears in a sort of global fugue state word salad.

"...and in the Pacific Northwest near Seattle police are reporting a rash of calls from people who say they saw lighted objects in the sky tonight...*CRACKLE*...got not idea what could have caused this rash of calls from so many people, some obviously upset...*ZZZZT*...has been recent sunspot activity that caused some communications problems but nothing like this...*CRACKLE*...will update this story as we get more information but for now...*ZZZZT*..."

Seymour switched off his radio, fingers trembling, went back to bed and pulled the covers over his head. Still he trembled, and still he was unable to sleep. But he lay motionless and breathed quietly, like a kid playing possum with his parents. He remembered the first time his parents sent him away to summer camp, the dark dark night when all the campers gathered around a huge bonfire to await the coming of Crowman, the sudden flareup of green flames, then the great swooping black-winged bird soaring closer and closer to the campers, terrifying them—screams, panic, someone grabbed a burning stick to scare the apparition away. Then hiding under his covers, staying totally still, frozen with fear and unable to sleep all night. Warm breeze puffing through the screened window—the hot breath of the lurking Crowman on his neck?

As he cowered in his bed, Seymour fairly jumped up when a blinding shaft of light burst through his window and into his small room. It penetrated the covers as if they were tissue paper, and he knew there was no point in trying to hide any longer. Slowly, Seymour lifted the covers from his eyes and peered into the horrific light that illuminated his room brighter than daylight, brighter than the moonlight outside.

He felt a presence near him, the same kind of feeling one sometimes gets when being watched from a distance—a vague, uneasy sense that one is not alone. His anxiety melted and he felt warm and peaceful. He was aware of a pair of large, black eyes scanning him. Then an arm raised up and he floated gently into the beam of light, out of the window, up high into the air. Serenely he went up into the ship and found himself again on a platform, but this time it was more like a reunion than a kidnapping. All about the rounded room, other people—humans—were stretched out on tables undergoing various procedures, in a seemingly unconscious condition but with their eyes open. As he lay on the table, helpless but unresigned to his powerlessness, a softly feminine creature with the same large black upturned eyes and dry looking grayish skin approached him. What was different was her head of fine, sparse golden hair and her ever-so-slightly raised, bare breasts. Like the others, she moved cautiously as if lacking in physical energy. But her luminous eyes and angelic hair made her seem—almost human.

She peered closely into his eyes, turned her head slightly to one angle as if questioning whether he remembered her. Although Seymour did, in fact, remember her as the young girl who had been paraded past him on his last journey into the ship, she now had reached a lovely adolescence and despite his seeming paralysis, he desired her. She gently drew one small hand down his chest and began touching his member until it was stiff and throbbing. Then, almost matter-of-factly, she climbed atop the platform where he lay motionless and straddled him, carefully dilating her small and obscure sex and slowly bringing him into her. Then she moved gently up and down a few times, while a half dozen of the others stood about motionless, peering curiously with their mute black eyes. Almost before it had begun, it was over and she climbed down, peered deeply into his face. Unable to speak, Seymour tried to wink at her. She nodded her head slowly, then turned and walked off and disappeared somewhere into the ovoid ship.

Once again Seymour floated on a beam of intense light down from the night sky and back into his room, into his bed where he fell fast asleep. He awoke early the next morning with no conscious recollection of the previous night's events. He did remember twisting the dial on his short wave radio, listening to static and then returning to his bed. When he showered, he noticed a thin trickle of blood from his nose, which soon stopped and he thought nothing further of it. Then Seymour got to work on the long-delayed deck.

CHAPTER 4

❀

"*I* don't see how we can balance the books unless we proceed with the expansion of the retail district, as the administrator has outlined." Zack's face was stern and sullen as he spoke before about 150 islanders who'd gathered for the council's second meeting. "I know this isn't exactly what any of us had in mind when we voted for secession. But I guess the realities of economics don't stay on the mainland any more than the tourists."

"That's right, Zack," Rex said. "But maybe it's too soon to know for sure whether we'll be effective in maintaining our rural character. This whole thing is really an experiment—just like the American Revolution. I don't see that this kind of minimal zoning adjustment threatens anybody. We'd be wise to encourage a balance of economic uses in town."

"Personally, I'd be very happy if we got some more galleries and maybe even artists' studios in town as a result of this amendment," Allison added. "There are currently two art galleries on Skagit Island. Even if we experience 100 percent growth, that's only four galleries! Is that too many? I don't think so, and I know a lot of other artists on the island who feel the same way."

A ripple of applause went through the audience. Allison smiled and waved at her supporters and fellow artists.

"I'm with the others on this," Cerise Bagoth said. "We need to develop our economic base a little more if we want to have the freedom to exist as a separate government. It's really kind of a classic dilemma: how do you grow the economy without killing the goose that laid the golden egg? The primary purpose of incorporation was to have self-determination. Now that we have it, we also have the responsibility to pay our own bills that goes along with independence."

"Just because we had our little revolution, doesn't mean we decided to abandon capitalism," chimed in Charlie Rector, with somewhat sarcastic tone. "The sooner we get started on this, the better off we'll all be. I move approval."

So in their first official action, the Island Council voted unanimously to allow limited expansion of the commercial district to include bed and breakfast, restaurant and other tourist-oriented activities—as well as a .05-cent sales surcharge—to a mixed chorus of applause and boos from the assembled crowd. In a mock ceremonial gesture, Wharton rose and handed each council member a small plastic fish. "Brain food," he explained. "We're all gonna need it."

Just as the council was about to adjourn, Seymour rose and came forward holding up one arm politely, like a student asking the teacher for permission to go to the bathroom.

"Seymour Creighton, a senior at the high school. I'm making a butterfly census in the Cemetery Hill area of the island for a paper I've been working on for about a year. I've found three different rare species of butterfly here on our island. We already know that butterflies are very sensitive to certain manmade pollutants such as toxic chemicals, odors and exhaust fumes. So I want to propose the creation of a butterfly habitat preservation zone running roughly from Cemetery Hill down to Red Creek—about five square miles. I have tons of research showing where the actual habitat is and what the species are, and I'd be happy to share it with the council."

Seymour wrestled awkwardly with a large, hand-drawn map of the island showing the area of butterfly habitat. Just as he succeeded in unfolding it, the floppy sheets imploded and cascaded to the floor with a "plop!"

"What exactly do you mean by a 'preservation zone'?" Rector inquired.

"A place with only limited contact with humans," Seymour answered. "In California, there's a town where the Monarch butterflies spend the winter after migrating from Mexico. They always come back to the same trees every year. And the city has designated that as a butterfly preserve. People can visit, but they can't actually touch the trees or disturb the butterflies. And they must be quiet. Butterflies hate loud noises."

"I assume the land you're talking about is private property," Zack said. "Are you proposing that we purchase the land and put it in open space?"

"Hmmmm…yeah, that would be cool. Or if the council doesn't have the funds maybe the property owners would consider donating it."

Wharton shook his head almost imperceptibly, while a couple of council members stifled a chuckle.

"Thank you for presenting your thoughts to the council," Zack said. "I'm sure we will want to look into this. Meeting is adjourned."

Somewhat hurt and confused by his reception at the council meeting, Seymour went home and reviewed his butterfly handbooks to see if he'd made some error in presenting his case. He quickly scanned the already-mentioned pages, mentally reviewing what he'd said. When he realized that he had said exactly what he believed to be the truth, he was even more puzzled that his serious concerns would be met with laughter and derision. He looked at his long, tapered fingers as he held the booklet. There was something strange and yet familiar in their shape…like, like…like the fingers of the woman on the ship. *If I'm one of them why do they leave me here like some kind of freak on this earth? What kind of stupid punishment are they trying to give me?*

Seymour opened his window to the dark night and looked longingly outside, up into the star-speckled heavens, and sighed heavily. Then, for the first time in his life, tears formed at the corners of his eyes and rolled down in creeping, warm rivulets.

"We gotta go fishing again." Zack cornered Rex at the doorway and started desperately into his eyes. "I'm not sure we're still friends."

"Don't be ridiculous, of course we're still friends," Rex chuffed. "But I'll still go fishing with you anyway. How about this weekend?"

"OK. I'll come by for you Sunday. This time we're gonna go to the lake so can swim ashore if anything happens."

"Sounds great. I'm not worried."

Allison returned to her canvasses with a newfound determination. What had once seemed quaint and curious about Skagit Island now seemed more each day to be stifling and deadening. Only through reaching a wider audience for her art could she hope to thrive spiritually. All would be well, she felt, if only she had a connection to a greater and larger world—a world that loved and rewarded her talents. If that were possible, then the isolation of the island would once again seem to be a nurturing cocoon rather than an ever-tightening noose around her neck. Although not conscious of her growing desperation, Allison increasingly found in her periods of creativity the only justification for her existence and shred of joy—aside from her relation with Rex. None of this had she shared directly with Rex, although he sensed a growing restlessness in Allison's thousand-mile stare and ability to quickly tune out those things and people that seemed to bore her. Since moving in with Rex, she had completed 24 paintings and begun a half-dozen more, Already, the gallery in Los

Angeles had taken 10 of her paintings. Like a racehorse just out of the starting gate, her stride lengthened with each day. So while Rex and Zack went fishing ("drumming," Allison called it), she painted ever-larger scenes of madness, murder and mayhem—all expressed abstractly and tangentially with dark colors matted with clumps of straw, seaweed and sanitary napkins.

Once launched into the cold, steamy early morning waters of Heron Lake, Zack and Rex shivered and huddled over their paltry bait boxes while they attempted to slide squirming, bloody words onto their rusty fishhooks by the dim light of an old flashlight.

"Godammit!" Rex howled into the still air as the fishhook plunged deep into his thumb, sending up a gusher of blood. He thrust his hand into the frigid water and swished it back and forth to cleanse the wound.

"Here, pour some of this on it." Zack handed him a flask filled with gin, and Rex did as instructed. "Natural disinfectant."

"Got a band-aide on this old piece of shit?"

"Just wrap this around it," Zack said, handing him a crumpled old handkerchief.

As they struggled with the wound in the dawn darkness, the boat rocked crazily from side to side. Rex instinctively moved to the center of the hull and lay down to stabilize the craft. In so doing, his backside became drenched in ice cold water as he lay, face heavenward, wondering why he'd agreed to another maritime adventure with Zack. On the horizon, he noticed a bright aura of light that seemed to be slowly shifting color—from orange to yellow to blue to white.

"Damn, is that the sunrise?" Rex mused.

"Where...oh, that? Hell no! That's south—not east. Wonder what the hell that is."

They watched as the light continued to pulse, then rise slowly into the dark sky until it moved directly toward them, increasing in size and intensity until there was a huge circular light directly overhead. There it stopped, hovered and rotated noiselessly.

"Let's get the fuck out of here, Zack! Start that goddam engine!"

While the men started in dumbstruck awe, Zack struggling to whip the outboard into life, the object continued slowly on its course overhead and moved north. Then it turned eastward and shot out of sight, leaving the sky dark once again.

"Start that fucker!" Rex yelled, and as he did the engine fired up. Zack led them quickly to shore, where they pulled the boat onto the bank, ran into the truck and raced home, skidding from side to side on the dirt road in the dimly lit morning. "Goddamit, don't kill us on this fucking road, man. Whatever it was, it's gone now. Let's get to a phone," Rex tried to interject some sanity.

"So who we gonna call—fucking Ghostbusters?"

"I'm gonna call the FAA and see if they have any reports of an unusual object in the sky. After that, I'm taking a hot shower and getting back into bed with my woman!"

Zack gave him a pained expression, and Rex felt badly for him. He put his arm on Zack's shoulder and patted him in a manly fashion. "It's OK, pal. Count your blessings. Sometimes it's better to be single."

"Can I get in bed with you two?" Zack asked with abandon. They both burst into wild laughter, fueled as much my their fear as by the cold senseless solitude of being born to go fishing at strange hours in even stranger circumstances.

"Wow! Did you see this?" Allison tossed the *ClamShell* onto the breakfast table. "Seymour is missing."

"What do you mean, missing? Disappeared?"

As he sputtered, Rex grabbed the paper and read the front page headline: "FBI joins search for missing island youth." He held the paper motionless in front of his face in silence while Allison cleared the breakfast dishes.

"That's too bad," he said. "Seymour is a really nice kid. Says here they don't have any clues or any apparent reason for the disappearance. What do you think of this?"

"If the FBI doesn't have a clue, I sure as hell don't either. Maybe he went into Seattle to find a prostitute and he's locked away in some motel fucking his eyes out!"

"Hmmm…not likely. A kid like that doesn't make enemies. He doesn't make friends either, unfortunately. You don't suppose some other teenagers did something to him because he's such a nerd?"

"I hope not. But it wouldn't be the first time something like that has happened. A while back, *The New York Times* ran a feature about women on death row in America. There's a woman in her 30s in prison in Alabama awaiting execution for murdering another girl when they were teenagers. She and her husband tortured the girl, injected her with drain cleaner, shot her and dumped her body in a ravine somewhere in rural Alabama. Both of them were sentenced to death."

"Omigod, how ghastly! How old were they when they murdered this girl?"

"About 17, I think. It was some kind of teenage rivalry thing that got out of hand.

Rex had to force the words from his throat. "Let's hope he just went out on an extended butterfly field trip and is still collecting specimens somewhere."

A solemn mood pervaded the next council meeting, occasioned as much my the fact that the brief civic honeymoon already was over as by the absence of Seymour, who had been scheduled to give a follow-up presentation on butterfly habitat and preservation zones. In his absence, Rex shepherded the item through the agenda.

"Despite the untimely disappearance of a most unusual and highly gifted student by the name of Seymour Creighton, we are committed to working through his concept," Rex said. "I've discussed this information item informally with the other council members individually and there seems to be a feeling that this is a good idea. We'd like to hear the administrator's report."

Wharton outlined the cost involved in purchasing the five-acre tract defined in Seymour's proposal: $1 million assuming the land were for sale, which it wasn't. The area impinged on three property owners' lands and included a streambed that fed Heron Lake. If the Island Council created a separate legal entity—similar to a redevelopment agency—to negotiate the purchase and preservation of the land, then property owners could be approached and offers extended.

"This is something we just can't afford, especially if we're borrowing money for our first few years of operation," Rector snorted. "It would be nice to preserve everything if we could, but we have to get our priorities straight. This government was set up to preserve the whole island from development at the hands of the county. I think that's an important enough mission for now. Maybe later we can consider this idea again."

"Would there be any legal liabilities if one or more council members were to make inquiries of the property owners about this proposal?" Zack wondered. "Just to see if they might be interested in donating some land."

"If council members approached the property owners individually, and as private citizens interested in the welfare of the community rather than as elected officials, I believe there would be no legal liability issues. But I'd caution council members against making any representations whatsoever on behalf of the Island Council," Wharton said.

"I would like to find out of there is any support from the property owners," Rex added. "If there is, then we could bring word back to the council and see where we go from there. Would that put us on the "Wanted" posters at the Post Office, Mr. Wharton?"

A good-natured chuckle rumbled through the meeting. "No, I believe that would be well within the law."

"Good," Allison chimed in. "And if we're successful, we'll call it the Seymour Creighton Butterfly Preserve."

CHAPTER 5

*B*y the time Rex' divorce was final, he and Allison already were planning their wedding. It would be in the meadow adjacent to the old cemetery, encircled by helium balloons in the shape of butterflies. Everyone on the island—living or dead—would be welcome. Their wedding was to be a celebration of the spirit of independence that had given birth to the new island government, as well as a celebration of their new life together. In a flourish of enthusiasm, Rex hired a string quartet from Seattle to perform for a mere $350. The musicians were grateful for the gig, and eager to negotiate down from the flat fee of $500. By throwing in ferry fares, meals and free passes to the Island Cinema—plus slightly exaggerated tales about the lush beauty of Skagit Island—Rex was able to give the wedding a touch of class and Allison renewed confidence in their union. Afterwards, they went to Portland by train for a long weekend. The ride down the coast was slow and peaceful, punctuated by flocks of bald eagles soaring over the Pacific Ocean and pleasant beach-strollers waving Norman Rockwell-style at their passing train. The comfortable steel womb of the passenger coach provided Rex and Allison with an opportunity to snuggle, giggle and smooch.

With its gothic stone buildings, closed-off downtown streets and "alternative" shops, galleries, restaurants and bookstores bathed in Northwest fog and California sunshine, Portland was the perfect place for a quick getaway. Allison found a thrift shop where abundant items awaited her artistic hand for inclusion in sculptures; Rex found a photo gallery that specialized in images of jazz musicians. At Allison's encouragement, he bought a poster-sized print of Dexter Gordon holding his saxophone over his crossed legs, gazing dreamily upward at the smoke rings that curled from his cigarette. Allison filled a couple of bags with small statuettes, polished rocks of various sizes and shapes, rusty tea canisters and god-knows-what. Sated with their browsing, they returned to their hotel mid-afternoon and fell into a happy lovemaking session.

When they awoke from a brief slumber, Allison put her arms around his neck and purred: "You're the only man I've ever man able to trust."

"Really?! How come?"

"You're the only guy I've ever known who could talk about feelings."

"Wow...thanks. Maybe being sober has something to do with it."

Allison bit her lip, and grew pensive.

"I want to tell you something I've never told anyone before."

"Sure, if you feel OK. I'll keep it confidential."

"When I was a college student living in LA, I was raped by three men at gunpoint. They stopped in their car while I was walking home late one night and asked directions, then pulled me inside and drove off. They must have held me captive for several hours. First one, then the other, while one held on me the whole time."

"Goddamn!" Rex roared. "How awful! How did you escape?"

"Well, somehow they pulled into a gas station for cigarettes or something and I managed to get out of the car and run inside. They scrambled into their car and took off."

"I'm so sorry, dear. If I'd been there I would have shot *them*! Did you go to the police?"

"Yes, and they arrested two of them the next morning. The other one was arrested a couple of days later. By the time the trial happened, I was living in San Francisco and had to go back to testify. It was terrible," she said, tears rolling down her cheeks.

"I'm amazed that you want anything to do with men at all."

"Not men—just you."

Rex kissed her on the forehead and squeezed her hands.

"Maybe that's one reason we get along so well," he said, thoughtfully. "I wasn't raped in the technical sense but I was emotionally violated and physically abused by my stepfather. He actually tried to strangle me a couple of times. Whenever I knew he was going to be around, I found some way to be out of the house. My mother, God bless her, in the throes of her own alcoholism seemed oblivious to it all. He took care of the physical abuse and she handled the verbal part. It was quite a family. It's a wonder I survived at all. My goal in life when I was a kid was to grow up and be big and strong enough to kill my stepfather. I'd probably have done it, if I hadn't gone to live with my father."

"When was that?"

"When I was 13 years old. My father's approach was to buy me a new suit and send me to cotillion—to get over all the years of hell by pretending they never happened. In those days, people didn't talk about domestic violence, child abuse and alcoholism. It got swept under the carpet with the broken whiskey bottles. It worked fine, for a while. I became a perfect gentleman, did well in school, had dates and got into a good college. But after graduation, I married another alcoholic and off we went on our drinking careers. I've only started to deal with some of my anger toward my stepfather, and toward my mother for allowing him into our lives—since I've been sober."

Tears slowly dripped down the corners of Allison's eyes. "My father was a mean-spirited man who sometimes hit, sometimes was abusive, but I never had to deal with anything like that. I know we must both have some anger inside at how we were treated."

"No doubt. The only answer that I know of is love," Rex whispered. "That's why you mean to much to me. I believe we help each other by demonstrating that love can overcome any sort of pain and disappointment."

Rex went to the window of the hotel room, pulled back the curtains and gazed across the landscape of Portland in the afternoon sunlight. In the distance, a train pulled out of the station where they'd arrived and began its slow serpentine journey through the city and out into the countryside. The same familiar pace of life—people coming and going, trains leaving and arriving, the sun rising and setting—was reassuring but suffocating. The familiar instinct to flee that had dogged him since childhood rose and filled his throat with an acrid venom. *Is this all there is? Does it all come down to a mere confluence of healing and hope with pain and despair. Where are joy and freedom? Probably not in this life, here on earth.*

"I don't think God put us on earth to suffer," Allison said. "I know that Buddha said 'life is suffering,' but I really believe some of that suffering we bring on ourselves by being too willful, self-seeking and demanding."

Rex turned to her slowly, and sat on the bed. "I agree with you. Let's go find a great restaurant and have some fun!"

On the train ride home, Allison snuggled close to Rex as they watched the afternoon sun set over the liquid gold of the Pacific. "I think I'm getting bored with the island," she said offhandedly.

"How's that?" he replied, puzzled.

"Oh, it's been a great place to retreat and to heal, and to get lots of art work done, but I'm getting really restless. Whenever I go to LA for a show, I feel the pulse of life and it makes me feel alive. Then when I come back to the island I feel like I'm going into hibernation. My whole body just kind of shuts down."

Rex peered silently out at the smooth water for a moment. "Yeah, I know that you mean. I wonder whether we have itchy feet because we just got married or maybe because we're both entering a new phase of our lives. I feel the same thing—especially after being in the city for a few days."

"It's odd, really, because I've gotten to know more people on the island since this whole political thing happened than in all the years before. It's fun being involved with that and what we're doing feels really important. Maybe I'm just a gypsy at heart."

"How long have you lived on the island?"

"Altogether...let's see...it's been almost 10 years."

"Just a little longer than me. When we moved here, I told Cynthia I thought it would take us at least 10 years to put down roots and get established."

"I really feel the need for a steady home but as I get older, my art work becomes more and more important to me. I'm just not nourished by other creative spirits on the island—or in Seattle, either. I feel drawn to someplace like LA or New York where there is a tremendous artist culture."

Rex' head began to race and he could feel fear rising in his throat—the feat of abandonment. "Well, I feel like I have a commitment to stick with the Island Council, at least until things are up and running."

"That's fine," she said. "I'm just letting you know how I feel. I would never do anything without talking to you about it. Whatever we do, we'll do it together. And there's no real urgency. I'll survive for quite a while the way things are, especially if I get to go to LA now and then."

"Maybe. But you have a point. There is a very fine line between the peace and quiet needed for artistic creation and the kind of isolation that strangles life and creativity. Sometimes I think everyone on the island walks that fine line and we cross over often without even knowing it."

Allison's eyes grew larger. "It's not only that, Rex," she said in a loud whisper. "What about all that weird stuff with Mr. Dragoneth? What the hell is that all about? I mean, I could sort of accept that as 'quaint' but then there was the kid disappearing and all. Doesn't that kind of spook you?"

Rex laughed heartily. "Yeah, I see your point. I guess if I hadn't been so wrapped up in all this politics, I would have noticed those things more. You're right—it *is* spooky. I don't know whether it's because it's Skagit Island or some other..."

"Where else have you heard of such things?" Allison's fright was now palpable.

"Hmmm...*Bizarre Tales* comic books?"

"Look godammit, I'm serious! This shit scares me and I don't like it. I want us to get the fuck off Skagit Island!"

Several passengers on the opposite side of the aisle turned their heads in Allison's direction as her voice grew louder. "Let's go to the diner and continue this conversation," Rex whispered, rising from his seat and extending a hand to Allison. Wide-eyed passengers gazed at them as they scurried out of the sliding metal door with a "pfoosh!" The rickety-rackety sideways jogging of the train acted as somewhat of a soporific. By the time they elbowed their way to a tiny seat by the window in the diner, the sun was just slipping below the horizon and night was in the air.

"I'm sorry I got upset like that," Allison said. "It's not your fault. We both chose to live on the island. I guess I'm mad at myself for not doing something sooner."

"That's OK. I understand completely. I often feel the same way. But I feel I owe the Island Council at least a year of my life so they can get things started on the right track. Does that sound like an impossibility to you?"

Allison wiped back a tear from her cheek. "I just love you so much, and I'm sorry for being such a bitch. Of course a year is fine...I'll be with you always." Then, regaining her composure with a faint chuckle under her breath: "But I may have to take a few trips to wild and crazy places like New York."

"That's fine! Maybe I'll just go with you."

"OK, then let's start planning our first trip. How does Christmas in New York sound to you?"

"Wow! I can't imagine...but I'm trying."

"Think of all the Christmas decorations, the special gallery shows, even jazz concerts. New York is ablaze during the holidays. We could have a ball."

"Maybe...sounds exciting. I've never done anything like that before. It's always been the Christmas tree with gifts, kids, cookies..."

"I know. But this will be our very own Christmas, together. Maybe we'll start a new tradition!"

Rex recalled a bitter cold Christmas from his childhood, shortly after his parents' divorce. One night in the frozen sleep between Thanksgiving and Christmas, Rex was amusing his mother, brother and sister around the Christmas tree with impersonations of cartoon characters when the doorbell rang. A well-groomed man in a blue suit stood on the doorstep with two large black bags in his hands and explained politely that he had selected this very household for a preview of the new edition of the Universal Encyclopedia. And could he come in for a moment to explain some of the features of this greatest event in the history of publishing? As his mother hesitated, Rex got wind of the conversation and pleaded with her to let the man inside. Reluctantly but good-naturedly, she opened the door and allowed the knowledge merchant to enter and unveil the wonders of his books on the sofa. For what seemed an eternity, he went over the features of the new encyclopedia, demonstrated the various indices and bibliographies, vouched for the credentials of the authors and editors who had completed this mammoth task. Rex watched with wide-eyed fascination as the slick, fresh, pungent pages unfurled images of the steamy Amazon rain forest, fat hippos in African rivers, stark Argentine cities and blonde Norwegian milkmaids. Sensing her son's growing excitement, Mrs. Armistead became uneasy as the salesman went into the various financial arrangements for purchase of this investment in the future of her children's education. Yearly, semi-annual, and monthly payment options were outlined, with the summary question: "Which of these plans would you prefer, ma'am?" Rex searched his mother's face as a tear dripped down her soft cheek. "None of them," she said, her voice cracking. "We can't afford it." And the knowledge merchant was shown the door, finally leaving with his heavy black bags once again sealed shut. Then his mother collapsed into a living room chair and sobbed openly. "It's OK, Mom," he soothed her. "We have encyclopedias at school and those weren't that good anyway." Her sobbing continued unabated, and Rex puzzled over whether he'd done something wrong to cause his own mother such pain. Some 40 years later, as if to atone for the disappointment that Rex obviously had felt, she left Rex all of her meager collection of books when she died. Most were best-selling novels from the 50s and 60s, a few fatuous self-help books, and a couple were art history texts from her college days. Of these, the only one he wanted and kept was the family Bible that had been his grandfather's. In the center were genealogical entries that reached back several generations, as well as newspaper clippings of important family achievements and obituaries.

"Maybe I'm old fashioned, but I have a hard time imagining Christmas anywhere but at home. We'll see," Rex said. "Speaking of home, I'll be glad to sleep in our own bed tonight."

CHAPTER 6

"*M*igod! Did you see that?" Rex waved his hand toward the windshield while almost running their car into the dark ditch on the way home from the ferry. "It looked like a poster with a picture of Seymour on it…something official-looking."

"Wow. Turn around and let's go take a look."

Before he could turn, they encountered another poster on a tree ahead of them and Rex carefully slowed to pull off onto the shoulder. Engine running and lights on bright, they approached the poster gingerly.

MISSING—REWARD FOR INFORMATION

Seymour Creighton, 18, of Skagit Island was last seen alive on the evening of October 20. When last seen, he was wearing a dark sweater, blue jeans, high-top tennis shoes, and a yellow windbreaker. Creighton is 6 foot 1 and weighs 150 lbs. He sometimes speaks with a stutter, and takes prescription medications to control a medical condition. Anyone with information regarding his whereabouts, or the circumstances related to his disappearance, is asked to contact the Federal Bureau of Investigation at (800) 765-8400, ext. 1252. Mr. and Mrs. Creighton, his parents, have offered a $10,000 reward for credible information about the disappearance of their son.

"Holy cats! What do you suppose…?" Allison sputtered.

"I don't have a clue, unfortunately. I wish I did. I just wonder if somehow he managed to piss off some property owners. Or…"

"Or what?"

"Or whether the developers who wanted to build the bridge might have had some reason for wanting him out of the picture."

"It kind of gives me the creeps to think that a nice kid like Seymour would just vanish off the face of the earth—especially in a place like Skagit." Allison's voice quivered.

"Well, we don't know that yet. It's still possible that he fell or something out in some remote part of the island, and was injured."

"I thought the police had already been all over the island with bloodhounds looking for him. What if he drowned?"

Rex stood up abruptly as if called to attention. "Come on…let's go. I don't like standing out here by the side of the road like this."

They drove on in silence in the shimmering moonlight until they reached the house. Rex felt depressed and listless, unable to get out of the car. But Allison's opening and closing of car doors jarred him back to reality. He felt pushed down by a huge weight of some kind, barely able to move. He just wanted to fall into bed and sleep for 100 years. As he climbed into his familiar bed, he threw one arm around Allison's warm body and wished for oblivion—total release from the world. He didn't care if he never saw daylight again. He was ready to join the world of Pittor Dragoneth and Seymour Creighton.

After a few days back on Skagit Island, Rex felt more centered than ever before. He wondered inwardly whether living on the island had robbed him of the competitive edge necessary for survival in the larger world. The coping mechanisms of a lifetime—combativeness, self-assertion, dominance and manipulation—had slipped away just as surely as his wife and his old, alcoholic way of living. Try as he might, Rex could scarcely whip himself into a frenzy over anything. The most he could manage in that direction was a steady focus of energy on a problem, situation or person that needed attention. But most of his spiritual and emotional energy seemed naturally channeled into a deepening sense of awe and respect for nature and God's handiwork. Knowing fully well that he could never earn a living by appreciating nature, Rex did hew to a discipline as a writer and managed to sell a feature piece to a Seattle magazine, as well as a humorous tidbit to a national women's magazine. For a while, he wrote steadily for a health and wellness newsletter. But ultimately all those projects ended—sometimes several at once—leaving him with the constant worry and aggravation of turning a dollar. He wanted some part of his old way of life again—the part that involved regular work and steady paychecks. But much of that old way of life—the parts that involved drinking and a sense of being held prisoner in his own life—he was glad to jettison. Allison, on the other hand, could scarcely keep up with the demand for her artwork from galleries. She worked steadily each day in her studio, often until late at night. She was please to be successful and left no doubt in Rex' mind that she expected he would happily do the same for her, if the economic tables were someday turned.

> *Consider the lilies of the field, how they grow: they toil not, neither do they spin.*
> *Yet Solomon in all his glory was not arrayed like one of these.*

Responsibilities of the Island Council provided him with a routine and a format for his days that helped to counterbalance the vagaries of freelance work. And when he wasn't actively engaged in either, their house was in constant need of painting repairs, replacement of rotten deck beams and the endless campaign against weeds in the back yard. It soon became evident to Rex that Allison did not need the same sense of connection to place that he craved. He wondered at her ability to be completely absorbed in her painting and often wished that he could command a similar commitment. And she seemed genuinely puzzled at his deep sense of belonging to the land, as well as his need for familiarity with the natural as well as human community of the island. While noshing happily on his rhubarb/ blackberry pies, Allison secretly was amazed that he was the only man she'd ever known who seemed to take such delight from cooking and domestic routines.

After writing to the property owners who would be affected by creation of a butterfly zone, Rex called them individually and arranged to come and talk with them in their homes. They seemed puzzled but genuinely delighted that an elected official wanted to meet with them and hear their views.

"Well, I don't know what I'd ever do with that extra acreage," said Agnes Wilson after talking with Rex for more than an hour. "The county told us years ago that we couldn't build on it, and so we never tried to sell it. Land's too steep. And now, with the terrible loss of that nice young man, I just feel like giving it up. I suppose I'd like to give it to the island, if the other property owners will go along too."

Jubilant, Rex gave her an enthusiastic hug. "Thank you so much! This will definitely help us when we talk to the other property owners. You're a gem! And you know that, if we get this special district created, then all of you will be entitled to special tax breaks by the county."

"Oh, I don't care about that at my age," the white-haired Mrs. Wilson croaked. "My children will get this land soon. I just want to do something for the island."

With that endorsement in his pocket, Rex then called on the other two property owners and received an equally warm welcome. The amount and location of the land in question was remote from their immediate concerns, and they too seemed pleased to be rid of it. Rex then drafted a report of his activities for review by the Island Council.

"I'm happy to inform the council that all three property owners have agreed in principle to donate a portion of their land to create the Seymour Creighton Butterfly Preserve," he announced. "Now, with the assistance of the administrator, we should be able to move forward with this project."

"Wait a minute!" boomed Charlie Rector. "Not so fast. I'm not sure the council should be taking property off the tax rolls when we're already looking for ways to create new taxes to keep ourselves solvent. It just doesn't make any sense."

"I agree with Charlie," Zack said. "It's nice to have butterfly zones and all, but what's next? Will we have special zones for the blue heron, bald eagle and muskrat? Our first priority ought to be to balance the books. Then we can start looking at these environmental things."

"Mr. Wharton, do you have any idea what the fiscal impact would be of removing these parcels from the property tax rolls?"

"According to the county assessor's records, the combined property taxes from these three properties last year amounted to $11,250," he reported. "Based on the acreage involved as a percentage of last year's revenue, I'd estimate a loss of about $3,000 in tax revenues if we create this district."

"Look, I'll donate $3,000 to the treasury to make up the difference," Cerise Bagoth threw in impatiently. "I don't have the money any more than anyone else, but I'll gladly take a portion of my trust fund and use it to pay the taxes. This is an important step for us to take."

"I agree," Allison said. "The amount of money involved is relatively small but the principle that we stand for environmental conservation is something that should define us and send a message to the rest of the world about Skagit Island. I doubt that we will get involved in saving herons or beavers. This is a special case."

Predictably, the council voted 3-2 to approve creation of the conservation zone and to negotiate the donation of designated lands to the district—the first official indication of a clear split along philosophical lines in its neonatal life.

As the council sought to nurture an economically viable community with no ties to the mainland but a separate and unique political identity, the bravado and enthusiasm of activists slowly faded into dogged determination in the face of increasingly difficult odds. Making the island economically viable was, in itself, a practically insurmountable problem. Especially since the Island Council had been born from a womb of red ink with a DNA-encoded mission not to defile the natural gifts of Skagit Island, finding any sort of compatible commercial base quickly became the top political priority. It soon became obvious to some council members—including Rex—that there could be no real progress on protecting the island from the encroachments of greedy mainland business interests without encouraging some locally grown commerce. And those same local business people would not sit still for the creation of such amenities as the butterfly zone unless there were an equal amount of progress in the business arena. Thus the economics that pervaded the mainland took root on the island with a ferocity that was startling to those idealists who imagined creation of a separate island government the road to utopia.

"You know that store on the highway that sells the funky furniture?" Allison asked Rex. "I noticed a 'for lease' sign in their window and found out from the owner that they're moving off the island. So the place will become vacant the first of next month."

Rex winced, as if taken by surprise. "We can't afford to lose any good businesses, just when we're trying to build the economic base."

"Well, I was thinking," Allison went on, walking airily about the room like a teenager rehearsing for a debutante ball. "The building has 1,800 square feet. That's a lot of space and it's right in the middle of town."

"Yes, and…?"

"It would be perfect for a combination art gallery and book store, maybe even with an espresso bar. And the rent is only $750 a month."

"That's good," Rex said, going back to his newspaper. "I'm sure somebody will snap it up at that price. It sounds like a good opportunity."

Allison plopped down beside him on the couch, causing them both to bounce up and down crazily for an instant.

"Someone?" she teased. "Someone?" She drew nearer to Rex and put her arm around his shoulder. "I was thinking maybe you and I would want to go into business."

Rex stood up and rolled the newspaper under his arm. "How much capital do you think it would take to get started?"

"Who knows? A few thousand, maybe. We could do some research and find out. I think it would be lots of fun—and we could probably make a few bucks."

"I'll admit it has potential, but it scares me. What if we don't make it? What if we lose our shirts?"

"We'll never know if we don't try, will we? There are risks in everything we do—from going into business to going to the dentist. If we had to, we could just use credit cards to raise the up-front capital we need to get started. If you're interested, maybe we could go speak with the landlord."

"Uh, OK, but first I want to look into the business climate here on the island so we at least have some idea of what we're talking about!"

The two existing "galleries" on Skagit Island consisted of a concerted garage in the home of sentimental landscape painter Ralph Kodai, open weekends as advertised by knee-high freestanding signs along the sidewalks of town, and a gift shop/jewelry emporium operated by the White Eagle arts center as a venue for members. As such, there was no commercial art gallery along the lines of what one might expect to find in Seattle's Pioneer Square. For that matter, there wasn't even a decent espresso house on the island. So the combination of art and espresso struck both Allison and Rex as inevitable. Rex obtained a sketch of the floor plan from the landlord and brought it home to study with Allison. The large storefront windows facing onto the main street seemed to guarantee a certain amount of walk-in business.

"Awesome! What shall we call it?" Allison said.

"What about Art a la Carte?"

"Or maybe, Coffee and Contemplation?"

"I'm just wondering whether we can get enough decent art pieces to make it interesting. Do you know anything about running a coffeehouse?"

Rex scratched his head. "Well, I worked in plenty of them when I was in school—as a busboy and waiter. I know of know about the economics of food service from the ground level. I'd have to learn how to make a 'double cap skinny decaf.'"

They burst into laughter, amused at the bold brilliance of their plan.

"How much is this venture going to cost us?" Allison asked.

"He wants $2,500 to sign a one-year lease. I'm guessing that with another $2,500 we could remodel the inside and get some equipment."

"I don't think so," Allison groaned. "The espresso machine alone could cost that much. I'd say we need at least $5,000 to remodel and equip the place."

"OK, so we max out a couple of credit cards. Then we pay them off right away. Hell, I've heard of people who put themselves through law school or medical school on credit cards."

"This is completely crazy, but I like it! Let's go for it!"

"We need to decide who's gonna do what. I assume you'll run the gallery and I'll take care of the coffeehouse...what do you think about occasionally getting musicians or writers to come and perform or read in the evenings?"

"Sure—as long as we screen them beforehand. I once went to a poetry reading where this enormous redheaded woman in tight pedal pushers stood up on a wooden platform and stomped her leather boots to the rhythms of John Dunne's "To His Coy Mistress.'

It was enough to make you never want to hear poetry read aloud again."

"Hmmmm. The philistines vs. the bohemians again. I suppose we need to remember we'll be running a business and our objective is to get people to come into the place. We may have to swallow our esthetic standards a bit. But I agree with you. The only thing worse than bad poetry is bad jazz," "ex said.

"Or bad sex."

"Indeed."

"But I have a better idea for a name. I think we should call it Seymour's. What do you think?"

"That's excellent. I like it better than anything with literary or artistic pretensions."

Together they tore out and rebuilt walls, configured a small kitchen with an espresso bar and put in freestanding walls to increase the surface area in the gallery where paintings could be hung. Above the gallery, fortuitously, a large skylight allowed natural light into the display areas. The effect was to create a museum-like atmosphere of openness. The old hardwood floors only needed a good cleaning and waxing, and their timeless strength of character shone brightly. Seymour's acquired an atmosphere of casual elegance and unhurried charm that was inviting. As the pungent aroma of coffee drinks wafted into the gallery area, drawing visitors into the café, espresso sippers could hardly wait to finish their drinks so they could visit the artworks. The two arms of the operation really complemented each other while giving people two sets of motivations for dropping by. The only missing ingredient—a community bulletin board—became apparent after a couple of weeks and was installed and quickly covered with business cards, notices of garage sales and kitten litters as well as tai-chi and aerobic dance classes. In an important way unexpected by Rex and Allison, Seymour's soon grew into a real community gathering place.

"I think we'll make capitalists out of you yet!" Charlie Rector said at an after-hours gathering of the Island Council following their meeting. "I'm proud to see we're generating some new businesses and revenues on the island."

"Artists are the most complete capitalists there are," Allison said. "We do our own work, alone, then go out and try to sell it. We usually do our own taxes and have all the same anxieties of any small businessperson. I have yet to meet the artist who doesn't appreciate the value of a dollar."

"Well, then," Rector said, bowing his head respectfully. "Maybe we could even get some artist/capitalists to consider voting Republican one of these days."

"Not likely. Ayn Rand is the only artist I've ever heard of who was a Republican. And she's been dead for years."

"Not artist," Rex corrected. "Propagandist."

"Did I tell you I pen a line of poetry myself now and then?" Rector grinned mischievously. "I've never told anybody—not even my wife."

Rex stood up abruptly and saluted with faux elegance. "My compliments. Perhaps you'd like to consider reading at one of our poetry slams?"

"Poetry slam? Is that like a mosh pit?"

Allison giggled under her breath.

"Naw. It's just a group of people who bring some of their work and share it with each other and whoever drops in that evening. Very informal, and everyone is very supportive. Our next reading is this Saturday evening. Why don't you come and bring your wife?" Rex said.

"OK, and I'll bring my son, Chris. He's a linebacker with the Huskies."

"*Chaque un a son gout*," Rex said haughtily, trying to piss him off. "Is he also a poet?"

"No, but he understands physics. Like the physics of one giant body crunching into another on the muddy football field." Rector smiled and looked around, pleased with himself.

"Excellent. We'll be delighted to have all the Rectors here!"

CHAPTER 7

❀

Seymour's was filled to overflowing with bearded, beret-wearing, beatniks with long silvery hair and young punks in black leather well before the poetry slam was to begin. Slender girls with long straight hair that hung over their foreheads held sheaths of typescript in their wispy fingers and studied their words intently, ignoring the espresso drinks that steamed in front of them—and the young men who plied a number of ruses to get their attention. Already the air was charged with the energy of sexuality. Males strutted and swaggered, gathering their bravado for a testosterone-fueled delivery of their immortal lines, while the women poets became withdrawn and reflective, scholarly in their inward concentration. Rex and Allison were pleased and excited by the turnout. Before the first word of poetry was recited, Seymour's already had sold more than 100 espresso drinks for cash revenue of more than $400.

A large, uncoordinated young man with long greasy hair wearing black leather motorcycle gear and heavy combat boots stomped to the podium and yelled loudly:

"My finger turned purple
When I pulled it out
Of the cash machine
And never got my card
From the talking cunt."

Then he thrust his fist high above his head, punching the sky defiantly: "Yeah…right fucking on! Right on, you bitches!" His display
of bravado was met with a chorus of booing and hisses, and he
smiled sardonically as he strode triumphantly offstage. "Faggot!
Trailer trash! Fuck you! The audience yelled back at him.

Allison glanced over at Rex, who seemed stunned by the sudden
explosion of bad poetry and even worse emotions. As their woeful
expressions met, both burst out laughing uncontrollably. The night
was young and the artistic tap had barely been opened—an entire
phalanx of poets awaited their moment at the microphone.

The ballsy biker poet was followed by a tall, fuzzy redhead in fish-
net stockings, a mini-skirt and black tank top whose demeanor was
as detached as his had been bombastic. She slinked to the micro-
phone and chanted in silken, sultry tones:
"Pres, Bird, Diz and Trane
Keep riffing in my brain.
These mystic souls afire
Like sparrows on a wire,
Showed us the way out
And *they* were way out—
Way out, way out, way out."
A ripple of applause caught her by surprise, and she dropped her
poetry to the floor. When she bent down to retrieve it, her pendulous
breasts bore witness to the magnificence of nature in all its perfec-
tion—and the applause grew even louder. Without losing her com-
posure, she smiled, bowed and walked slowly back to her table. Rex
rolled his eyes at Allison.

Chris Rector, sitting hunched over a small table like a gorilla at a
tea party, dropped his coffee cup on the table with a loud clang and
grew beet-red as he fumbled to clean up the spilled coffee. With his
close-cropped hair, buffed body and clumsy lack of social graces, he
looked as out of place as a whore in a revival meeting. Charlie Rector

stood, as if to divert attention from his son, and walked up to the podium. The café grew strangely quiet.

I hope you'll bear with me," he said self-effacingly. "I'm not a professional poet and have never read anything of mine to a group before. But I guess you could say that, as of tonight, I'm 'out.'"

Whistles, cheers and applause thundered through the room.

"This is a little poem I wrote a while ago. I've never read it or showed it to anyone yet." His nervousness was apparent.

"There was a young maid from Minnesota,
Who wouldn't fool around one iota.
Her morals were impeccable,
And really quite respeccable—
Once she'd met her quota."

The room remained eerily silent as Rector folded his poem neatly, tucked it into his pocket and returned to his table. When Chris Rector pulled out his father's chair, a faint ripple of applause arose. It swelled politely, then quickly died down to nothing. After more than an hour of readings—from the absurd to the downright embarrassing—the poetry slam began to disintegrate. Rex made his way quickly to Rector's table. "Would you consider letting us publish your limerick in an anthology from tonight's reading?"

"Ah, sure. If you really want to." Rector's discomfort was painful to witness.

"It's just going to be a photocopied record of what was read here tonight—nothing too fancy. We're hoping to do this every time we have a slam. We'll sell them for a dollar and give some copies to the library. It's just our way of promoting the arts."

Rector stiffened his back righteously. "Excellent idea. Count me in."

As they finally closed the café after midnight, Allison and Rex walked arm-in-arm to their car, exhausted. They drove home in serene silence. "I guess we should assume the role of facilitators and promoters of the arts—not judges," Rex mumbled. "If I were to judge what was read tonight, I'd say about 98 percent of it was dog shit."

"Yeah, I know what you mean. I guess this is a fine example of how elitism in the arts operates," Allison said. "I'm sure to the people who read, their poetry was wonderful and heart-felt."

"No doubt. Maybe Robert Frost was right in that poem of his where he rambles on about not wanting to silence anyone's song. Remember that one?"

"Yep. It's very democratic, of course. But art and politics operate according to different principles. Just look at some of the appalling 'art' that came out of the Soviet Union—Dmitri Shostakovich not-withstanding, of course."

"Well, we *are* running a business and it's good for business to do these kinds of things," Rex sighed. "Jesus! I never thought I'd hear myself say that!"

"As the Reverend T. Lawrence Shannon says, 'We live in two worlds—the real and the fantastic.'"

The poetry slam triggered something that smoldered deeply within Rex. Although in his youthful innocence he'd written simple, song-like lyrics about winter stars and young love, shortly after college Rex had relegated his poetic efforts to a dusty cardboard box and never looked back. There was more than frustration to this abandonment of a part of himself that felt so vulnerable and naked. A rising sense of shame and inadequacy had driven Rex to the conclusion that he had never written a single worthwhile line—poetry or prose—and likely never would. So in the same way that he'd put aside his adolescent fascination with motorcycles and outboard hydroplanes, Rex had scuttled any poetic ambitions. It was not unlike his sudden abandonment of the piano when he was even younger. When he was a young lad shortly after his parents' divorce, Rex had been all but adopted as a surrogate son to his grandparents, whose only child was his mother. His grandfather Wyndham Bolton, a good-natured and hard-working family doctor, loved football, good whisky and scooting about on the Piankytank River in his outboard skiff—which he referred to as "maneuvers." His maternal grandmother Lucy had been a nurse at St. Luke's Hospital in New York City when she met Dr. Bolton during his residency. But in her youth, Lucy Wickham had sung opera on the radio in her hometown of Niagara Falls. So when Rex danced wildly about the house to the same "nigger music" that black domestics listened during their workdays in the homes of White Piedmonters, Dr. Bolton reacted with impatient anger while his grandmother recognized a kindred musical spirit and arranged for Rex to study the piano.

Weekly lessons with "Miss Minnie" at her prim Victorian townhouse in downtown Piedmont and daily afternoon practice sessions at his grandparents' house thrilled and satisfied Rex' love of music. Each half note, or pencilled chord annotated in the margins of his practice book, became his own personal treasure. Each afternoon after school, Lucy rewarded Rex with milk and cookies as well as praise when he finished his practice session. And he loved performing in a recital of Miss Minnie's students that involved four boys at two pianos banging out a lugubrious "Volga Boatmen."

But at the same time, his grandfather was relentless in his pursuit of Rex' football career. Dr. Wyndham even bought Rex a football jersey with the same numbers (22) as Charlie "Choo Choo" Justice, one of the college gridiron idols of the 40s and 50s. Rex despised everything about football—the painful and ill-fitting shoulder pads and awkward pants, the physical crunching that most often left him lying on the ground with a mouthful of dirt or someone's cleated shoe, or both, and the shouting and competitive demands of the coach. During his years as a student at St. Anthony's School, he grew to hate football with such a fury that he sometimes slipped away from practice sessions and his in the thick woods behind the gymnasium. When word reached his mother, an interview was promptly arranged with a child psychologist. Dr. Wyndham began applying even more pressure on the young Rex to become more "manly." The result was that, in order to keep peace in his fractured family and convince himself of his own worthiness, Rex decided that playing the piano was for "sissies" and a frivolous waste of time for a young man of his serious ambitions. He thus stopped lessons, stopped practicing, stopped visiting his grandmother in the afternoons. In so doing, he traded lonely long-distance rides on his bicycle into the country for milk and cookies; solitude for the warmth and tenderness of his grandmother; shame and determination for fun and esthetic joy.

In much the same way, Rex had turned his back on poetry as frivolous and nonproductive when he decided to become a journalist. Newspaper writing was "real," earned money, made a difference in the world. Poetry was "puff," subjective, personal in the worst sense, and a foolish waste of time. Rex felt that his transition from writing poetry to news writing marked his transition from boyhood to manhood.

But now it once more called to him. The simple eloquence of recovering alcoholics and addicts sharing their experience, strength and hope in meetings had struck a chord inside him. He began to listen for the nugget of poetry in the testimonies of sober drunks, and he often found it. He also found it in a few spiritual writings wisely stripped of rhetoric and verbosity, focused on just the right words to express the inner vision. As his journey into truth and honesty deepened, so did his rejuvenated love of poetry. Emboldened with his newfound passion, Rex even wrote a poem—his first in more than 20 years. After he'd finished, he looked it over, decided it was sentimental rubbish and threw it into the burning wood stove. But a seed had been planted, even if it hadn't yet germinated. He pulled down his dusty volumes of Keats, Milton, Browning and Chaucer and disappeared into the realm of fantasy. Their words were a healing balm for his soul, and he feasted like a starving leper placed before a banquet table.

"You won't believe this! We finally have all three parcels signed, sealed and delivered for the butterfly preserve." Dudley Wharton was fey, practically hyperventilating into the telephone.

"Wow, that's amazing," Rex replied. "I assume you'll be making a report to the council at tomorrow's meeting?"

Definitely, but I wanted to let council members know individually beforehand. I think this is a real feather in our cap."

"Maybe you could include in the agenda item something about a discussion of a dedication ceremony to honor Seymour Creighton. He's really the whole reason this came about. Maybe we can get his parents to come...I don't know."

"I'll list it as an information/discussion item. That way everyone can speak their piece, and the council could also open it for comments from the audience, if they want."

"Do we have our first quarter report from the Department of Revenue yet?"

"Yes, as a matter of fact it just came in this afternoon. Looks like we're about where we projected—maybe a tad more taxes than we thought."

"It's because of the poetry slam!"

Wharton exploded with laughter. "Maybe that's right. I hadn't thought about it until now!"

On the designated Saturday at 11 a.m., the entire Island Council and about 200 islanders gathered on the high grassy south hillside that sloped down into Giggling Creek to dedicate the Seymour Creighton Butterfly Preserve. To the east, a thicket of pine and madrona trees cast a wide shadow across the meadow, but the seats had been cleverly arranged to catch whatever sunlight filtered through the forest. A small wooden platform had been erected on the north side of the clearing, hard against another stand of evergreens. After an expression of gratitude by the chairman of the local Sierra Club, Rex rose to make a formal dedication of the open space.

"We all know why we're here today. We're here because we love this island and want to protect it from being spoiled—by us or by anyone else. I can see the faces of many who worked hard during the bridge fight and the incorporation struggle to help give us some control over the destiny of out island and our community. Thank you all for your efforts!

"Your Island Council has been working hard to accomplish what we all set out to achieve more than a year ago. We've made good progress at building an economic base that is consistent with our character as a rural island, knowing that we need to be self-sustaining to keep Skagit Island out of the hands of those who would exploit it. Recently, we had an unusual opportunity to acquire some land for open space through the generosity of three property owners, and because of the vision of one of our youngest citizens.

"Seymour Creighton—many of you know him well—is a young man is singular vision and unusual dedication to this island. This preserve was his idea, and will bear his name. Most of you know that Seymour also worked hard to help create our Island government, and that he had a particular interest in the butterflies that live here on our island. I'm sure that if he were here today..."

Rex caught sight of something moving in the woods nearby, and stumbled over his words. His gaze became riveted on the nearby brush, which moved as if someone were pushing their way through the undergrowth. As he stared, so did the assembled crowd. Pulling himself forcibly back to his notes, Rex sought to continue.

"Deer season must have started early this year!" he quipped, to an appreciate round of laughter. "As I was saying, if Seymour Creighton could be here today I'm sure that he would appreciate what we've..."

Another ruckus in the brush brought sounds of crunching branches and someone breathing loudly, and Rex once again interrupted his speech as all eyes turned toward the mystery in the woods.

From the brush emerged a tattered and bruised Seymour Creighton himself. He paused when he saw the crowd, removed his glasses and scratched his head.

"Ladies and gentlemen, I don't believe what we're seeing here is an illusion—and we certainly did not plan this," Rex sputtered. "Seymour, is that you?"

Seymour approached slowly, nodding his head. Rex jumped off the podium, ran over to him and embraced him warmly. "Seymour! Where on earth have you been? Are you OK? We thought something terrible had happened to you!"

"I'm, uh, OK I think," Seymour said, dazed.

"Where have you been?"

"Just looking around for butterflies. It must be hibernation time because I haven't found any yet. Who are all these people?" Seymour squinted as he looked toward the audience, most of whom were now standing and staring in open-mouthed disbelief.

"Come on over here with me, Seymour," Rex said, pulling him toward the podium. "Fellow islanders, please welcome Seymour Creighton!"

Incredulous islanders began clapping slowly, then louder as they witnessed Seymour in the flesh before their eyes.

Into the microphone so all could hear, Rex said: "Seymour doesn't know yet that we are here to dedicate this open space as the Seymour Creighton Butterfly Preserve. I think this young man deserves our congratulations and appreciation, but I suspect he'll need to go to the clinic right away to be checked over. Seymour, we're proud of you and we missed you."

As he spoke, Rex noticed one of the two island emergency rescue vehicles arrive at the dedication site with red lights flashing. Unceremoniously, he walked Seymour toward the ambulance and helped the crew load him on a stretcher into the rear. Then Seymour once again disappeared.

"I'm speechless," he declared upon his return to the podium. "Why don't we just observe a moment of silent gratitude for this preserve, and most important for the safe return of Seymour? Thank you all for coming."

"Seymour Creighton, 18, male, no history of psychiatric illness. Brought to Island Clinic with mild dehydration, some confusion, apparent (radiation?) burn marks on forearms. Possibility of amnesiac or psychotic episode. Does not remember last several weeks, except that he was "looking for butterflies" somewhere on the island. No recollection of kidnapping or violence. Patient unaware that he had been reported missing. No evidence of physical trauma, except for burn marks. Recommend thorough psychiatric evaluation and work-up. Transferred to Harborview by ambulance following police interview."

Frank Bleeker, MD, scratched his bald head as he read over his chart notes. Somehow it did not all add up. Although the facts were as stated in his notes, there was no logical thread to hold the pieces together. After 20-plus years of practice on the island, he'd seen domestic abuse, drug and alcohol abuse, self-abuse and stoned stupidity in abundance. But there seemed to be no category of his experience into which Seymour Creighton could be fitted.

"What d'ya make of it, doc?" Sallie Henson, RN, had the officious, in-your-face manner of a hardened nurse manager, which she'd been for more than two decades before transferring from a large Seattle hospital to the Island Clinic. She stood in Bleeker's doorway, arms akimbo, as if to confront him.

"Unusual, very unusual," he replied softly, so his voice would not carry outside his office. "I'll be anxious to see what they come up with at Harborview."

"Hmpff! He probably just ate the wrong mushrooms. Kids these days..."

"Miss Henson, I'd appreciate it if you'd show some professional demeanor. Do you realize that you are creating legal liabilities for everyone in this office by not respecting confidentiality?" Bleeker's voice quivered with anger, although it was still subdued.

Taken aback, the stocky nurse blinked and shook her head remorsefully. "Sorry, doctor. You're right. I'm way out of line here. I won't discuss this with anyone."

Then she left for a waiting patient and Bleeker did not see or speak with her the rest of the day. When he went home at night, his exhaustion was palpable. He munched on a cold piece of fried chicken from the refrigerator as he undressed for bed, turned on the television to watch an all-night movie, and snuggled next to his sleeping wife, Caught in mid-reel, the movie was a 1950s sci-fi thriller about the visit of a flying saucer to save humans from destroying Earth with nuclear weapons. As Bleeker dozed off to sleep, his fatigued brain tried to make some sense of the unearthly phrase "kleng tagbo udon nikta" that reverberated through the dank night air from the TV.

"You got home late last night," Bev Bleeker smiled as she held a steaming cup of coffee next to her slumbering husband's Sunday morning nose. The aroma of fresh coffee finally lifted his head out of the covers, then the fog from his brain. He sat up in bed and sipped it with relish.

"Sorry about that," he said hoarsely. "We had a crush of patients late in the day, and then we had to be out of the building for about an hour while the state environmental people looked around."

"Looked around for what?" Be asked, propping herself on the bed next to him.

"Well, you know the clinic is built on a former ICBM missile launching site," Bleeker coughed, "The missile silos were filled in with dirt years ago, but someone wrote a letter to the state about possible radiation contamination. So they had to send a crew out to check on radiation levels."

"The clinic is built on a missile site?!"

"Yeah, I told you when we moved here years ago. You don't remember?"

"No, I don't," she replied curtly. "I remember you said something about the clinic having been some kind of government facility before it became a medical clinic."

"Well, I think it's a bogus complaint probably dreamed up by a hypochondriac patient and a hungry lawyer. Oh, and then we had the Creighton kid come in, so that took extra time."

"The Creighton kid? You mean Seymour?"

"Yeah. Apparently he just wandered out of the woods while they were having the dedication ceremony for that butterfly place. He was somewhat disoriented, a few scratches but otherwise OK. Said he had no idea what had happened...he'd been out hunting for butterflies, or something. Oh, and he had these funny burn marks on his forearms. Dandiest thing I've ever seen. Sent him over to Harborview."

"Never a dull moment...want some breakfast?"

CHAPTER 8

❀

Seymour paced up and down the narrow, fluorescent-lit corridors of the psychiatric ward like a corralled impala, scratching his forearms where dry itchy scabs had formed over the burned areas. In that cauldron of Thorazine-zonked zombies, twitching schizophrenics and withdrawn paranoiacs, Seymour blended in like just another of the mental casualties of modern life. Except for a low dosage of Valium, he'd been offered no medication for the first 48 hours of his evaluation period. Each time he traversed the corridor, he passed by the room of an autistic young woman who rocked herself back and forth on the floor curled into a tight fetal ball. Another room where the door was just ajar enough to permit a quick view inside presented an even more disturbing sight. A muscular, tattooed, unconscious young man was lashed tightly to his bed with leather straps and an IV tube inserted in his right arm that was covered with bandages its entire length from a razor-slashing suicide attempt. Seymour strode frenetically around the nurses' station in his neverending loop of futility and then went back down the corridor again. The nurses ignored making direct eye contact, but occasionally peered up from their charts as he passed to check on his level of agitation.

"Mr. Creighton," barked the officious head nurse on one of his passes. "Dr. Laroque will be coming to see you soon. Maybe you'd like to wait in your room?"

"Who's Dr. Laroque?" Seymour had stopped in his tracks at the sound of her voice.

"He's Chief of Psychiatry. He wants to talk to you about your experiences and find out what we can do for you."

"My experiences? Like watching butterflies?"

"Yes, that too. He'll explain it to you. Just make yourself comfortable in your room, OK?"

Seymour returned to his room and stretched out on his stiff, narrow bed. At last, a profound sense of exhaustion overcame him and he fell into a deep slumber. White everywhere, like a blizzard. *White room, white light, white table…except those black eyes, floating in the whiteness. No talking, no words, just the eyes and everything white. Where's my stuff? Are we out of school? There's ice on the bridge—be careful! So cold and white everywhere.*

"Mr. Creighton?" The voice seemed to float into his dream of whiteness.

"Huh?" Seymour raised his head and rubbed his bleary eyes.

A tall, lanky bearded man in his 40s smiled graciously and nodded his head. "I'm Dr. Laroque. May I come in?"

"Yeah…must have fallen asleep. Come in, doctor."

"How are you feeling?" Laroque's steely blue eyes seemed to penetrate into Seymour's soul.

"Scared. I'm not sure why I'm here. Am I crazy?"

"No, you're not crazy. We want to help you try to remember what happened so we can sort it out and see where we go from here. You've gone through a terrible experience."

"I have?"

"You don't remember anything at all?"

"Like what? What am I supposed to remember?"

"Well, according to the calendar, you've been missing for 33 days. Does that seem like a long time to you?"

"No. I mean, yes. Well, I'm not sure. You see, it doesn't seem like I've been missing at all. I just went out to look for butterflies and…and then I was there in the woods at that park and all."

Laroque's eyes grew expressionless. "Because of your disappearance, and because of the burns on your arms and loss of memory, I'd like to suggest something. Have you ever heard of sodium pentothol? It's a drug that is sometimes used to help people remember things."

"Yeah, I saw a movie once where these Nazis were trying to get some secret information out of this American GI who was captured. And they tied him down and shot him with that truth serum…"

Laroque chuckled. "Well, that's how most people think of it, I'm afraid. But it's more like something to help you relax and remember. It's really quite harmless when administered correctly. I'd like to suggest that we try that approach to help you remember what happened."

"How long does this take?"

"Oh, maybe a couple of hours including the time it takes for the drug to wear off."

Seymour got up from the bed, walked to the window and peered out at the thick fog on Elliott Bay. "Then can I go home after that?"

"That depends partly on what we find, what your parents say, what the other doctors here say. We're trying to help you, Seymour."

"OK, I guess so."

As the drug seeped into Seymour's bloodstream, he felt pervasive warmth throughout his body and a sense of profound relaxation overcame him. Residual fears and anxieties slipped away into nothingness, and he knew a strong kinship with Dr. Laroque: they were kindred spirits on a strange journey into darkness and truth. Whatever strange occurrences had befallen him, Seymour knew that together they could untangle the mystery so he could once again be whole.

"Seymour, tell me something about butterflies," Laroque began in a soft tone of voice. "How long have you been interested in them?"

"Aren't they beautiful? I think I've always wanted to be a butterfly, ever since I saw one land once when I was a little kid out playing in the yard. It was gold, and black and white. When I tried to touch it, it just flew away and I wanted to follow it. I had dreams about that butterfly...about riding on its back up to the moon."

"So you've wanted to fly for a long time?"

"Oh, as long as I can remember. I tried to build a little airplane once when I was a kid—this kind of contraption with wings attached to my bicycle. I was gonna see if I could race down a big hill and then just glide on my wings off into the air."

"What happened?"

"The wings fell off when I got going pretty fast. It wasn't very well designed because I don't know how to design a butterfly wing. But I kept on dreaming about butterflies all the time, until I found a book on them and I got a pair of binoculars and went out into the woods..."

"Were you looking at butterflies just recently?"

"I wasn't looking for butterflies...I was just outside walking in the woods, at night. It was so dark and quiet, I was thinking 'I wonder where all the butterflies are?' when I saw some kind of light overhead. I thought it must be an airplane...some kind of airplane...so I kept right on walking. Didn't hear any airplane noises, though."

"Where were you walking?"

"I was up near the Island Clinic, in the woods near there, because you can look all around and see Seattle and the airport and everything. But it was dark in the woods where I was walking, and quiet. Until I saw this light."

"What does the light look like?"

"It's getting bigger and brighter and closer. Really huge now, right overhead! I'm just standing in the woods, crouched behind a tree, but it's coming right down near me and I'm scared...it's just this huge disk with different-colored lights and some markings on the bottom. Then there's a searchlight that shines out of the thing right in my eyes, and I'm moving toward the thing, toward the ship and going up."

"Like a butterfly?"

"Like a butterfly...going up, floating up toward the light. I'm floating in the dark, I can see the lights of Seattle and all around the Sound. I'm going inside the ship now...everything is white. They're got me on a table and they're looking at me with those black eyes...questioning me without speaking."

"OK, Seymour. What do they want? What are they asking you?"

"I'm not sure...they're putting something like metal inside me...oh shit! You can't do that!!! STOP IT!!!!!" Seymour thrashed about on the bed, waving his arms and whipping his head back and forth. Laroque put a hand on his shoulder, but Seymour continued out of control. "NO...TAKE THAT THING AWAY!!! STOP IT!!!"

Dr. Laroque picked up the telephone and said: "Dr. Strong to Room 319, West Wing...Dr. Strong." Within moments, a crew of panting, muscular orderlies and residents crashed into the room, restraints and hypodermic needles at the ready. They pounced on Seymour, held him down on the bed, injected him with Demerol and tied his arms and legs to the bed as he slipped into total unconsciousness."

"I'm gonna have to answer to the medical review board for this," Laroque muttered under his breath, shaken. "Danger to self or others...violent and uncontrolled...use of restraints justified."

When he came out of the anesthesia, Seymour remembered nothing. He awoke hungry and confused, trying to sort out the whirlwind of the previous 48 hours. Inside the institutional regimentation of the trauma hospital, Skagit Island seemed remote and dream-like. Seymour shivered briefly, then felt a sudden acrid warmth flood the pit of his stomach. Like a butterfly pinned to a display board, he was trapped. Gingerly he crept from his bed and poked his head out into the dark hallway. An old patient in a disheveled robe ambled aimlessly down the corridor, but otherwise there was no one around. Quickly he threw on his clothes, found a moment when the hallway was empty, then dashed to a side exit and ran at breakneck speed down the filth-stained concrete stairs to the crowded lobby, where he pushed open the heavy fire door and burst out with a wild abandon at last onto the street. Outside the hospital, a collection of the insane, drug-addicted and otherwise hopeless street people milled about coming and going from visits to the psyche ward, VD clinic and detox unit. The air was perfumed with the sweet, oily stench of diesel exhaust from the shuttle vans that carried this Amazon of human misery for medical care, and from the unwashed bodies of patients whose illnesses had left them unable to perform even the most basic self-care. Seymour ran down the street away from the hospital, turned left after a block and ran downhill seven more blocks all the way to the ferry dock to get the next boat back to the island. By the time he reached the ferry terminal, his chest felt like it would explode and his breath came in great, heaving gasps. As he ran up to the ticket counter, he watched the passenger ferry pull out from the dock and disappear in a great churning rooster-tail westward toward Skagit Island.

"Jes' missed it!" The large-boned black woman in the ticket booth moved with a slow, deliberate pace that would have been maddening if Seymour hadn't already been overcome with a sense of futility. She handed him his ticket and change with an indolent indifference.

"When's the next boat leave for the island?" Seymour struggled to get the words out between gulps of air.

"'Bout an hour and a half from now. You can wait over there." She pointed to a large circus-like tent that served as the passenger waiting area. Seymour found a seat on the pew-like wooden bench and picked up a copy of the daily newspaper. The front page was dominated by a four-column photo of Rex Armistead standing in front of the White Eagle Arts Center, over the headline:

'Skagit struggles to balance the books after incorporation'

It was another in a long series of mainstream press accounts of island life that served up Skagit and its residents as some sort of loony-tunes diversion for the sensible, hard-working folks of Seattle. The underlying assumption seemed to be that the flakes on Skagit Island deserved whatever bizarre fate they brought down upon themselves. But Seymour pulled up his shoulders when he read this paragraph: "Despite its shaky fiscal start, the Skagit Island Council was able to set aside approximately 300 acres of open space as a butterfly preserve, through the generosity of three island property owners. The parcel has been designated the Seymour Creighton Butterfly Preserve, in honor of an island youth who has catalogues many of the butterfly species on the island and who mysteriously disappeared last month."

So I'm still missing? Maybe I should stay missing!

Seymour threw the newspaper into the recycling bin and walked out onto the loading platform, straining his eyes to get a glimpse of Skagit Island. Its green wildness was just visible on the horizon, and he yearned more than ever to be home. The waters of Puget Sound were wind-whipped and choppy—the ride home would be bumpy. Seymour loved the violent up and down motions of the powerful passenger ferry as it sliced its say through the whitecaps, slapping hard against the waves and churning mightily. Once aboard the boat, he quickly slipped into a profound slumber with his head bathed in warm sunshine from the large, plate glass window. When the ferry bumped into its slip on Skagit Island, Seymour awoke with a start, scampered off and up to the bus stop where he caught a bus directly home, went straight to his room and pulled out his butterfly books.

In his field sketchbook, he made a pencil drawing of the ship that had taken him up into the sky. From its circular base radiated a flurry of fine lines, signifying the strange power that had lifted him upward into the night air. Then he sketched the inside of the ship as he remembered it, with the small table and the small creatures that stared with large black eyes into his face. Another sketch showed a close-up of the tools they had used to poke and prod his body, including a strange angled metal arm that had somehow been inserted into his nose and made crunching noises inside his head.

CHAPTER 9

❀

"**A**ccording to these projections, we will still end the fiscal year *another* million bucks in the red." Rex threw down the heavy sheaf of Island Council papers on the table where Allison sat and sipped tea. "We could have 15 new art galleries on the island and still not be able to pay our bills!"

"I thought we had a five-year plan to get out of debt?"

"We do, but it doesn't presuppose going further into debt each year. What I'm saying is, things are getting worse despite our efforts. That stupid newspaper article didn't help much, either. It just puts more pressure on us."

"I told you on the train what I wanted to do." Allison spoke flatly, and squinted her eyes as she sipped the steaming tea. "You're taking this too personally. It's not just your responsibility. Everybody on the island has a stake in this."

"Oh, I know that…but I feel a special responsibility because I've been one of the main movers of this whole thing. I feel a sense of obligation to see it through and not abandon everyone when the going gets tough. I suppose Zack and I ought to talk this over, the way we used to do."

"Why don't you give him a call? I think your friendship could use a little repair."

Rex leaned over and kissed Allison sweetly. "Thanks. That's why I married you—because you're so sensible!"

Rex drove to Zack's house and found him sitting on the living room floor, a large jar of pennies in front of him and a pile of loose coins on the floor, bundling them into $1 paper rolls. Zack smiled broadly when he saw Rex, motioned for him to take a seat.

"What's up, buddy?" Zack said as he resumed his counting.

"I just decided that we should go fishing again, or maybe hunting, or something," Rex began awkwardly. "I was looking at the council packet and I got so bent out of shape that I needed a break."

"You mean the budget stuff?"

"Exactly. It's beginning to feel as if we've put a noose around our necks."

"Well, I'm not sure about the island, but *I* sure am up against the wall."

"How come?"

"Haven't had any work for almost six months, and here I am rolling up my pennies to pay the light bill. I'm thinking of selling the house 'cause I can't pay the note any more."

"Shit, man, don't do that!"

Zack nodded his head slowly as he continued rolling and counting. "Trying not to, buddy."

"This is a rough time for all of us," Rex sighed. "What do you say we go for a ride in my truck? Maybe we could go fishing off the pier over on the eastside?"

Zack paused and looked blankly into space. "OK. I could use to get out of this house for a while. A little fresh air would do us both some good."

"Yeah, and then after we get back I'll help you roll."

"Deal!" Zack said as he painfully drew his gangly frame upright and grabbed his coat. Rex followed him to the basement, where they gathered fishing rods and reels and a baitbox, then back to the kitchen where Zack pulled a package of frozen squid out of the freezer and plunked it into the box.

"This is the only stuff that always works," he said to himself. "Good for salmon, rockfish…"

"Don't you think we should bring a knife or something to get the bait out of the ice?" Rex wondered.

"Right here!" Zack smiled as he slapped the bayonet-sized knife lashed to his leg in an aged leather scabbard. They clambered into Rex' truck and headed for the pier.

Ensconced at the end of the dilapidated pier with their poles drooping into the frigid waters of Puget Sound, the two old pals drew in deep draughts of bracing air and relaxed at last. Rex cringed as Zack popped open one of his ubiquitous cans of warm beer and took a big swallow.

"I've had a helluva time finding work here myself," Rex said. "I thought it was because I'm a carpetbagger."

"Carpetbagger?!" Zack laughed heartily, then became convulsed in a smoker's hysterical coughing fit. "Naw. It's just some hard times for lots of folks now. Economy's slowed down, plus I don't go off-island for jobs any more."

"Have you considered going back to fishing—I mean profession-ally?"

"If I was 30 years younger, I'd be out there pulling in king crabs now. That's a rough business and most of the guys are done by the time they're in their late 20s. I did that years ago, made a lot of money, then spent it all. All I'm good for now is just odd jobs and such. Got no education, no family…"

"Well, hell, Zack! You're starting to snivel. It doesn't become you." Rex nudged him with his best AA tough love technique. "You'll find something soon, I'm sure. Don't give up five minutes before the miracle happens."

"Shit," Zack snarled, opening another can of warm beer. "It *would* take a miracle to get my life back in order now."

"I'm going to an AA meeting tonight here on the island. Wanna come with me?"

Zack looked as if someone had stepped in a cow pie, his nose scrunched up and his eyes squinted painfully. "AA?! You're in AA? What the fuck for?"

"Yes. I haven't had a drink for more than a year. It's the best thing that ever happened to me. I'd love it if you'd come and just check it out." Rex was in earnest, but Zack wanted none of it.

"You must think I drink too much, huh?"

"Hey, that's for you to decide. I just know that a lot of the 'problems' that I drank over for so many years just evaporated when I stopped drinking."

"That simple, really?"

"Well, there's a little more to it than that. But we say AA is a simple program for complicated people. Everybody thinks they're unique when they first come through the doors of AA. Then we discover that we all have the same problem and can help each other."

"Yeah—that God crap. I know all about that. My ex-wife tried to get me to go to AA years ago. I'm not real crazy about Bible-thumpers who have been goosed by the Lord."

Rex laughed out loud. "Bible-thumpers? Hardly!"

Zack put his arm around Rex' shoulders, slurped another gulp of his beer.

"OK, buddy. I'll go with you to that stupid AA meeting—so long as I have the right to leave at any time."

"Of course. We don't have any rules in AA. We just have suggestions and the 12 Steps. You'll see. It's not like any other group you've ever known before."

"That's good," Zack grunted. "I'm not wild about groups. What's this about steps...?"

"The 12 Steps are the core of the program. They're kind of a synthesis of Zen Buddhism, Christian mysticism, Jungian psychology and common sense. We contrast them with the 10 Commandments of Christianity. They're not commandments—only suggestions based on what we've found keeps alcoholics from drinking."

Before Zack could ask another question, he felt a tug on his fishing line and instinctively tugged back on it. "Think I got something," he announced calmly as he began to wind in his tackle. As the line drew near the surface, they could see a large croaker wiggling and trying to swim away. Zack pulled the line onto the pier and laid the squirming fish down.

"Wow! That's a good one," Rex said. "Are you having me over for dinner?"

"Why don't we go to your house and share with your wife?"

"Such a gentleman! Of course. But I need to catch something before we leave."

"Here…catch this!" Zack tossed the just-freed fish to Rex. It spun and wiggled through the air, but he snared it in his arm, football-style, and wrestled it into the cooler. "Not bad, for a California boy!"

Rex found Allison intensely dabbing paint on a large canvas in her studio when he awoke and wandered around, coffee mug in hand, to find her. At times like this, the most he could hope for conversationally would be a few well-timed grunts, and an occasional sideways glance as her work held her in thrall. He stole up behind her and quietly pecked her on the side of her neck.

"Oh, hi! What did Zack think of the meeting?" She was pert and very focused.

Astonished at her sociability, Rex sat down on a rickety wooden footstool and took another gulp of strong coffee. "I'm not sure," he said vacantly. "He seemed fascinated by AA but I'm not certain he thinks alcohol is a problem for him."

Allison continued painting in silence. The morning sunlight created a mosaic of long shadows and erratic splotches of spilled paint hues on the floor. The effect was mesmerizing. Rex wanted nothing more than to float into one of his wife's canvasses and disappear into a great crest of color and another dimension. The peaceful, healing energy that radiates from anyone engaged in a creative act gave Rex access to a deep joy. Nothing mattered except that they were together at this moment, in this spot of sunshine, while this canvas was being painted. Time itself became a mere contingency.

"Does he want to quit drinking?" Allison asked without looking up from her work.

"Well, he wants his life to change but I just don't know whether he thinks sobriety would do anything to change things. He's been out of work for a while, drinking, going more and more into debt. Seems like things may be worse for him than he lets on."

"I hope he decides to get sober. He's a nice man."

"I know it. This goddamn disease kills a lot of people."

"Wait a few days, then ask him if he wants to go to a meeting with you."

Seymour's father stormed into the house and slammed the front door shut. "Is he here?" he demanded of his wife. "I got a call at work that he'd taken off from the hospital without speaking to anyone."

Mrs. Creighton rose from her reading, her eyes wide as saucers. "Don't be too hard on him, Bill. He's a frightened young boy."

"Well, he's a *frightening* young boy. What kind of freak are we raising?"

"Seymour's not a freak, dear, he's just different."

Bill Creighton snarled and looked anxiously about. "Is he in his room?"

Without waiting for an answer, he marched to Seymour's room, wrenched open the door without knocking and walked in to find his son asleep at the desk, his butterfly atlas at his side.

"Get up, boy! You've got some explaining to do."

His eyes were red with fury as he shook Seymour by the shoulders.

"Whaa...?"

"What makes you think you can just leave the hospital without telling anyone? Don't you realize you've caused us enough worry already? What's the matter with you, anyway?"

Exhausted by his ordeal, Seymour was slow to respond to his father's entreaties and rolled his eyes as he tried to focus.

"Already people are laughing at us behind our backs for your asinine stories," his father resumed with a vengeance. "It's been in the newspapers, now it's hurting my business. Nobody wants to buy insurance from someone whose son is a whacko! Stand up when I'm talking to you, son!" As he spoke, a blue vein bulged grotesquely in his neck.

Seymour struggled to get upright, but before he could rise out of the chair the first blow hit the side of his head. Then the other fist hit him again, and he lurched forward. The top of his head crashed into the computer screen, shattering the glass and his skull and sending Seymour down onto the desk into a slumped, immobile heap.

"Bill! Bill! What are you doing?" His mother reached the doorway just as her son dropped down, and she ran frantically to save him. "Seymour, darling!" She touched the top of his head, which was bloody and encrusted with tiny bits of glass from the video tube. "You monster! Look what you've done!"

"Awright, awright," he grumbled. "I'll get an icebag."

"No, not an icebag…call 911. He's unconscious and barely breathing. Quick!!"

Once again, Seymour was carried to the medical center by ambulance. But this trip was different. This time the diagnosis was swift and certain: death caused by massive cerebral hemorrhage and cranial fracture. Bill Creighton was taken into custody on charges of manslaughter and incarcerated in the Skagit County Jail. Lois Creighton left to stay with friends in Seattle and ingested large quantities of Valium. The Creighton home was encircled by yellow police tape and the driveway closed by police barricades with flashing yellow warning lights. And then islanders began to talk.

VOLUME III

Penance

CHAPTER 1

❀

"If we reduce the size of our police force from three to two, cut back on hours at the library and postpone road repairs, we can trim enough from our budget to pay the interest on our bonds. And then, if we're lucky enough to get more tax revenues, we can start to pay off the principal. Conceivably, we could still have our startup debt paid off in five years if we institute these cuts."

Dudley Wharton pushed himself back from the table at Seymour's Café that was littered with papers, cold remnants of breakfast and random scribblings on the paper place mats. He stared at Rex openly and with an aspect of total vulnerability that was somewhat alarming. Rex scanned the budget once again, then stared vacantly out of the window while a large, red-tufted woodpecker made his way noisily up to a pine tree. His eyes were puffy from lack of sleep, his manner distant.

"Is this sort of thing normal when you start a new town?"

"Not usually. But this isn't just any town. There are many variables…"

"This is gonna be a septic tank explosion."

Wharton chuckled briefly. "I hope not!"

"The only way we were able to sell the idea of an island government to the fiscal hardliners who were perfectly happy being part of the county was to convince them that we could deliver the same—or better—services for the same—or less—taxes. If we do this, then we've reneged on our promise."

"Yeah, I see what you mean. That's one reason why it's so hard to get a new municipal government off the ground. The first few years can be tricky."

"Tricky? I'd advise you to start looking around for another job, son. That's not a threat—just a word of caution."

"Well, maybe the other council members won't feel so negatively about it and will get behind a plan to temporarily cut services. It's probably the best shot."

"I sure hope so. I'll do what I can to grease the tracks before our meeting. But even if the council buys it, what about the community? That's where the real heat will come from."

"Could I suggest something?" Wharton was growing obsequious. "Perhaps if you gave some sort of economic report—some kind of projection for how we could get more tax revenues—it would help balance off the bad news I'll have."

"Sure," Rex said sarcastically. "I'll just say we were wrong to defeat the bridge and maybe we should go back to the state and ask them to build it because it would bring us so much business. Then we could really make our fiscal nut!"

After his jarring meeting with Wharton, Rex drove slowly out to the butterfly preserve. He parked his truck near the highway and hiked up into its rolling green hills above the creek bed. Although there weren't yet any butterflies, the area was peaceful and quiet. Jays and crows happily swooped from tree to tree, without interference from humans. *We may fail to create a human sanctuary, but Seymour has done something for the butterflies. Some small corner of this island will remain pristine, no matter how badly we screw everything else up. Thanks, Seymour…thanks from me and the butterflies.*

As he sat on the hilltop overlooking the stream Rex envisioned this tiny piece of land surrounded by legions of internal combustion engines spewing fumes into the atmosphere day and night, choking and poisoning the lungs of Earth. And there was really nothing to stop the onslaught. "Progress" and prosperity demanded the complete despoliation and exploitation of every natural resource on the planet. As the lust for more wealth spread, nations and armies would fight each other for the remaining supplies of oil and any other fuel to keep the engines of commerce running. And perhaps in some future millennium, humanoid space travelers would visit the burnt-out toxic waste dump called Earth and marvel that it ever supported life.

Rex wiped a tear from his eye as he climbed back into his truck. The strangeness of the whole situation, his life for the last few years, made him tremble with fear. He felt like a lost child as he slowly drove home, dragged himself into the kitchen and made a cup of strong coffee. *Gotta see about getting some meds...feel like I'm in a box.*

As he sipped his coffee, Rex flipped through an IRATE photo album from the incorporation drive and found Seymour's face—beaming with simple, child-like glee—in practically every photo. For the first time, he realized just how much Seymour had contributed to the effort by his enthusiasm, his persistence, and his good spirits. And he hated himself for secretly feeling that the youth was somehow just a little *too* strange.

He decided he owed it to Seymour, if not to himself, to see that not only the butterfly preserve but the entire island remained as the group had intended when its members set off on their zealous crusade. Something that Seymour couldn't verbalize very well, but that he obviously felt passionately in his heart, drove Rex beyond his sadness. He would find a way both to increase the tax revenues and maintain the sanctity of Skagit Island. The two really weren't mutually exclusive, but rather mutually interdependent.

With a new determination in his eyes, and a trembling hand, he wrote down on a notepad his steps to achieve this goal: "Meet with Seattle business leaders; find a way to promote the arts and artists;

work with realtors to find suitable space for galleries and advertise in greater Seattle; plan some kind of annual event to draw people to Skagit to sample arts and crafts." He nibbled on the end of his pen, then continued: "List the butterfly preserve in conservation magazines, include on hiking trails."

Then he thumbed through his copy of Alcoholics Anonymous, and re-read the section on *Working with Others*.

"Your job now is to be at the place where you may be of maximum help-fulness to others, so never hesitate to go anywhere if you can be helpful. You should not hesitate to visit the most sordid spot on earth on such an errand."

Council chambers were eerily still as islanders filed in and packed the small room wall-to-wall. Council members sat heads down in seeming concentration on their paperwork as the muted tension simmered. Only once did Zack raise his head to furtively survey the room and, spotting no one with whom he could exchange an easy smile and a wave, he quickly turned back to his agenda. The setting reminded Rex of an imbroglio he'd once covered as a reporter, when a community antipoverty agency was on the brink of implosion as it struggled with ethnic, political and social cross-currents on its board of directors. There was a seething rage beneath the placid surface that made the fragile equanimity of the crowd somehow deeply threatening, like a bottle of gasoline left out for hours in the hot desert sun.

Once again, Wharton outlined the fiscal picture. Once again, he tried to remain upbeat as he presented the alternatives. Once again, islanders looked stunned and incredulous—like children who've just ripped open a brightly-wrapped Christmas gift to discover it wasn't what they wanted at all. A sense of battle weariness pervaded the gathering, and Rex drummed his fingers nervously on the table until Allison kicked him under the table to make him stop.

"We've raised taxes on the business district, tried to get new retail in here, and now we're faced with cutting back on out level of services." Charlie Rector shook his head sadly, as if he'd just witnessed a particularly egregious instance of child abuse. "How could our projections have been so wrong?"

"You know as well as anyone else here, Charlie, that when we first discussed formation of a new island government we knew that experience would be the only true measure of how well we were doing," Zack said. "How many of us thought we'd be building a surplus our first few years, anyway? This is a disappointment, but not the end of the world or the end of the island."

When the public hearing opened, a lineup of speakers assembled.

"My husband and I live at the end of Witchazel Road. Sometimes we don't see a police car in our area for two or three days at a time. Will this cutback mean we won't get any police protection at all?" Retired schoolteacher Rosalind Timm's gray bun of hair quivered along with her voice as she spoke.

"What's your address, ma'am?" Rex asked briskly. "You should be getting more frequent patrols. I'll have the administrator look into it."

"My children use the library a lot on weekends, because I commute into Seattle for my job and that's the only time I can take them. Are you talking about eliminating weekend hours?" Attorney Benson Heidler stood stiff and tall, his liquid blue eyes penetrating.

"No, sir," Allison answered. "Our initial proposal is to cut four hours of service on Sundays only. I hope that won't inconvenience you and your children too much."

"I've been waiting four years to have the arterial that leads from the highway down to our property resurfaced," Jeffrey White lamented, hunched over and trembling with Parkinson's Disease. "The county told me two years ago it was on their list. They never got it done. How long will I have to wait?"

"Sir, you won't have to wait more than another year," Rex answered.

Old Man White raised his head up as far as he could and peered querulously into Rex. Eyes. With a good-natured chuckle, Rex hastily raised his right hand: "I swear it!"

After they got home and fell exhausted into bed, Allison said wearily: "It feels like we're running this island on nothing more than fantasy."

"Fantasy Island! I like that," Rex blurted out. "Maybe we could market it!"

Zack returned home to a dark, empty house. Using the headlights of his idling truck to see, he wrestled the garage door open and then pulled inside and parked. The cluttered garage was a microcosm of his life—a chaotic, sprawling aggregation of power tools, random engine parts, seashells, and old cheesecake calendars still hanging on the wall. None of it mattered any more; he felt strangely detached from everything. Zack lit a cigarette and rummaged behind his workbench until he found his long-hidden six pack of warm beer, a remnant from his defunct marriage. With shaking fingers, he pried open a can and guzzled it down. As the warmth spread from his stomach to his brain, then throughout his bloodstream, Zack knew what he had to do. He tossed the empty can on the concrete floor with a "clunk" and popped open another. Then he reopened the garage door, backed the truck down the driveway and returned to the garage. He found his large container of kerosene, stored for heating emergencies, opened the cap and tipped it over, spilling a river of the smelly fuel across the garage. Then Zack walked slowly to the door, took another hard drag on his cigarette and flicked it directly into the kerosene, which ignited with a sudden flash. He quickly closed the garage door, got into his truck and drove off, watching in the rearview mirror as flames engulfed his house. Zack kept driving until he reached the fishing pier, where he got out his pole and dipped it in the water while finishing off the sex-pack. When he got cold and had not felt a nibble for a long time, he packed his gear into the back of the truck, curled up on the front seat under a dirty tarpaulin and slept.

"Why don't you just come and stay with us for a while?" Rex said, putting his arm around Zack's shoulder to calm his distraught friend. "You don't have any business sleeping in your truck! I'm sure the insurance company will offer to pay for a place as soon as they make an inspection."

Zack's bloodshot eyes spoke more of alcohol than of fire. "If I could maybe stay here for a few days…"

"Aw, hell, Zack! You can stay here as long as you want. You know that!"

"Maybe there's some work I could help with around the house, to pay you back."

Sensing his friend's discomfort, Rex paused. "Well, Allison's been saying for quite a while she wants to clean and paint her studio. Why don't you talk to her about that?"

During his brief stay, Zack neither drank nor attended any AA meetings. Stoically, he acted the part of the aggrieved innocent. At Allison's direction, he moved all of her studio materials into a portion of the garage where he was staying and set about doing remedial carpentry to replace rotted beams and siding in the studio. Alone with his work, his cigarettes and the radio, Zack felt somehow purged of the past as a new sense of hopefulness about the future crept into his consciousness.

With $100,000 from the insurance, I can build my own place for about half of that and put the rest in the bank. Tell the credit card companies to kiss my ass. Work whenever I want. Best thing ever happened to me.

While Zack grew more confident as his work progressed, Allison grew more impatient without a place to paint. And as Allison became more miserable, she found more creative ways to discharge her frustrations onto Rex. Areas of unpleasantness included his employment status, their financial plight, the isolation of the island, the time wasted during painting of her studio, and the seeming dead-end that was once a dream of island independence.

Zack was completing the trim around the windows one afternoon when the Skagit Fire Marshal accompanied by a deputy sheriff drove up the bumpy driveway, parked and knocked on the door.

"What's up, Barney?" Zack asked pleasantly.

"May we come in? I've got some bad news, Zack. Looks like we're gonna have to charge you with arson. This is a warrant for your arrest."

Zack dropped his paintbrush and gulped.

"Come with us."

Transported to the Skookum County Jail, Zack soon found himself in a large holding cell surrounded by shifty-eyed con men, smelly vagrants and angry street blacks. On one of the bunks, a tall, lanky, dark-haired Eskimo-looking fellow sprawled insouciantly as if to advertise the fact he'd secured one of the highly prized beds. With more than 30 men in the cell, and only 10 bunks, priorities became: 1) find a bed to sleep in, 2) telephone a friend, relative or attorney to arrange release, and 3) stay out of the way of the dangerous-looking criminals. A head-shaved young black man returned every few minutes to the pay telephone of the wall near the sliding steel bar doors to place a collect call to his mother, who still wasn't at home. Zack sat disconsolately on the cold concrete floor and stared blankly at the tiny window slits more than 12 feet from the heads of the men. The windows were brown-stained and looked as if they hadn't been cleaned in 20 years. Through his thick head, he tried to remember Rex' telephone number and several times he lurched for the telephone after the young black man had slammed down the receiver. But when he got to the phone, he could no more recall the number on Skagit Island than he could believe he'd ever be free again. So he sat in frozen desperation on the floor—withdrawn, silent, terrified.

"Whaddya in for?" asked a pear-shaped white man of about Zack's age.

Zack wanted a cigarette and a beer desperately. Instead, he got this freakish outcast standing over him, looking down. Without looking back, he mumbled: "Arson."

"Oh, pssshhht! That's nothing. You can beat that one easy. Got a lawyer?"

Zack shook his head slowly.

"I know a guy who's a good one. Gotten me outa some real jams. Oughta give him a call. I'm Sam. What's your name?"

"Zack. Nice to meet you." He looked up and extended his gnarled hand warily.

"Got any money?"

Zack looked surprised. "No. They took everything when I was brought in here."

"I mean, money to hire a lawyer. This guy's good, but not cheap."

"What does he charge?"

"Depends on your case. Probably not less than a grand, though."

"I suppose I could manage that, if he's as good as you say. What's his name."

Danny Aiello. He's in the yellow pages. This guy is unbelievable."

"Thanks. I'll be sure and look him up."

"Say, are you a fisherman? You kinda look like a guy I knew once in Ballard."

"Just a weekend fisherman. I mostly do carpentry and odd jobs on Skagit Island."

"Wow! That's an expensive place to live, huh?"

"I guess so…in more ways than one." Zack's voice cracked as the words moved over his throat. Then he lay down on the hard, cold concrete floor, closed his eyes and fell asleep.

"Dinner" was served at 4:30 p.m. on square plastic trays. It was a lugubrious admixture of tasteless meatloaf drowned in a pasty gravy, mashed instant potatoes, frozen vegetables barely thawed and tapioca pudding. Ravenous, Zack shoveled a mouthful down his gullet, only to realize how repellant the food actually was. He covered his tray with a paper napkin, got up from the floor and joined the circle of pacing men. In other cells, he could hear men moaning and shouting their disgust with the meal. Something inside him was now wound as tightly as a precision watch spring. His body moved from its store of animal flight energy—not from any healthy need for exercise. By pacing in circles, Zack became dulled to his surroundings and somehow derived a sense of accomplishment, no matter how transitory or absurd. The still air of the cell reeked with the body odors of the men, their fear, their diets, their diseases, their nicotine-fouled lungs. The fresh ocean breezes of Skagit Island seemed a world away.

The muscle-bound young black man with a surly, confrontational attitude strutted around the cell also, warily watching Zack and occasionally stopping to try once again to reach his mother on the pay phone. Each time, when he was unable to make the connection, he slammed the receiver down violently into its cradle and resumed his strutting—with an intensified sense of rage and frustration. "Motherfucker!" kept tumbling from his curled lips as he strode around with fire in his eyes. The other prisoners cut him a wide berth. Zack stood at one of two urinals in the bathroom, and noticed out of the corner of his eye the swaggering approach of the street tough. Although he tensed inside, Zack tried to keep cool. With a faint smile on his face, he glanced over at the figure standing next to him.

"What the fuck wrong with you, honky? Never seen a black dick before? You some kind of motherfucker faggot?"

"Nope. Sorry." Zack zipped and zapped. He found a corner of the cell where he could crawl under a small steel picnic table and be somewhat unnoticed by the other prisoners, curled up and tried to sleep again. As he started to doze, he again heard the voice of the black prisoner, now filled with a pleading, pitiful fear.

"Mamma…Mamma…Mamma! You don't understand, Mamma. I didn't do nothin'. Why you can't come and get me outa here? I *know* you done bailed me out before, Mamma. But this time I didn't do nothin', Mamma. *What?!*"

He once again slammed the phone down, uttered a desperate curse under his breath and resumed his pacing. Zack closed his eyes and pretended to be asleep. As he did so, he noticed a huge dust ball rolling across the concrete floor toward his face.

CHAPTER 2

❀

"**W**e've gotta get him out of that godawful jail before something bad happens to him," Rex declared as he paced in the kitchen. Allison sat slumped indolently at the table, staring out of the window.

"Something bad has *already* happened to him," she mused. "I was kind of getting to like the peace and quiet around here."

Rex fixed a cold glance on her. "Zack is my friend. I have to do whatever I can to help him. I'll go an get him out of jail if you're not interested."

She rose and put her arm around his waist. "You're cute when you get pissed off. I didn't really mean it. I guess I just wish the whole thing had never happened. I agree that we should help him out. But I can't go to the jail with you because someone is coming this afternoon to look at some of my paintings."

Rex stroked his chin. "This is probably the most important AA call I've ever made. This guy's life is on the line and he may not even know it." As he approached the door, he paused and turned back to her. "You don't suppose I'm just enabling his disease, do you?"

"Well, maybe. I think we should set some time limits and ground rules for him when he comes to stay with us. That's the only way we can avoid giving him permission to stay stuck in his alcoholism."

"Like, what did you have in mind?"

"Like, one condition of his staying here is that he goes to 90 AA meetings in 90 days," Allison ticked off the familiar litany of early sobriety. "And that he gets a sponsor—not you or me. And that he gets a full-time job and pays us rent."

"Yeah, I know you're right. Maybe we should tell him that if he slips in any of those areas he'll have to move out."

"As much as I hate the expression 'tough love,' that's what it takes sometimes."

Rex kissed her and they held each other tight. "Thanks for helping me to get my feet on the ground. I needed that."

Bond for Zack Beale was set at $70,000, which meant that a cashier's check for $7,000 would win him release from jail. After negotiating the check, Rex had $32.17 remaining in his checking account. He approached the clerk at the county jail and tried to affect a pleasant demeanor. Hers was a cigarette-stained, wind-etched face that responded to nothing so subtle as a smile.

"Case number?" she asked indifferently.

"Uh, I'm not sure. The prisoner's name is Zack Beale. B-E-A-L-E."

An ominous silence filled the small cubicle as she scrolled down her battered computer screen. Without taking her eyes off the monitor, she recited terms and conditions: "I need a certified or cashier's check in the amount of $7,000 made out to the county treasurer's office."

Rex handed her the oversized check, which she placed in a drawer chock full of cash and checks. Then she wrote out a receipt and handed it to him, at last making eye contact for the first time.

"When will Mr. Beale be released?"

"Soon as the DA sends someone down here. Probably in about an hour."

Rex used the time to walk up the steep incline of Yesler Avenue to the Seattle Area Intergroup headquarters of Alcoholics Anonymous, where he bought Zack a copy of the "Big Book"—otherwise known as "Alcoholics Anonymous"—and gathered up free pamphlets and a schedule of meetings in the Seattle area. The walls of the pioneer-era building were coated with decades of amber-colored cigarette smoke residue, and the place smelled like an ashtray that hadn't been emptied for about six months. He quickly made his way outside and walked further up the hill. Standing atop the promontory overlooking Elliott Bay, Rex could imagine the thudding sound of gigantic logs as they thundered down the skids to be loaded onto cargo ships, past the raucous bars on First Avenue with their cheap beer, wild talk and easy women when Seattle was a jumping off point for Klondike gold rushers. "Skid Road" was now a tony shopping district where tourists brushed past drunken Indians with bloodshot fire in their vacant eyes, and the melancholy stench of poverty and madness followed the bustle of commerce like the unburied doppelganger of a guilty past.

He gripped the AA literature like a drowning man would clutch at a life jacket and made his way slowly back down the hill to the jail. After a quick stop for a meal of pancakes and eggs, Zack and Rex boarded the ferry for the island. Zack seemed to relax at last as the fresh marine air washed over the upper deck.

"You know, when I was drinking I had this recurring nightmare that I was in prison," Rex said. "It was really scary. Sometimes I woke up in a cold sweat. It wasn't jail—this was prison, for something horrible like murder—and I was never gonna get out." He paused for a moment. "But since I've been sober, I haven't had those dreams any more."

"Believe me, I sure as hell never want to go back there again."

"Back to jail, or back to drinking?"

"Neither one. Neither one."

"Well, you need to get a sponsor, a lawyer and a job right away. I can't help you with the first one, but I may be able to help with the other two. You realize you're living with a couple of recovering drunks and we've probably tried every excuse and ruse in the book ourselves?"

"I know, but that's good because I need someone to kick me in the ass."

"Consider yourself kicked, pal."

Zack put a cigarette in his mouth, paused for a moment, then put it back in his pocket. "Gotta stop this addiction, too."

"Especially on the ferry! If one of the crew sees you smoking while we're underway, you're liable to go right back into that hellhole I just got you out of."

Zack relaxed and drew a deep breath. "It's so great to have friends. I mean, I really feel like you and Allison are almost family."

"Thanks. We're just a couple of drunks trying to stay sober one day at a time. But I have an ulterior motive, too. It's no fun to go fishing all alone."

"All right! Let's get out my boat and go for a little expedition, shall we?"

"Tomorrow's good for me. Maybe Allison will even join us."

Zack screwed up his leathery face into a comical look of pain. Rex burst into a belly laugh and slapped his friend on the shoulder.

"Hey, just kidding…lighten up! There's not a chance in hell she'd go with us. She hates fishing. It'll just be you, me, and the seagulls."

As they scampered off the clanging steel ramp onto the dock, Zack at last lit his cigarette. "I'm sorry. This is my one and only smoke today. By the way, that reminds me…have you ever wondered about that kid Seymour Creighton? That whole business is just a little weird. First all the talk about an abduction, then the murder. People in Seattle must believe everyone on the island is nuts."

"We are," Rex said flatly. "We'd have to be nuts to want to live on an island in the first place, don't you think? I mean, what normal person would want to live in such a remote place and have to deal with the ferries whenever they want a new pair of shoes, for Christ's sake?"

"I just hope we can get ourselves out of the red soon. That might help the rest of the world to take us a little more seriously."

"Ah, fuck 'em. Who cares what they think?"

"This is true," Zack reflected as he took another deep drag. "The crazier they think we are, the less likely they will be to try and live here."

"Exactly."

Rex helped Zack to get settled in his room, then headed for the studio to check on Allison. But before he left, he turned to Zack.

"There was a guy at the AA meeting yesterday who said he needed some help with his landscaping business. I wrote his name and phone number down somewhere...believe it was Phil something. Maybe you'd want to give him a call."

"Thanks. I'm gonna be giving lots of people calls, starting tomorrow morning."

Allison greeted Rex with a kiss. "Charlie Rector called you while you were in town," she said. "He seemed anxious to talk to you about something."

"Did he say what?"

"I'm not really sure, but with Charlie you can make a safe bet it has something to do with either money or business—or both."

"That's funny," Rex said. "He's never called me before. I don't think we've ever held a conversation outside the council meetings."

Allison wiped her brush and laid it down gently on the easel, eyeing Rex seductively. "I sold two paintings."

"Wow! That's terrific! We should celebrate."

She drew closer and pushed her firm breasts against him, eyes riveted on his.

"OK, let's." Allison reached down and unzipped his trousers, put her hand inside and began stroking him. Rex quickly forgot about Zack Beale, Charlie Rector or the vagaries of island governance. When he was quite excited, she carefully zipped him back, took him by the hand and led him upstairs to the bedroom. She locked the door, took off all her clothes and got into bed. Then she beckoned to him to join her.

As they approached a feverish climax, a horrendous gunshot boomed nearby. The sound briefly reverberated off the trees and echoed back into the house.

"Jesus, what the fuck?!" Rex sputtered as he leaped out of bed.

"Hurry back," Allison said faintly as she rolled over.

As he descended the staircase, Rex thought he could smell gunpowder downstairs. He followed the scent all the way to Zack's room, and banged on the door. Zack swung the door open with a smile on his face and a shotgun in one hand.

"What the hell is going on?" Rex demanded.

"Oh, those goddamned crows drive me crazy this time of year!" Zack threw the rifle down on his bed and motioned for Rex to enter. "Every spring they cluster in the trees and carry on this ungodly racket. Only thing that works to get rid of them is a good blast from the old cannon."

Rex gulped. "I see. Well, I don't think you should be firing your shotgun here on our property. It's too dangerous, the neighbors will complain, and it scared the shit out of us. I suppose you'll just have to put up with some crowing if you're gonna stay here."

Zack looked crestfallen. "I didn't mean any harm. Honest. I guess I'm just in the habit of doing whatever I please at my own place, and didn't stop to think. I'm sorry."

"I'm a little perturbed that you brought a shotgun into the house and didn't tell me. I assume you have a license for it?"

"Oh, hell yes. I've had this popper forever. I use it to go bird hunting every year."

"Do me a favor, pal? Put the shotgun away and don't shoot it any more while you're here. OK?"

"OK. That's fine. Maybe I'll just get some earplugs when I want to sleep."

"Yeah, and get some for me too, OK?"

Allison was sitting up in bed with a pout on her lips when Rex returned.

"The fucker fired his shotgun at a bunch of crows! Can you believe that?" Rex said. "I'm afraid this is really gonna test our friendship."

"He scares me sometimes," Allison whispered.

"Yeah, me too. Of course, we were never scary when we were getting sober."

"Very funny. I never carried a shotgun, Rex."

"He's harmless, really. Zack has just lived alone on this island for too long. I think living here with us where he has to be accountable to other people will be good for him. He's like a big, overgrown kid."

"Tom Sawyer goes to AA!"

"Look, we made a deal with him. I think we owe it to him to hold up our end of the bargain. Zack probably can't say it, but I think he's desperately lonely more than anything else."

"OK, but if I see or hear that stupid shotgun again he'd out of here quicker than a scalded dog."

The normally ebullient Charlie was sullen and downcast when Rex found him sipping a cappuccino at Seymour's Café.

"We got our butts in a sling, Rex." Charlie was not a man to mince words.

"How so?" Rex felt strangely uninformed and vulnerable because of Charlie's directness.

"I've lived on this island for almost 40 years, my kids grew up here, and I love this place. I can remember when there were still a few berry farms in operation. Nowadays, the only strawberries are in the produce section of the market. And they're all from California."

Charlie's sudden digression made Rex squirm, but he maintained his composure. *When will this asshole ever get to the point?*

"I was one of the people who screamed the loudest about the bridge deal," he continued, oblivious to Rex' discomfort. "And I've worked like hell to try and get this new deal we got going here off the ground." Charlie frowned and shook his head. "But we gotta face the facts."

He looked around the room, quaffed down the last drops of coffee, and coughed loudly. "We just ain't making it, pal. We're broke. We started out broke, we're broke now, and we're gonna stay broke until the next ice age."

"Of course," Rex jumped in. "We've known that for some time. But the council agreed on a plan to deal with it. As you saying the plan isn't going to work?"

"I'm saying that I've been approached by a group of people—a very influential group of people—here on the island who think we should cut our losses."

"How?"

"They want us to go back to Skookum County. Disband the island government. Cancel the check. Call the experiment a failure."

Rex gulped as his stomach did a flip-flop. "What?! That's…that's not even legal."

"Sure it is. If they put something on the ballot, the voters approve dissolution of the island government, then we go back to the county by default. Just as simple as that."

"Jesus. This is incredible. Just when I thought we were getting somewhere. I appreciate your bringing this to my attention so we can discuss it at the next council…"

"I won't be there to discuss it, Rex. I'm resigning to lead the push to put this thing on the ballot."

After a stony silence, Rex said calmly: "That's your right, Charlie. I don't think you'll ever get it on the ballot, personally. Got any recommendations for someone we can appoint to fill your unexpired term?"

With a huff, Rector pulled himself up from the table and pushed his chair in. "Afraid not, Rex. I'd advise you to join us. You're paddling in a sinking ship, son."

Despite his bluster, Rex felt anxious. About Zack's precarious condition. About the discontent festering on the Island Council. About Allison's deepening involvement with her art and the connection it provided her with a life outside Skagit Island. As he left the café, Rex wondered whether it had been worth the struggle to organize islanders to fight the state, then the county, to achieve independence. He was reminded of the southern slaves who were "liberated" by the Emancipation Proclamation and the Civil War, only to discover just how hollow a victory their "freedom" was without any education or any means to earn a living apart from the colonial slave system. *Freedom is just another word for nothing left to lose.* Somehow he felt abandoned, like a small child alone and terrified. For the first time in his sobriety, he considered taking a drink. The image of a cold, crystalline glass of tequila with a fresh lime on the lip popped into his mind. But then he thought again of Zack, and of his children, and knew a drink would be out of the question. An AA meeting, however, wasn't.

CHAPTER 3

✿

$\mathcal{A}$s he made his way back to his car, Rex noticed bright yellow posters stapled to a line of telephone poles along the highway. So he stopped to read one:

"TOWN MEETING–Friday, 7 p.m., Skagit Grange Hall. Come and learn the truth about why our island government can never succeed. It's time for Skagit Islanders to take charge once again. Success?—yes. Secession?—no!"

A bitter rush of anger made his skin tingle. Rex could visualize Charlie Rector with his squat little body reaching up to post the fliers, and his soul blackened with hatred. Now he could add betrayal to his list of resentments. When he got home, he went directly to his desk, pulled out his AA notebook and began writing. When he'd finished his inventory of hateful feelings and written them all down, he realized that fear was the root emotion that underlay all his other destructive feelings—fear of losing control, fear of losing prestige, fear that the island would be delivered into the hands of those who would ruin it, fear of looking like a fool.

For the first time, he got on his knees and prayed. He begged to have his fear removed so he could live free of resentments. When he finished, Rex felt lighter and somehow purged, more willing to simply let events unfold naturally without trying to force them in the direction that his will dictated. Then he went for a walk on the beach alone, and found rounded stones that he could skip across the relatively calm water just as he'd done when he was a child. As each stone skipped, then sank into the dark depths, Rex gave it a name. One was hope, another fear, yet another anger. One by one, he tossed his attachments into the icy waters of Puget Sound and was happy to leave them there.

When he returned to the house, Rex felt positively buoyant. He could hardly remember a time when he felt so light, so free, so fresh and willing to try something new. *Is this what they mean when they talk about being born again?*

Allison met him on the back walkway as she left her studio and headed into the house.

"What are you grinning about?" she asked, genuinely perplexed.

"Charlie Rector has given me a great gift. He has just made me realize that my life—our life—will go on no matter what happens on this island."

Allison cocked her head suspiciously. "Have you been abducted, too? This doesn't sound much like the same guy who left the house this morning. What happened?"

Rex put his arm around her waist and they walked slowly together. "You know how we say in AA that God sometimes speaks to us through other people? Well Charlie Rector—completely unbeknownst to himself—has made me aware of what's really important to me. And it's you—us! I'm really powerless to decide what happens to Skagit Island in the long run."

"I'm glad you feel that way, but are you forgetting how hard you've worked for this thing? I'm not sure that a pink cloud over losing something you care about and struggle for is really quality sobriety. Just go slowly here, hon. If Charlie Rector and his little band of morons want to take the island and give it back to the county, it's gonna hurt. And we'll both be pissed off!"

"That's true, but it's not us or our lives that are at stake here. Sure, we'll be upset and disappointed. But we have each other and we're sober. We'll find our way."

"Never had any doubts," Allison said, patting him on the butt.

"This isn't the only island in the world, you know."

"I know. But this is the island where you and I decided to make our home. I just think we need to go slow here. Let's stay cool."

"You can't tell me you've always felt this place is a paradise on earth," Rex observed dryly.

"Got news for you, son. There ain't no such place. Anywhere there's people—which is just about everywhere—there's problems. I've blown off steam sometimes when I get aggravated. But you need to know that I'd do that anywhere. I say we stay put and see this thing through."

Rex was more than a little surprised. He'd fully expected Allison to have her bags packed before he could finish his first sentence. His childlike enthusiasm quickly wilted.

"You're right, of course," he said with a serious expression. "I guess my old geographical cure mechanism just started kicking my butt before I knew what was what. I'm sorry if I made a fool out of myself."

"No apologies necessary," Allison said firmly. "Maybe that's why we're in each other's lives—to call each other on things when they come up."

"What do you say we both go to Charlie Rector's meeting? Maybe we can bring Zack, and we'll all learn something."

"OK, but we can't all three go because that could be construed as an illegal meeting of the Island Council."

"Right. Then *we'll* go, and tell Zack when we get home."

The Skagit Island Grange Hall was filled with the musty odor of bodies and stagnant air when they entered its raw-beamed interior. In numbers, the assembled crowd was sparse—no more than 20 people. But they were island natives mostly from pioneer families, and

Rex recognized them only because he'd seen their faces on a Skagit Island Historical Society float during a recent Strawberry Festival parade. This was a prickly group, unsettled and unsmiling. Charlie Rector sat at the front of the row of steel folding chairs, whispering into the ear of another man and gesturing with one hand that clutched a sheaf of papers. They slipped into the hall quietly and took seats at the rear, trying not to attract attention.

"Well, it's Rex Armistead and his lovely wife Allison!" Charlie had spotted them just as they sat down. He rose and moved toward them, a shit-eating grin on his face. "Welcome to out little revolutionary cell, folks!"

All heads in the room were now focused on Rex and Allison, and both wished they'd never come.

"Why thank you, Charlie. You are always the perfect gentleman." Allison overwhelmed with her flawlessly saccharine missile shield.

"You folks may not like what you hear tonight." Charlie's demeanor had become grave.

"That's OK, we can take it," Rex answered. "I thought we might learn something. Maybe even change our minds."

"Hah! I doubt that, but you're welcome to stay."

"I just want to ask you, and everyone else here, a question. About a year ago, most of us were together at a hearing to defeat the bridge. We were all united in wanting to protect the island from development and exploitation. Now many of those same people are here to participate in the very thing we were fighting. Why?"

There was a moment of silence, then fuzzyheaded architect Craig Wysham stood up. A lifelong islander, he was a tall and imposing figure.

"Here's why: we can't pay our bills. It's kind of like when you saved up to buy your first car, Rex. If you were like me, you worked and saved and then looked around at all the flashy cars—the Jaguars, Corvettes. Even the used sports cars that wouldn't run cost too much, so you settled for a funky old Plymouth that would get you where you wanted to go. And in the process, you learned how our economy works."

"But we've just started, and we've got plans to develop the tax base," Rex said. "That takes time. I don't think we've given this idea of independence a fair shot. What do you suppose the Founding Fathers thought after the Revolutionary War when the country was broke, with huge war debts and a struggling economy? Did they beg to be taken back under the British crown?"

Charlie Rector's face became a contorted washrag of disgust.

"Look," Charlie said angrily. "I'm sure all of us are here because we chose to live on the island. If we tax ourselves right out of our homes, then we'll lose the island faster than if we let the bridge go up, or go back to the county. Understand?"

"Yes, we both understand perfectly well," Allison said. "I personally feel a little disappointed in some of you folks who are my friends. I thought your convictions were stronger than that. Maybe this isn't the community we thought it was. Maybe we should just go back to the county and forget this whole business."

Rex and Allison rose and walked out of the Grange Hall in silence. As they walked to their car in the black night, they listened closely for any sounds of voices from within. But there was no sound, other than the soft hoot of a night owl in a distant pine tree.

As he parked the car in the moonlight, Rex leaned over and softly kissed Allison. "I love you, dear. We'll get through this. Maybe it's only growing pains. They could put this thing on the ballot and it could be voted down. We just have to wait and see. This is when we should be setting an example of conviction, don't you think?"

"Yeah, I suppose. It's kind of funny that a couple of drunks would be in the position of trying to provide some leadership. The only thing I can do is just stay sober, one day at a time. They're gonna do what they're gonna do."

They approached the silent house, dark except for a light glowing in Zack's room. Rex' spirits rose at the prospect of talking with his old fishing chum.

"Let's go tell Zack what happened," he said.

"You guys can talk. I'm going to bed."

Rex kissed her again, then trundled downstairs to Zack's room. He tapped gently on the door, but there was no answer although the lights were on. Several more knocks went unanswered, so he slowly pushed the door open.

Spread out on the bed before him like the picnic feast of a psychopathic butcher were the decapitated remains of Zack's corpse. The bulk of his head had been blown completely off by the blast of his shotgun, which lay on the floor beside the blood-soaked bed. Bits of bone and flesh were splattered all over the far wall, and the whole room reeked of blood and gunpowder. Rex gasped as if he would retch. Then, finding his breath again, he shrieked so loudly that Allison ran downstairs in a flash. She stood at the doorway for a second, then turned and ran upstairs to call the police.

The coroner's report showed no alcohol in Zack Beale's blood at the time of his death. Nor were there any symptoms of gross organic disease. The cause of death was listed as: "Self-inflicted gunshot wound to the head. Subject had history of alcoholism and depression." Rex and two other men from AA took his ashes out to Puget Sound in a small fishing boat and released them into the northbound currents. "By tomorrow, his ashes will be spread from Skagit Island half-way to Hawaii," said Bill Overby, skipper of the funereal vessel. They spent the trip back to the island in bitter self-recrimination.

"I should have agreed to be his sponsor when he first got sober," Rex said.

"Yeah, I guess I could have reached out more to him and gone to meetings with him," Bill lamented.

"Zack always seemed like a nice guy, but I never bothered to get to know him. I wish I'd gotten his phone number and called him." Kevin was positively morose.

"Maybe he was just tired of living," Rex said. "He didn't have any family—no wife or children, no home really. Maybe he just wanted to…to have it all be over."

At a memorial service on Shipwreck Beach, Father Larry McCollom from St. Patrick's Cathedral in Seattle delivered a requiem and led prayers for Zack. As a fellow recovering alcoholic and Jesuit priest, Father Larry knew as well as anyone the fine line between madness and lucidity that drunks in early recovery usually walk. The diminutive priest called on the assembled crowd to have compassion and forgiveness for Zack, and to see in his struggles their own.

"Zack Beale had to find the light through a tragic act of self-destruction," he said slowly. "For too many of us alcoholics, this is often the case. But the miracle of AA and recovery is that God will save our sanity, our health and our lives if we let Him have His way with us. We must have what is sometimes referred to as revolutionary patience. Those of us who are willing to be patient and give ourselves fully to our higher power can discover the light of divine love and service right here on earth. The third step of out program makes all this possible, when we turn our will and our lives over to the care of a higher power. May God bless Zack Beale in his journey, and may God bless each and every one of you in your recovery."

CHAPTER 4

❀

*F*or Charlie Rector and his forces, Zack Beale's death was a signal that victory was nearer. They redoubled their efforts to galvanize islanders to their crusade. Preachers used the sad economic condition of the island as a moral lesson in overcoming adversity. According to their individual views of the world and their lifetimes of conditioning—emotional, intellectual, cultural—islanders took different attitudes toward the latest political winds to sweep Skagit Island. The common view among the younger generation was that corrupt capitalism had triumphed once again and that return to the county represented the most odious form of capitulation. The merchant community, although in number the smallest interest group on the island, organized meetings, spent money on advertising and direct mail, and generally drowned out the voices of any dissenters by volume and repetition. Many commuters who saw in the move toward independence an affirmation of their decision to live on the island were disheartened by the turn of events but disinclined, whether through lack of energy or commitment, to get involved. And most oldtime islanders shook their heads and went on about the business of their lives as if none of the huffing and puffing mattered. Thus was the precious unity and cohesiveness of the island lost.

Sensing a sure thing, county bureaucrats began to rub their hands together at the prospect of once again tapping into the island's tax base. With continued growth and residential expansion in Skookum County to the south and on the western side of Puget Sound, the board of supervisors was stretched thin to balance its budget with the increased demand for more libraries, police services, roads and parks. The pulsing heart of capitalism required that more lifeblood in the form of tax revenue flow through the body politic to nourish its growth spurts. And thus continued the cycles of urban sprawl that generated the very style of life loathsome to many Northwesterners and symbolized by sneering references to Los Angeles—freeways turned into parking lots, rising crime rates and street violence, and a sickening spume of pollution hovering in the air above the cold waters of the sound.

"It's funny," Allison chuckled bitterly. "I actually had designed some pretend money from the 'Bank of Skagit Island' that I thought maybe the chamber or somebody could use to help promote tourism. That was before Charlie Rector got up on his high horse."

Rex smiled laconically. "I'd love to see it. Maybe we can use it to live on while we're trying to sell the house."

Allison disappeared from the kitchen and returned with an outsized sketchbook. She flipped open the transparent cover to reveal the full-sized images of startlingly realistic-looking currency in five and 10-dollar denominations. The image at the center was a blue heron standing peacefully in a serene and shallow tide, with an unearthly light from a full moon spilling over everything.

"Wow…those are beautiful! How come you never showed them to me?"

"I guess I was saving them for a little surprise to give the Island Council. But then Zack died and all…think I should give them to Charlie or someone?"

"Hell no!" Rex boomed. "Don't give that prick anything. Let's keep them as a little souvenir. I'm serious about selling the house. I think we should leave. I've just had about enough."

Allison closed her sketchbook and returned it to her studio in silence, then came back and sat beside Rex.

"Are you sure? We won't be able to run away from greedy, stupid people by moving somewhere else."

"Oh, I know that," Rex said with good-natured irritation. "There's just too many ghosts here—of every kind."

"I've always wanted to live in Mexico."

"Me too. I love it there. The people are wonderful, the pace of life is human."

"Won't you miss your children?"

"Of course! That's what airplanes are for. We'll come back every so often to visit everyone. I love the idea!"

A black cloud darker than any shadow cast by the ill-conceived bridge plan eclipsed the island's already-dim prospects, in the form of a pending decision by the State Department of Corrections. Ominous flyers posted overnight around town announced a public hearing on the planned parole to Skagit Island of a registered sex offender. As if that weren't disturbing enough, the posters contained in their center—like a bull's eye in a shooting gallery—a grimy prison mugshot of the tough black man named Purvis Leaper who had served six years in the state penitentiary for sexual predation on children. According to state law, correctional officials had to schedule and advertise at least two public hearings in any community where a convicted sex offender would be released, and the first hearing was set for the Skagit Presbyterian Church at 7 on a Thursday night. Warring forces in the re-ignited battle over incorporation quickly laid down their hatchets and came together to meet this latest threat from beyond the waters of Puget Sound.

The flyers said that Leaper, a 36-year-old man from Kent, had been convicted of two counts of child molestation and one count of child rape six years previously, had served his time without incident and was deemed by correctional authorities to pose no more than "minimal" risk of re-offending if released on parole. The flyers announced in cheerful bureacratese that he was engaged to be married upon his release to a white woman who lived on Skagit Island—as if that would calm the fears of a group of 9,000 geographically isolated white people, many of whom had fled the inner cities to live and raise their children far from the likes of people like Purvis Leaper.

"We got a real problem on our hands," Charlie Rector said to Rex one day in the market, with his usual gift for subtlety.

"You mean...with the community split over the council?" Rex liked to play Candide to Charlie's Pangloss.

"No, for Christ's sake! Don't you read? I mean this goddam sex pervert nigger the state wants to shove off on us!"

Rex quickly glanced around to see if anyone he knew was within earshot.

"Oh, yeah. What's the problem? The state will do what they want anyway."

Charlie shook his head as his face became beet-red. "I just don't understand you, boy. I tried working with you on the council, I tried telling everybody I know to give you a chance even though you're from California. Now I'm not sure..."

Rex shook his head along with Charlie. "You can run but you can't hide. Do you know if Skagit has ever had a sex offender before?"

"Are you kidding me? Do you think I'd choose to live here if I knew we had that kind of scum here?"

Rex smiled enigmatically. "You know, Charlie, you sound just like some of the people I grew up around in the South. I guess being black doesn't help this guy's case any."

"You don't think this is about skin color, do you?"

"Umm…yes, I do think it affects people's attitudes."

"All I can say is, I hope you are at the hearing along with every-body else from the council so the state doesn't get the idea we don't care about this." Charlie's face was so red that Rex thought he'd explode.

"Oh, yes. I wouldn't miss it for the world."

The church was packed pulpit to pantry with sweating, heaving white bodies when Rex arrived. The simmering stench of hatred hung heavily in the air like a pathogenic cloud, although the crowd was subdued almost to the point of silence. He tried to slip inside, but could just get far enough through the front door to catch a side-ways glimpse into the chapel where three dour representatives of the State Department of Corrections sat at a table, looking away from the fixed gazes of the crowd and shuffling papers on the table before them. The Presbyterian pastor had offered his services for the evening as "moderator" in a bid to provide a visible semblance of civility to the proceedings.

A small, bouncy man given to Sunday outbursts of divinely inspired ecstasy that involved thrusting his arms straight up into the air and shouting "God is love," Reverend Peter Parshall also was uncharacteristically grave in his demeanor. He stood in front of the pulpit, which had been moved off to the far right side of the podium, holding a microphone in one hand and raising the other as if to both calm and welcome the visitors. Slowly, his shit-eating smile sank and he began to cough. Red-faced, he coughed louder and louder until he had to leave to room to get a drink of water. He returned armed with a long pole with a metal gizmo at the end for opening high win-dows. This he thrust into the upper reaches of the A-framed chapel and began to crank to allow some fresh air in. Gradually, the thick air thinned and diluted the pheromone-charged cloud of fear that poi-soned the air. Rex finally drew a refreshing breath.

After the introductions, welcomes and bureaucratic recitation of statutes and procedures, the meeting was thrown open to questions from the floor. According to the rules of the meeting, comments were considered "informational" and would not necessarily get a direct response. The panel had agreed only to make "closing statements" at the end of the meeting that would address some of the issues raised, in general terms.

Jason W., as he was known in AA, was a tall, pony-tailed, motor-cycle-riding, middle-aged architect hipster with an iron handshake that could make a man writhe in pain. His steely blue eyes could in the span of a single sentence express anguish, fear, anger and humor. His deep voice was as solidly wooden as his physique. He was a man's man, and one of the unofficial "leaders" of AA on the island. He stood in his seat and his hands trembled slightly with an excess of adrenaline as he fixed his gaze on the panel of flak-catchers.

"We live just on the other side of some undeveloped property between our house and the school where my daughter is in the sixth grade. The children have a pathway through the woods—a short-cut—they take to school. According to your maps, this shortcut would take them directly behind the house where Mr. Leaper would be living."

Jason paused for a moment that seemed endless.

"How would you feel if your child was passing behind the house where a convicted sex offender was living? Would that be OK with you?"

A low grumble rolled through the crowd.

"Listen to me," Jason continued. "If this man is released onto this island and so much as touches any of my kids, I'm coming to Olympia to find each and everyone of you."

Red-faced and smiling sardonically, Jason was enveloped in a din of cheering, shouting support from other islanders. He gracefully lowered his lanky frame back into the packed pew. Energized by Jason's in-your-face challenge, the assembled mob rose one after another to voice their discontent. Like a feverish contagion, fear infected everyone in the church with its urgent, atavistic bloodlust.

As it spread from speaker to speaker, fear turned the air rank and stagnant, hot with the breath of a hundred heaving vigilantes. Rex could finally take it no more, and stumbled outside to gasp for fresh air. Up in the clear night sky, a satellite zoomed across the stars. Unconsciously, he raised his hand in a salute. "Hi, Zack," he said under his breath.

Weary with the whole business, he turned to leave but spun around when he felt a firm tug on his shoulder.

"Where you goin'? It's just getting interesting!"

Jason stood triumphantly on the front porch, gazing down at Rex.

"I think I know how things will go from here," he said faintly. "I don't think there's much I could add. You made some very good points."

"I didn't tell them the whole story." Jason grinned like a little boy with a snake in his pocket. "I've got about 50 feet of heavy rope in my garage, and several cans of gas."

Rex shuddered. "Maybe you won't have to use it, Jason."

As he drove home, the words of a black politician rang in his ears: "If you black, you gonna die by southern rope or western dope."

Zack's downstairs room had become, *de facto*, off limits. Not unlike the sick rooms of tuberculosis patients in a previous century, the space had the unmistakable pallor of death about it. Although Rex and Allison had hardly acknowledged it, they avoided Zack's room in the slightly magical expectation that somehow, sometime, they might come home and find him there slouched across the bed reading Puget Sound tide charts. They hadn't even sorted through his meager possessions, which consisted of a box of shotgun shells, a chest of tangled fishing gear, two fishing reels, a grocery bag filled with grimy baseball caps, and several boxes of personal mementos such as photographs, letters, souvenirs, Bolivian coins, cigarette lighters. On the night table next to the bed was a well-thumbed copy of the "Big Book," also known as "Alcoholics Anonymous," with pages of names and telephone numbers scrawled in the back pages. They were remnants of a hard life, but one lived honestly and with no small amount of dignity.

The house was empty when Rex arrived; he lay in bed awaiting Allison and listening to the occasional bleat of a foghorn on the sound. A brisk wind had risen and it drove tree branches against the windows in a steady thrashing sound although there was no rain yet. Somehow the restless wild night comforted him, and he closed eyes peacefully after remembering Zack in his prayers.

CHAPTER 5

❀

*T*he next issue of the *ClamShell* carried an account of a suspicious fire at Bill's BBQ, the only black-owned business on Skagit Island. The front of the restaurant had been destroyed by a fast-moving blaze, suspected of having been set since most restaurant fires generally start in the kitchen area. The blackened storefront still gave off occasional plumes of smoke and an acrid aroma when Rex and other members of the Island Council went for an inspection.

Shaking his head, Charlie Rector turned to the fire chief. "Was there any kind of note or anything else that would make you think this is a hate crime?"

"Nothing specific, except the timing and nature of the fire. It came the day after the hearing on the sex offender parole, and it certainly points to arson. This looks like a gasoline burn," he said, pointing to the charred and smoldering façade.

"So have you notified the FBI?" Rex wondered.

"Yes. They're sending a couple of agents over here tomorrow."

"Jesus! Just what we need when we're trying to build up the business community!" Charlie kicked the charcoal embers in disgust.

"How the hell do you think Mr. Washington feels about this?" Rex shouted at Rector. "He's lost a restaurant and his livelihood and he may not reopen because he'd terrified. And all you can think about is your own wallet?! I'm ashamed to be on the council with you, Charlie!"

"Then why don't you just resign, Mr. California Man?"

"Not before I bust your fat ass!"

Rex lunged for Charlie, fists gathered into hard battering rams, but was restrained by the fire chief. "Hold on, boys. Cool it off. This ain't worth getting thrown in jail over."

"You don't care about anybody but yourself, do you Rector?" Rex continued.

"Well, it just so happens that a majority of the island feels the same as I do—this whole incorporation thing was a ridiculous idea. And pretty soon you'll be just another jerk from California with no voice and no power. Just wait."

Rex pulled free from the huge arms of the fire chief and glared back at his tormentor. "Fuck you, Rector!" he shouted. "We'll just see about that!"

Allison quickly grabbed him by the arm and scurried him back to the truck.

"That settles it," she sputtered. "We're leaving this island."

Rex' heart felt as if it would explode, and his blood ran hotly through his head. When he could catch his breath, he wiped the sweat off his brow in a quick motion.

"If we leave then they'll win. They'll get the bridge, the cutesy-poo tourist town and the whole thing. We can't let them get away with that!"

"There's nothing we can do to stop them at this point. We're outnumbered."

"I've never been one to run from a fight before. It just doesn't feel right."

"Think of it as not running from a fight, but maybe going someplace where we can live in peace."

"Humpfh! That's why I moved here in the first place. It just seems so…futile."

"Yeah, probably it is. It's just something we have to accept."

Rex rolled his eyes. "OK, OK. Spare me the AA flogging, will you?"

"Wow…you *are* mad, aren't you?"

They drove on in silence for a while as Rex practiced deep breathing. He caught a glimpse of Allison from the corner of his eyes, and her face was drawn into a tight knot or worry. Once home, they walked in silence into the kitchen, where Rex flopped down at the table with a long sigh.

"It's so strange. We both came here more or less searching for the same thing. We've lost friends and loved ones, and now we're losing the place we thought would be our sanctuary. I'm starting to feel a little like a Gypsy."

"But we found each other," Allison smiled. "That's worth something, isn't it?"

Rex pulled her close to him and kissed her. "You're right. Home is wherever we are, as long as we're sober and trying to work the program. I'm such a fool. Always I focus on the 2 percent of any situation that doesn't agree with me and ignore the 98 percent that's terrific."

"How would you like to focus on the 98 percent of me that needs your touch?"

"Yes. Zat is qvuite possible," he said with his best mad Nazi scientist demeanor, as he led her upstairs by the hand. "I believe zat vould be qvuite zerapeutic, nein?"

After they made love, Rex went downstairs to the darkened kitchen to find something for dinner. He switched on the miniature tabletop TV for light as well as companionship while he made an omelet to share in bed with Allison. The Seattle newscast featured a "standup" of a breathless young woman in trench coat posed in front of the burned-out Bill's BBQ, reporting that the state had at last issued its decision to release Curtis Leaper to the island—against the ugly backdrop of racism and violence symbolized by the fire. "This quiet island is now on edge and residents are quite angry about the state's decision," she reported urgently and baselessly. The crass superficiality of the whole presentation soured his stomach, and he wrenched the tiny TV from its socket and threw it into the garbage. "Fucking imbeciles," he muttered as he turned the eggs on the soft moonlight.

Quietly he put two trays down on the bed and waited to see if the aroma of hot food would stir Allison. When she snorted her deepening commitment to sleep, he switched on a bedside light and began eating noisily, clattering his silverware and glass. Finally, she raised her sleep-matted blonde head from the pillow and squinted at Rex. "God, what are you doing?"

"I got so hungry, I made us some dinner. You needn't eat if you aren't hungry."

Allison grabbed the other tray and sniffed the omelet. "This'll do for an appetizer. Such a good hubby!"

Rex gobbled down his food and slurped hot coffee.

"I think you've finally convinced me. You and the boob tube."

"What on earth are you talking about?"

"I agree that we might be better off somewhere else. I think I've about reached the end of my rope."

Allison nodded silently, pensively. After a long pause, she said: "It's a big step."

"So what? I'm up for an adventure."

"Well, I've already developed a pretty good deal with the gallery in LA. I could live anywhere and do my artwork."

Rex scratched his head nervously. "Yeah, and I need to buckle down and focus my energies on selling some magazine pieces and not spend so much time caught up in stupid political battles. I guess living here has been a transition for us both...it's where we met each other, too."

"Oh, you love politics. Admit it!"

Rex gazed silently out of the window for a moment. "Truth is, I really miss my kids. And it doesn't look like I'm gonna be able to see them unless I'm somewhere near Connecticut. Cynthia's made it quite clear she doesn't intend to move back to the West Coast."

"Ever lived back there?"

"Where…Connecticut? Nope. The closest I've ever been is Piedmont, when I was growing up. But it's close to New York, isn't it?"

Allison chuckled. "Oh, yes, quite close."

"I've always had this fantasy about living in New York. Even if it's only for a while."

"So where are your kids?"

"Darien."

"Not more than a couple of hours from the city."

"It sounds like you know the area well."

"I thought I told you I went to the Art Students League when I was in college. I lived in New York for a few years back in my flaming youth."

"Think you could live there in your smoldering middle age?"

"Sure, if we could smolder together somewhere!"

"That is quite possible." He kissed her sweetly on the cheek. "Qvuite pozzible."

The next issue of the *ClamShell* carried two front-page stories read by everyone on the island, and about equally loved and hated:

Elections Department Schedules Vote on Skagit Island Independence

Sex Offender Can Live on Island, State Corrections Officials Decide

"Godammit!" Charlie Rector threw the newspaper across the room and picked up his cell phone. Frantically, he dialed a number, drummed his fingers nervously on the table and sighed heavily several times as he waited.

"Max?" he shouted into the phone. "We got a huge problem, buddy-boy. We need to get a VIP group together and go see the governor—pronto! What? Of course not! Why should they listen to a bunch of hicks out here on Skagit? We need to get some people with deep pockets together…know anybody who contributed to his campaign? OK, get him over here and let's get started."

Then he went to his desk, opened the drawer and pulled out a World War II vintage .45-caliber sidearm, stuffed it into his baggy jeans and stormed outside. The island was shrouded in a thick, foggy mist as evening crept up on its sloping banks, and Charlie felt the moisture on his hot face as a soothing balm. His hands, sweaty and cold, clutched the pistol tightly. He seemed to draw strength and courage from the cold steel and smooth oaken grips on the gun's handle.

Charlie walked briskly in the direction of Heron Beach, although brisk walking for him looked like nothing so much as a duck waddle. But the determination was evident in the midst of awkwardness. About two blocks from his home, the road dropped down abruptly in a series of hairpin curves toward the beach. At that time of day, the only people on the road were late arriving commuters and those forced for some reason to drive either to town or to catch a ferry. Only the steady roar of the surf broke the quiet darkness as it washed against the rocky beach.

He untied and flipped open a heavy wooden beach access ladder. It hit the sand with a solid thump, and he carefully lowered himself sideways down the steps. Feet firmly planted at last on the beach, he paused and drew in a few deep, slow breaths. A cloud-lined moon shone dimly on the Olympics and the water in the last second of the evening was black and powerful. Charlie walked down the beach away from the access trail to a point where he would be hidden from a direct line of sight by fallen trees and the sculpted recess of a small cove. There he drew out his pistol, unlocked the safety, and cocked the firing mechanism.

A horrific explosion rang through the darkness, and he could see a tiny blip on the surface of the water where the bullet entered.

"Fuck you, Rex!" He fired twice more in rapid succession. "Fuck you! Fuck you!"

Then he swung around and pointed the gun at the base of a fallen tree and fired again. "Fuck you, nigger pervert! Stay off our godamned island!"

Charlie then emptied the magazine in a frenzy of rage, firing up into the air at a passing helicopter, then at the beach, the moon.

Then he stood silently, heaving in great gasps of air as his over-heated body drew in the cool breeze the same way a hot engine would suck in air to cool its cylinders. As his heart shifted to a slower pace, he looked down at his pistol and noticed that his hand was trembling. He quickly thrust the gun back into his pocket and headed back for the roadway. In the brief time he'd been on the beach, the tide had moved in just enough that he had to walk through the rising surf as he slogged toward the trail. By the time Charlie had reached the edge of the beach, his shoes and feet were soaked to the skin and he was desperate for the comfort and light of his home. He muttered in an incoherent, smoldering rage as he swaggered, wet and smelling of gunpowder, up the hill toward his waiting wife.

CHAPTER 6

❁

*A*llison was working in her studio when she heard the throaty roar of a sports car in the driveway. Since usually the sound of a vehicle approaching meant nothing more than a lost motorist, she continued splashing paints and ignored the sound. But moments later came an insistent, methodically tapping at the front door and Allison knew her afternoon concentration would be broken. Making her way hurriedly through the house, she swung open the front door to behold Cerise Bagoth, dressed neatly in a purple jumpsuit with white books. Every hair on her graying head was neatly in place, and her eyes sparkled with excitement. Allison, wearing a paint-spattered apron, brushed back an errant lock of hair with the back of one hand.

"Excuse me for dropping by unannounced," she said. "I was just out for a drive in the neighborhood and thought I'd come and see if you were home."

"I'm so glad you did," Allison lied. "Please come in. I was just about to take a break anyway. Would you like some tea?"

Cerise stepped briskly inside with the poise of a woman who knew her place in the world and how to maneuver in any social situation.

"That sounds wonderful! I really hope I'm not interrupting anything."

She followed Allison into the kitchen, and stood gazing about the house.

"This is really quite lovely. You and Rex have certainly done a lot of work here. I'll bet you're going to miss this place."

Allison looked up, startled, then turned back to her tea making. "Yes, I'm sure we will. We've talked about it, and decided we can always come back to Skagit. Do you prefer sugar or honey for your tea?"

"Just a little honey would be great." Cerise lowered herself into one of the large oak chairs and surveyed the small, framed watercolors that adorned the kitchen. "You are so talented!"

"Oh, those? I did those in a class that I taught at the White Eagle and Rex liked them so much he insisted on framing them. I'm not that crazy about them, actually."

Cerise paused, taking in her words with a sip of hot tea. "It hasn't been easy for you two here on the island, has it? Especially after Zack's death."

"Not really. Rex hasn't been able to find any full-time work—just a little freelancing here and there. I've been doing OK, but most of my work has sold out of galleries in New York and LA. And the politics here has been rough."

"I'm sure. It's rather discouraging, isn't it?" Cerise had the empathic gift of a Jewish mother, both affirming and soothing the slings and arrows of an outrageous world in a single sentence. "You two are smart young people. There's no future here on this island for people like you with talent and ambition. You should go out into the world, then maybe come back later."

"I think we would have stuck things out for several years, but this backlash with Charlie Rector and all…"

"Isn't he too much? That man belongs in a rocking chair on the porch of a beaten up old gas station of a dusty road somewhere in Georgia!"

Allison bowed her head slightly, imagining what Rex would say if he were there to hear Cerise's remark. But she held her tongue.

"I'd love to see your studio, if it isn't an imposition."

"Oh, sure. But watch your step. There's wet canvasses and tubes of paint and turpentine all over the place!"

The exciting aroma of fresh paint greeted them as they entered the studio. Allison had left a light shining brightly on her work-in-progress, an abstract dreamscape full of swirling colors and nightmarish blues and crimson.

"Wow! That's powerful," Cerise said.

"Oh," Allison chuckled. "I never know exactly what I'm gonna do until I get started. This thing just started taking shape the other day. I have no idea what it is, yet."

Cerise strolled slowly about the garage studio, surveying the piles of paintings.

"You must have enough work here to fill three galleries!"

"I try to stay busy. Lately I've been lucky. My work has been selling pretty well."

"I thought I wanted to be an artist once," Cerise said wistfully.

"Really? Why didn't you?" Allison seemed genuinely amazed.

"Oh, I got married right after I finished art school. My husband was one of those workaholics who wasn't around much. We did well, financially, and had two children. When our second child, Matthew, was born with cerebral palsy, he couldn't handle it and started seeing someone else."

Allison shook her head in a gesture of world-weary sympathy.

"I held on for a while and pretended that everything was just fine. But the loneliness got really bad. He just wasn't around to be with me or with the children. I finally got fed up and realized that I could be all alone when I was single and not have to worry about him. So got divorced."

"I'm so sorry…"

"That was years ago, and it seems so far away now. Eventually I remarried and moved here with my second husband. He also had plenty of money, so I never really had to work. I suppose I got lazy. I love to see other people's work, but I know now that it's too late for me to start an art career."

"Nonsense!" Allison boomed. "There are tons of artists who started in later life—and I'm not just talking about Grandma Moses, either"

They shared a gentle laugh.

"I love visiting with you, although I'm afraid I'm taking too much of your time."

"Don't be silly, Cerise."

"I guess if I hadn't had children it might have been easier to become an artist. But I'm sure it's tough whenever and however you do it. Anyway, I love being around artists and supporting them. That's part of the reason why I came over here today."

Allison looked puzzled.

"I'm wondering whether you and Rex have given any thought to selling the coffeehouse when you leave?"

"To be honest with you, we haven't even discussed it much. We've been so focused on getting our house sold and making plans to move. I think we both sort of assumed we'd just close it down and take a loss."

Cerise waved her hand, as if warning. "Oh, please don't do that. The coffeehouse means so much to people here on the island. It's a wonderful place for people to meet, and I love going there to be with the art crowd. Would you consider selling it to me?"

"Wow…uh, sure. I really had no idea what it might be worth or anything. We aren't making much money with it, you know. Just enough to pay the bills and a couple of employees. After we opened it, we decided we didn't want to spend our entire lives running a small business."

Cerise smiled contentedly. "Allison, I don't need to make any money from the coffeehouse. It would just be a way for me to have a good connection with the community. After my husband died a few years ago, I've been looking for something to do that would help fill the hole. Nothing has really worked. But I know that when I'm there, I feel good and it makes me happy."

The simplicity of Cerise's statement, and her directness, momentarily left Allison speechless.

"I can speak to Rex about it tonight," she said. "See what he has to say."

"Wonderful! Now I really must be going and let you get back to work."

Both Rex and Allison experienced the distortion of time that precedes major change: the sense of being pleasantly paralyzed at the prospect on onrushing events mingled with the nagging frustration of trying to extricate one's self from the daily tedium that has constituted the rhythm of daily life for so long. Weary from a day of making phone calls to New York and trying to finish business with the quickly-deteriorating island government, Rex came home and collapsed into his favorite chair.

Allison greeted him at the door with a warm hug and a kiss. As she unbuttoned his windbreaker, he noticed her radiant smile.

"Looks like you must have had a great day!" he opined.

"Well, yes. It hasn't been bad. You'll never guess who came over for a visit."

"Mmmm..." Rex screwed up his face in an exaggerated burlesque. "Santa Claus?"

"No. Cerise Bagoth. She wants to know if we're interested in selling her the coffeehouse."

"Selling...? Why would anybody in their right mind...?"

"She's not in her right mind, of course. She's a very generous, kind-hearted woman with tons of money and she just wants to help us."

"Well, that would be great. But I have no idea what to sell it for. I'd just be grateful if she wants to take over the lease."

Three days later, a certified letter from Cerise's attorney arrived. It contained an offer to buy the coffeehouse and all its equipment for $15,000. Rex and Allison accepted a cashier's check in that amount and deposited it in a certificate of deposit so it could not be spent for at least a year, and so they could get on with the business of planning their move.

"I've got this incredible idea to help us build the tax base." Charlie Rector quivered with excitement as he walked unannounced into Dudley Wharton's office. Everybody in the whole world knows about those funny lights we've been having on the island, and practically everybody in Seattle has read enough about Skagit to wonder just what kind of place this is."

Wharton fairly crouched behind his desk, as if ready to drop on the floor to protect himself against nuclear blast.

"So, I was thinking we could develop some kind of mystery tours of Skagit Island," Charlie said, moving one hand in a deliberate, dream-like way. "Come and see the lake where mysterious lights have haunted islanders. See the place where people have disappeared for days, then suddenly reappeared."

He dropped his hand quickly. "Can't you see it? Doesn't it just make your blood curdle?"

No, you make my blood curdle.

"That sounds like a terrific idea," Wharton said in his best, bureaucratic, ass-kissing mode. "It would be a quick and easy way to add some tax revenues. Wouldn't require any infrastructure, or any specially trained work force. Are you thinking the city would some-how sponsor this?"

"Aw, hell no! You must think I'm nuts, son."

Yeah.

"I'm talking about pure free enterprise here. This might just be the kind of thing that would help us to get over this hump. I mean, I wanted the special election on the ballot as a last resort. We have, oh, maybe six months to still try and see if we can make this incorporation work. Then if we still can't balance out books, I'll be the first one to lead the parade to dismantle the whole kit and caboodle. But at least we can still give it a shot."

"So do you know anyone who might want to try this mystery tour thing?"

"You're looking at him!"

Charlie's idea took root with the feverish intensity of a summer weed after a rainstorm. There would be silver, skin-tight costumes for the tour guides. Their heads would be covered, too, with silver helmets that would obscure their human features. High school kids, with their gangly bodies, could serve as tour guides in the summer months and lead visits to the lake where lights had been spotted. A couple of rowboats launched from a simple wharf would complete the minimal investment. The revenue stream would be strong and sudden, with only a small amount taken out for advertising and salaries. Skagit Island would be the beneficiary, and Charlie himself the entrepreneurial hero. If things went just right, perhaps the island government could be saved—and Charlie become its second mayor. After all, Rex Armistead would be long gone and could not mount an electoral campaign.

Magical Mystery Tours of Skagit Island!

CHAPTER 7

$\mathcal{B}$usiness at Skagit Town Hall ground to a halt in anticipation of a vote to dismantle the infant municipality and crawl back into the waiting, greedy arms of the county. Dudley Wharton spent his days openly printing out copies of his resume and mailing them all over the United States, Police and firemen spent most of their idle time—which was most of the time—idly discussing their future. Aware of the political and policing paralysis, teenaged hot-rodders roared up and down the Skagit Highway at even higher than usual breakneck speeds, endangering lives and limbs. The library was the only vestige of town government that seemed to function, and its bulletin board was posted to overflowing with political flyers for and against the upcoming special ballot measure.

Disgusted and disillusioned, Rex and Allison entertained offers on their house and began reading *The New York Times* on a daily basis. Everything had changed. Somehow the sleepy island had morphed into a microcosm of everything they both had sought to escape when they came there despite their best efforts to protect it against corruption. The horrible human hologram of greed, power and racism had encompassed the deep green quiet of Skagit Island and transformed it from a sanctuary to a snakepit. Rex likened the situation to that of the Tar Baby in *Uncle Remus*: the more Br'er Rabbit struggled, the more enmeshed and embroiled he became without realizing that he himself was the source of, and solution to, his problem.

The hot real estate rumor was that voters would soon approve the special ballot measure that would drive market values up. Thus the best time to buy anything on the island was right now. And they found the rumor profitable. Within a week of putting their house up for sale, Rex and Allison had two offers that topped their asking price, which set off a minor bidding war between the two would-be suitors. Finally, tired of the daily intrigue and haggling between themselves, their realtor and the two potential buyers, Rex and Allison decided to accept the highest offer and, with Allison's consent, put an end to the madness. They then had 30 days to vacate their house, find a place to live in New York and move. Signing the sales document made everything shockingly real, and they shared a wound borne of a sense of loss that preceded their actual leave-taking. To dull their mounting sense of bereavement, they got busy with plan and hotel reservations for a trip to the East Coast.

"I don't know if I can move fast enough to survive in New York," Rex fussed.

"Don't worry," Allison assured him. "Before you know it, you'll be caught up in the energy of the place. What did Thomas Wolfe call it? The 'manswarm'?"

"Yes, he did. I'm surprised you knew that."

"I *can* read, you know!"

"Of course…I didn't mean that. I just never knew you cared about Thomas Wolfe."

"Don't be ridiculous, Rex. Doesn't everybody know his work?"

"I'm afraid not. Not outside universities, anyway. We should re-read 'Of Time and the River' before we move to get us into the mood for New York."

"Can you speed-read? I mean, it's something like 1,000 pages long!"

"No, and I wouldn't want to speed-read Thomas Wolfe. Let's savor him and share what we find when we read it."

Just the day before they departed for New York, voters on Skagit Island did as anticipated and approved the special ballot measure by a two-to-one margin. To avoid hassles at the polling place, Rex and Allison had mailed in their ballots a week earlier with "no" votes. A sense of sad inevitability helped to push them forward when they hesitated and tried one last, fruitless time to breathe some life into their dead dreams.

On the plane, Rex chuckled. "Charlie Rector will be insufferable now."

"He's always been insufferable," Allison corrected.

"Do you suppose anyone ever tried to stop the commercialization of Manhattan Island the way we fought for Skagit?"

"Yeah…the Indians. Look where it got them."

Once they got settled into their hotel just off Central Park and went out to stroll the city streets, Rex and Allison were filled with a palpable electricity. They rode the subway downtown and went through the Guggenheim and Metropolitan, then went to the Village for shish kebabs and live jazz. Afterwards, they got a taxi back to their hotel and fell into a profound, exhausted slumber. The next day was a bright, sunny fall morning filled with sun-baked warmth but crisp around the edges, and the cool air of autumn. They ordered poached eggs, croissants with blackberry jam and giant pots of coffee from room service, then sat on their beds munching and gazing out the window at the swarming world below.

"God, I love it here!" Allison said with a mouthful of pastry. Rex nodded enthusiastically, as he also gobbled.

"Maybe we should spend some time today looking at places for sale or rent?" he said, assuming the role of responsible parent.

"OK, we can go to SoHo. That's where all the artists are. There's tons of lots and galleries everywhere. I think you'd like it."

"Great. And I want to find a good kosher deli."

"What's your problem, son? This is NEW YORK!"

The city challenged them at every step. There were subway and bus schedules to decipher, restaurants to sample, entire neighborhoods to probe. And always the crowds on the street presented an endless, onrushing stream of humanity. Rex recalled taking the train from Piedmont to New York in his senior year of high school, to attend the Randall's Island Jazz Festival. He particularly recalled Dizzy Gillespie joking from the bandstand: "This place is so bad, they had to name it twice—New York, New York!" Indeed.

After a few days, their excitement was tempered on an evening stroll back to their hotel by the discovery on the sidewalk of a young woman's body lying atop a collection of battered garbage cans, blood dripping down onto the pavement. Before they could fully comprehend the scene before their eyes, police sirens screeched their approach. Rex and Allison gingerly continued their walk for a few more blocks.

"Drugs?" Rex mumbled.

"Who knows?"

"I'm so anxious to see my kids."

"Naturally. Why don't you call them and see if you can arrange a visit?"

"Would you want to meet them?" he asked shyly.

"I think the first time you should just go and visit. After we get settled someplace, then we can have them over."

Rex ran his hand quickly across his face. "Yeah, getting settled. That's gonna be interesting."

"How so?" Allison tossed her clothes on the bed.

"I mean, everything here is so expensive. My god!"

"Well, after you get that $200,000-a-year copywriter job with J. Walter Thompson, the sky's the limit."

"Un-hunh, I should be getting that any day now." Rex turned on the TV and plopped into bed wearily.

"Look, it's not the end of the world if we have to rent for a while. Lots of people I know rent lofts in old warehouses and convert them into studios and living spaces. No reason why we can't do that—if we can find any lofts that haven't already been taken."

Then she snuggled up close to Rex, and they gave each other little lovebird kisses. She could feel his body relax, and she scratched the back of his neck.

"When you go see your kids, I'll talk to some of my friends and see what they know about places to rent. I'm sure we can find something we like. Let's both try to turn this over and stop worrying, OK?"

"Yeah, how quickly I forget. I'll try."

Rex took the train to Connecticut, riding up the shoreline against the crush of commuters. He stopped in New Haven briefly to change trains, then continued on to Darien. His heart was filled with anticipation and trepidation, for he had no idea what Cynthia's mood would be or, for that matter, whether the children would be angry with him for having been so long absent from their lives. The steady rocking motion of the machine and the clattering of the wheels along track seemed to offer him comfort.

As the train drew slowly into the station, he jumped up from his seat when he saw Cynthia and the children waiting on the platform. Tears streamed down his cheeks as he stepped off and walked toward them.

"Daddy! Daddy!" they shrieked, running toward him as Cynthia stood back, a faint smile on her face. Rex wrapped his arms around them, hugged and kissed them each one, then started to laugh with joy.

"Thanks for bringing these sweeties with you," he said to Cynthia with a quick turn of his head.

"Oh, they wouldn't let me leave home without them. Do you have some bags?"

"Just this one," he answered distractedly, slapping his tattered suitcase.

In her inimitable safe, defensive style, Cynthia drove the same station wagon they'd shared during their life together on Skagit Island. It struck Rex as strangely out of place in suburban Connecticut.

"I've fixed up the spare bedroom so you can stay with us if you'd like," she said matter-of-factly.

"Well, I guess I just assumed I'd be getting a hotel room…"

"Stay with us, Daddy! Stay with us!" came the chorus from the back seat. Rex chuckled again, then turned to look at his children once more.

"OK, I'll stay with you. But you have to let me read you some bedtime stories."

"Yeahhhhh!!!!!"

"From a quick sideways glance, Rex noticed that Cynthia seemed a bit heavier and more relaxed than he remembered her.

"Are you enjoying living here in the country?" he asked awkwardly.

"Oh, yeah. I have a horse and the kids can play outside every day. I love it."

Somehow, her protestations seemed a bit overstated and therefore dubious.

"So, I hear you're happily remarried?"

"You know me…I'm not the kind to stay single forever. What about you? Anyone special?"

"Nobody I'm planning on marrying, if that's what you mean."

Rex focused his attention on the children, trying to feed the hungry maw of their paternal neediness. There were bedtime stories, tickling, and laughter. Once the youngsters were put to bed, Rex noticed a light on in the kitchen and found Allison sitting at the table, reading a newspaper.

"They've really missed you," she said softly.

Rex pulled out a chair and sat down next to her. "And I've missed them so much." After a lip-biting pause, he continued. "I...I've felt badly about how I treated you, especially when we were on the island. I was selfish and insensitive. And wasn't much of a husband or father. I realize that I hurt you—and the children. I don't ask your forgiveness, unless you want to offer it, but just want to let you know how much I regret..."

"Oh, yeah, the AA amends stuff." Cynthia waved her hand dismissively. "Don't give me all that crap, please. You don't have to apologize and I don't have to forgive you. I guess we both made some bad choices."

There was a hardness in her manner that Rex had not known. He felt alone and somewhat ridiculous until he recalled a passage from the "Big Book" that cautioned recovering drunks not to expect miracles—or, indeed, anything—from those they'd injured during their drinking career when they attempted to make amends. In a moment of silence, he remembered how sweet and innocent their love had been at first, before booze put those feelings to sleep and then to death.

"OK. I just had to tell you, that's all. I hope that someday we can be friends."

Cynthia gave him a look of cynical disbelief, the corners of her mouth upraised in a sarcastic smile.

"I really mean it," Rex persisted. "I've always know you are a good person, and I really want to be your friend even if I have to earn it. And it certainly would be better for the kids if we're not at each other's throats all the time."

Touched by his earnestness, Cynthia softened. "OK. I can accept that. Let's be friends."

He leaned toward her and gave her an awkward, sideways hug that felt wonderful, then quietly slipped off to bed.

The children were more subdued, but seemed contented the next morning. Rex fixed his fabulous lighter-than-air pancakes for a huge breakfast before they headed off to the train station. On the platform, he was once again gripped with the pain of imminent loss as the train slowly pulled in.

"Next time, you all can come and visit me in New York. Sound good?"

They nodded their assent, and he hugged and kissed them a final time. Then he waved from the window of the train until they were out of sight, and finally slumped into his seat in a sweet melancholy. For the first time since his divorce, Rex allowed himself to imagine a happy future for his children that included him. He visualized wonderful museum trips, ice skating in Central Park, concerts and shopping. It pleased him to think of his children as adored objects of his affection, constantly involved with his new life. As the train picked up speed, Rex knew that he and Allison had done the right thing by moving to New York. Skagit Island had barely left a trace in the memories of his children, and now seemed so distant even from him that is was like a dim relic from some long-forgotten past.

"I've found this incredible loft for rent just off Houston Street!" Allison practically leaped upon him as he got off the train in Penn Station. "It's owned by an artist who's going to live in Europe and he may decide to stay there and eventually sell. We've gotta go see it first thing in the morning. He said he wouldn't let anyone else have it until we've both had a chance to see it."

"Great."

Sensing Rex' subdued mood, Allison tried to calm herself. "How were the kids?"

"Just fine. It was so great seeing them. I didn't realize until then how much I'd missed them. I asked them to come and visit us in the city as soon as we have a place."

"Of course…I can't wait!" She kissed him hard on the cheek as they rode back to the hotel in their cab. "I think this is a really good move."

Once in their room, Rex threw his bag on the bed, kicked off his shoes and began flipping through the Sunday newspaper. "I guess you haven't had any reason to check the real estate ads, huh?"

"No, not really. Mostly I've been walking around in SoHo, checking signs for rent and talking to some of my old friends."

Rex buried himself in the paper and disappeared into a shroud of silence, while Allison puttered about. "Migod!" he said at last. "Have you seen this?"

He opened the paper, folded it in half, and laid it on the bed for them both to read. A large feature story with a photo of Charlie Rector dominated the national news section:

SEATTLE JUDGE MAY VOID ISLAND ELECTION AS UNCONSTITUTIONAL

SKAGIT ISLAND, WA—On this remote island in Puget Sound near Seattle, feisty residents decided almost two years ago to take their destiny into their hands. They voted to split away from Skookum County and form their own independent island government.

But their bravado came at a price—a price many islanders were no longer able to pay. So two weeks ago, they voted in a special election to dismantle their fledgling government and return to the county because lagging tax revenues threatened to scuttle the new government before it got started.

"I was a big supporter of independence for Skagit Island," said Charlie Rector, a member of the Skagit Island Council and architect of the petition to return to county government. "But the our fiscal projections turned out to be all wrong. We barely have enough money to pay the rent on our so-called Town Hall."

But all that has been thrown into legal limbo by a decision last week in Skookum County Superior Court, Judge Gwendolyn Harper issued a temporary restraining order against making any changes based on the election results, pending a hearing on constitutional issues raised in a petition filed by island attorney Pittor Dragoneth.

In his action, Mr. Dragoneth seeks to void the election results as unconstitutional on grounds voters were not given adequate information in the voters pamphlet to make an informed decision, that voting machines functioned improperly and the vote itself was not counted accurately.

"Once these issues are taken into account, and all the votes are counted fairly, it will be obvious that these election results are invalid," according to Mr. Dragoneth's petition, who also successfully sued the Washington State Transportation Department several years ago to stop construction of a bridge across Puget Sound.

Open-mouthed, eyes dilated, Rex and Allison looked at each other in disbelief. Then they chuckled, belly-laughed, and finally fell on the floor with great whoops of hysterical laughter that went on forever.

0-595-22092-4